Foolish
Undertaking

Also by Mark de Castrique
Dangerous Undertaking
Grave Undertaking

Foolish Undertaking

Mark de Castrique

Poisoned Pen Press

Poisoned Pen Press
6962 E. First Ave., Ste. 103
Scottsdale, AZ 85251
www.poisonedpenpress.com
info@poisonedpenpress.com

Printed in the United States of America

In memory of my mother,
Marianne, aka TOOTSIE

Acknowledgments

I'm indebted to K'Sang Bonyo of the Catholic Social Services Refugee Office in Charlotte; Ellen Dubin, Director of HIAS in North Carolina; and Pat Priest, Director of Lutheran Family Services in Greensboro, for their information on the Montagnard people. Thanks to Detective William DeMille of the Boston Police Department for his expertise and to Steve Greene for his invaluable guidance throughout the creation of this book. I'm grateful to Cullie and Sylvia Tarleton for letting me use the Julian Massi bedroom in their mountain home, and to Kathy Moore for searching for gristmills I could grind into words.

Writing for Poisoned Pen Press is a privilege made enjoyable through the support of Barbara Peters, Robert Rosenwald, and their staff. Thanks to my agent Linda Allen and to those many booksellers who share my mountain community with their customers. I thank my wife, Linda, and daughters, Melissa and Lindsay, for honest critiques, and my father, Arch, for the funeral home anecdotes that keep Barry on his toes.

Preface

Foolish Undertaking is a work of fiction. The characters and events are fabrications suggested by contemporary life in the mountains of western North Carolina. However, the roots of this story are also embedded in a place halfway around the world and at a time nearly forty years in the past—the Central Highlands of Vietnam during the War in Southeast Asia.

This is not a book about that conflict, but a story drawing upon the courage and loyalty of the indigenous Montagnard people who aided and protected U.S. servicemen at great risk to themselves.

Regardless of how history may judge the Vietnam War, the Montagnards deserve to be more than a footnote. Lest we forget, their struggle against persecution and subjugation by the Vietnamese government still goes on, as commerce, not communism, now threatens their homeland and their very existence.

Chapter One

Uncle Wayne appeared to be praying. He was on his knees at the edge of the sidewalk, dressed in a navy blue suit and bending low before the front columns of our funeral home. The glow of the late afternoon sun rimmed his white hair like a halo.

In the backseat of my jeep, Democrat whimpered his concern. Then my uncle scooted to his left and revealed a flat of blue and pink petunias. The man was planting flowers.

Democrat scratched at the window impatiently. I honked the horn warning Uncle Wayne his petunias were in immediate danger of being trampled under by the four paws of a five-month-old cyclone. As I pulled into the driveway of Clayton and Clayton Funeral Directors, Uncle Wayne stepped up on the front porch where the yellow lab's greeting could do the least damage.

I kept Democrat on a short lead and steered him away from the temptation of freshly dug dirt. "Aren't you a little overdressed for gardening?"

"I wore the suit because you said we had dignitaries coming. I didn't want them thinking we aren't as good as a big city funeral home."

"And the petunias?"

"Hardware store had them on sale. Buy one flat, get one free. Couldn't resist. Thought they might liven up the place. I'll put some here and the rest along the back driveway." He looked at his purchase and scowled. "But they're kinda puny. Need to get them in the ground."

"I'll plant them if you don't have any old clothes here."

He clucked his tongue like he was scolding me at age five. "I can have them planted in less time than it takes to change. I'll be careful." He crouched down and planted his bony knees in the center of the frayed LC of an old WELCOME mat.

"But we're not receiving guests tonight. Visitation's not till two tomorrow."

"Archie Junior came by saying there'd be movie stars and even a general, and there's no telling when they might come by."

"Archie Junior doesn't know what he's talking about." Archie Donovan Junior had been a schoolmate of mine and had gone into his father's insurance business. He always had some scheme guaranteed to make a fortune. So far he was batting a thousand—all strikeouts.

"Then I don't have to rush." Uncle Wayne continued to dig.

"That's right. And you don't have to be out here in a coat and tie. People will think you sleep in that undertaker getup."

My uncle chuckled. "But isn't that the way we do our planting?"

The front door opened and my mom stood on the threshold, a red-checked apron covering her plump body. She and Uncle Wayne shared a head of thick white hair, but where Mom barely broke five feet, her brother was over six and thin as a rail.

"Barry, I saw your car. Are you here for supper?"

Democrat whined and strained against the leash, anxious to greet the woman who ruled the kitchen. "For supper and for the night," I said. "If that's all right."

"Fine. Anybody else coming?"

"No, but tomorrow promises to be hectic. I'd just as soon be here in case we get any last minute questions. Mr. Eban's causing quite the stir."

"Celebrities." Uncle Wayne jammed his trowel into the dirt.

"I read the article in today's *Vista*." Mom frowned at Uncle Wayne. "He was quite the hero."

"He didn't even clean under his nails," Uncle Wayne mumbled.

My mother sighed. "The poor man had cancer, Wayne. He was in no condition to worry about his nails."

I could feel a sibling squabble brewing and knew that both Mom and Uncle Wayne were reacting to the pressure of conducting a funeral service attended by a group of out-of-towners, including a U.S. senator. "I'll take care of them."

"Already done." Wayne never broke the rhythm of his troweling. "Used a toothbrush and Soft Scrub. Ink's what it was."

"Do they look okay?"

"Of course. You know that's part of our reputation. Mr. Y'Grok gets nothing less." Wayne mispronounced the Y as *why* instead of a long E.

I looked at Mom, who rolled her eyes. We'd both heard Uncle Wayne extol the virtues of our meticulous grooming of the deceased. He'd even suggested a motto for an advertising slogan: "Clayton & Clayton—Where every body cleans up nice." Fortunately, my mother always had final say on our marketing materials.

"Y'Grok," I said, emphasizing the E sound. "And the Y sorta means mister."

Wayne just grunted and kept digging.

"I'm going to bring Democrat around to the back." I gave a tug on the leash. "Don't want him thinking the front rooms are no longer off limits."

Mom started back in the house. "You can let him loose in the kitchen. I've got the gate across the top of the stairs."

I had to drag Democrat a few feet past Uncle Wayne and his wilting petunias until the dog realized we were heading for the back porch. Then I had to struggle to keep him from pulling me over. Obedience school couldn't come soon enough.

When Mom mentioned the gate was across the stairs, I knew my father was up in either his bedroom or the den. The toddler's barrier served a dual purpose. It kept the dog from making a sudden appearance that could startle Dad, and, more crucial, it kept Dad from wandering downstairs and out of the house.

Democrat's claws made the kitchen's linoleum floor sound like a snare drum. I grabbed his collar to hold him still. "Would you rather I put him in the backyard so he won't be underfoot?"

My mother turned from the sink where she was snapping string beans. Something simmered on the gas range, and the air was rich with appetizing aromas. No wonder Democrat was hyper. "It's after five," she said. "We'll eat in about thirty minutes. Why don't you take Democrat up to see your father?"

I lifted my squirming puppy and carried him over my shoulder like a burlap sack of feed corn. At the top of the stairs, I stopped at the gate and called out, "Dad, it's me, Barry." I could hear some song playing on The Nashville Network. Music videos and cartoons were the extent of my father's TV attention span. "Dad," I repeated. Alerting him that you were about to enter his space seemed to reduce his spontaneous anxiety.

As I unlatched the baby gate, I heard the faint response, "Barry?" and couldn't tell if Dad was questioning whether it was me or whether "Barry" was an unfamiliar word. With his Alzheimer's, he had good days and bad days.

My father sat in his easy chair with a half glass of iced tea on the end table beside him.

I stepped in front of the screen and gave a little wave. "It's me, Barry."

He looked up and smiled. "Barry," he repeated. Then the smile broadened into a grin. "Democrat," he said. Today was a good day.

The puppy wriggled at hearing his name. I set him on the floor and he bounded into my father's lap, both of them oblivious to the fact that Democrat's days as a lapdog were over.

"Do you want your tea?" I pointed to the glass.

He shook his head and I made sure one less item could be knocked to the floor by Democrat's tail.

"Then I'll take this down to Mom."

Dad nodded, but his mind was on the adoring dog licking his face. As unruly as Democrat was, he had a sense that something was different about my father. Democrat heeded Dad's short commands to get down or jump up much better than anyone else's. My girlfriend claimed he was a good candidate for a pet therapy dog at the hospital where she was a surgeon. Canine candy stripers are eagerly awaited by kids in need of cheering up.

Downstairs, Mom set out four places at the kitchen table. "Wayne's going to join us for supper. He couldn't resist my rhubarb pie."

"Rats. Less for me."

"I baked two. Wayne only knows about one."

I gave Mom a grateful kiss on the cheek. "Dad and Democrat are guarding each other. I'm going to check on Mr. Eban." I opened the door to the business part of our funeral home. "Give me about a five minute warning."

The embalming room, which we always referred to as the operating room, was on a separate wing of the house. The body of Y'Grok Eban lay on the stainless steel table discreetly covered by a sheet. I folded the sheet back to his waist and examined Uncle Wayne's work.

Y'Grok had been around sixty, a Montagnard from the central highlands of Vietnam. I didn't know much about Montagnards, other than they had been staunch allies with the U.S., particularly in support of our Special Forces troops that had operated in the central highlands during the war. My friend, Sheriff Tommy Lee Wadkins, had direct experience with their courage. "They saved my sorry ass," was his succinct comment.

According to Tommy Lee, the man lying before me had been instrumental in getting a number of downed pilots and ambushed platoons to safety. Soldiers don't forget those who laid their lives on the line for them, and news of Y'Grok's death had spread rapidly through the military veteran's community. No less than a U.S. senator, a three-star general, and a Hollywood movie star had planned on attending this funeral.

I lifted one of Y'Grok's hands. The skin around the nails was a little lighter where my uncle had scrubbed them, but it was less noticeable than ink stains.

When preparing a body for burial, we were sensitive to having the deceased look as natural as possible for the comfort of the family. If we didn't know the person, a recent photo was our best aid. We had no pictures of Y'Grok and were unfamiliar with the ethnic subtleties of the Montagnard race. Tommy Lee had told me they had darker skin than the majority Vietnamese population. They also lacked the skin folds around the eyes common to most Asians. This man looked more like a dark skinned Polynesian. Uncle Wayne had been careful to control the concentration of embalming fluid so that the skin didn't appear discolored.

I slid the sheet away from his thighs to check the incision points where the fluid had been injected. The cuts were neatly sutured. Then I noticed a tattoo on his right thigh. *Viet* was handwritten and the number *2000* centered above it. Both would have been upside down if the man were standing. I lifted the sheet from the left leg and discovered more tattoos. The word *Nam* and a circle of letters were upside down on that thigh. I moved the leg for a better look.

"Barry?" Mom's voice came through the intercom. "Would you get your father? Supper's on the table."

I replaced the sheet and turned out the light.

After a full meal, complete with two slices of rhubarb pie, I spent a quiet evening watching cartoons with Dad.

A little after ten, I closed the door to the guest bedroom. The shelves along the wall still bore some of the trappings from when the room had been mine—model cars, sports trophies, and school pictures. Democrat had a dog cushion on the floor at the foot of the bed. I kept him with me so he wouldn't be tempted to wander into my parents' bedroom. The last thing I needed was Mom or Dad tripping over a dog if they got up during the night.

I slipped between the cool sheets wearing only my underwear. Early April was still too soon for sleeping with open windows, but in a few weeks, I would enjoy a night breeze laced with the scent of honeysuckle. With such pleasant thoughts, I fell asleep.

Democrat's whine pulled me back to consciousness. I checked the clock radio. 2:55 a.m. "Democrat," I whispered. "Quiet." The puppy whimpered at the reprimand and started scratching the door. He had never acted that way before, even at my cabin, where plenty of wildlife roamed outside the walls.

I got out of bed, concerned that he might be desperately trying to adhere to his housebreaking training. I could hardly discipline him for an accident if I refused to let him out.

Not bothering to dress or grab a robe, I followed Democrat into the hall. He pawed at the webbing of the child's gate. I didn't want him to outrun me down the stairs, so I picked him up and released the latch spring.

The kitchen table and counters were barely visible in the moonlight. As I walked across the cold linoleum, I heard a scraping noise coming from the operating room. Democrat gave a sharp yip.

If we had burglars, I didn't know if I wanted to confront them, or start shouting to scare them off. I decided to investigate further before waking Mom and Dad.

The back hallway to the operating room was pitch black. I stepped slowly, keeping my eyes on the moonlit seam of the door ahead. Democrat yelped again, and I thought I heard a footstep. When I reached the door, I hesitated. The only sound was the infrequent drip from a worn faucet.

"Sshhh," I whispered, and set Democrat down. Then I turned the doorknob. I eased into the room, quickly searching the shadows for an intruder.

I flipped on the overhead light. I was afraid of who might be in the room. I was stunned by who wasn't. Y'Grok Eban's body was gone. The empty table registered for a split-second, and then Democrat lunged past me. Before I could move, someone slammed the open door into my head, knocking me backwards. Democrat gave one growl and then a high-pitched yelp. The puppy's body flew across my field of blurred vision like a football kicked through the goalposts. I staggered toward the doorway, a shout for help rising in my throat. A dark figure came from nowhere, blocking my retreat. A black ski mask hid all but the pale bridge of a nose and cold brown eyes. I threw up my arms to ward off another blow.

I never saw my attacker's hands move. A lightning punch to my stomach scattered my solar plexus in a thousand directions, and the call for help transformed into a whoosh of air as my lungs emptied. I struggled forward, trying to get past the attacker to the outside door. I saw a shimmer of moonlight reflecting off the curve of a dark metal fender. Cold air hit my face and I desperately tried to fill my lungs. Then my feet tangled with an unseen barricade on the threshold to safety. In an instant I knew I was walking on top of a body.

Two hands gripped my shoulders and spun me around. The world kept spinning as the assailant threw me back into the room. I saw a flash of silver rushing toward me and felt the impact of the embalming table smashing against my forehead. I clutched at the cold stainless steel surface but my hands skidded along, unable to stop my momentum. I fell to my knees, my lungs burning and blood blinding my eyes. Then a burst of white light exploded in my head.

Chapter Two

"Barry?"

From somewhere above came the frantic voice of my mother. I opened my eyes and saw the blurred pattern of a worn hardwood floor. Splotches of red broke the tongue-in-groove lines. I tried to speak but all that came from my mouth was a groan.

"Don't try to move. An ambulance is on the way."

An ambulance? For Y'Grok? But he's dead. Then my head cleared enough for me to feel the pain and I realized I was lying facedown on the operating room floor in a pool of blood. My blood.

"Democrat?" I whispered.

"He's okay. His barking woke me. Someone shut him in the supply closet. I've put him in the hall."

I heard a pitiful whine and scratching at the door. I felt like I'd been run over by an eighteen-wheeler, but I couldn't just lie there. I struggled to my knees and blood dripped into my eyes. I'd hit the table hard enough to split my forehead. The gash was painful to touch.

I explored the back of my head and discovered an ostrich had laid an egg. The throbbing lump seemed on the verge of hatching.

Mom was leaning over me, her face etched with concern. "I called Tommy Lee and Susan."

"Get me a chair. I feel woozy."

"Maybe you should just lie there till the ambulance arrives."

"No. If Tommy Lee gets here first, he'll draw a chalk outline around me."

Mom brought a straight-back chair from the corner and set it behind me. "Want me to help you?"

"Just steady the chair." I crawled backwards on my hands and knees, eased to a crouch, and then raised up enough to fall into the seat. Mom grabbed my shoulder to steady me as the room spun around. I took a couple of deep breaths.

Mom looked at the blood on the floor. "If you're okay to sit, I'll clean this up."

"No. Don't touch anything. This is a crime scene."

Her hand trembled. "Oh, Barry, you could have been killed."

I heard the distant wail of a siren. "Put Democrat in the backyard. Keep him away from here. Then we're going out in the hall. I don't want the paramedics destroying any evidence."

"Yes, dear." She patted my arm. "You've never stopped being a policeman, have you."

"I guess I can't help it." As Mom turned to go, I added, "And don't say anything about Y'Grok Eban."

Mom closed the door, leaving me alone to stare at the empty table. In the eight decades of Clayton and Clayton's history, no one had ever lost a body. We weren't a dry cleaners or shoe repair shop giving credit for missing items.

The siren grew louder. This would be a trip the EMTs would remember. How often does someone get transported from a funeral home back to the hospital?

"You might have a slight scar, but in a few years, people will think it's another wrinkle." Susan Miller clipped the suture and stepped back to admire her work.

My forehead tingled from the numbing injection. The only consolation was gazing into Susan's beautiful brown eyes as she stared at her patient. Then her concentration softened and I became Barry the boyfriend. She leaned over and kissed me gently on the lips.

"Nice bedside manner," I said. "We'll have to do this more often."

"Dinner and a movie are more my style. I'm adding them to my bill."

Susan was remarkable—a general surgeon whose specific skills had quickly broken down any doubts the mountaineers might harbor against a woman doctor. After all, she'd grown up in these hills and could as easily talk to a backwoods moonshiner as a bank CEO. Her talent went beyond medical competency. She treated her patients as people first.

I'd met Susan at the graveside service for a seven-year-old girl. The child had fought a losing battle against a malignant tumor Susan had done her best to remove. Susan had shared the family's grief and as she knelt by the small coffin, I could tell that her tears flowed from the deep well of her heart.

I'm attracted to a woman with a keen mind and independent spirit. Sometimes, that independence can be too much. I know. I have one ex-wife as proof. And Susan and I have experienced our rough spots. The prior December I'd unearthed the body of a murdered man who turned out to be her old boyfriend. That discovery uncovered details about Susan she'd wanted buried forever. The fallout nearly destroyed our romance. But when two people care for each other, they should find a way to keep the spark alive. We were searching.

I cautiously touched the back of my head. "Anything I should do for this nugget?"

"Rest easy. But try to stay awake all day. You've probably got a concussion."

I laughed. "Rest easy? I just had a body stolen out from under my nose."

Susan walked over to a table in the corner of the small emergency treatment room and started writing on her clipboard. "That's why we have a sheriff, Barry, and that's probably why Tommy Lee's sitting out in the lobby." She looked up from her paperwork. "Are you ready to undergo his treatment?"

Before I could answer, the gray curtain masking us from the central nurses' station was whisked aside. A young man in a white lab coat entered. He nodded at me and then walked close to Susan. "You didn't need to come in. I'm on call."

The man looked like he'd been on call for about forty-eight hours. His dark eyes were embedded in even darker shadows, and the stubble on his face threatened to become a beard.

Susan laid her hand on his wrist. "Barry's a good friend. I would have come in even if the Surgeon General were on call."

The doctor looked at me as if I were another dog threatening his territory.

I broke the silence and held out my hand. "Barry Clayton. I had a little accident."

"Ray Chandler." His handshake was firm. "Well, you're in good hands."

"Oh, they're great hands."

Susan looked annoyed. I could mark my territory as well as the next dog.

"Nice to meet you." With no further comment, Chandler left the room, snapping the curtain shut behind him.

"Who's he?"

"A third-year resident. He helps cover for the clinic. He's good."

"And he knows it. Wonder if he's related to Raymond Chandler, the mystery writer?"

"All I know is Ray's from Akron, Ohio."

"Home of the soapbox derby. Let's hope Dr. Chandler's not moving too fast. His wheels look a little wobbly."

Susan slipped a sheet of paper off the clipboard. "You're one to talk. I'm releasing you, but you'd better cool your jets for a couple days. Want a ride?"

I looked at the clock on the wall. 5:10 a.m. This wasn't going to be a day to cool my jets. "I'd better talk to Tommy Lee. Can he come back here? It's more private than the lobby."

"Sure. But if they need the room, the nurses will boot you. I'll send him back."

"Go home and get some rest. Don't say anything about the missing body. We hope to recover it without a media frenzy. And Susan, thank you."

"Always a pleasure to stitch you up. You're my walking resumé." She stopped at the curtain before leaving. "Where're you going to be?"

"At the funeral home."

"Good. I'll call you later."

I slid off the examination table and retrieved a brown grocery bag from a corner chair. When the EMTs had arrived at the funeral home, I sent Mom hurrying for my clothes. Riding in an ambulance to the hospital in my underwear was one thing; going home in Tommy Lee's patrol car was another.

I was trying to navigate my jeans under the skimpy hospital gown when I heard a gravelly voice.

"So, you finally got caught with your pants down."

Hopping on one bare foot, I pivoted as best I could. "As usual, you got your facts wrong. I got caught with no pants at all."

Sheriff Tommy Lee Wadkins grinned. "I might have let a prisoner escape once or twice, but never a body."

Tommy Lee grabbed my arm to steady me as I fastened my jeans. His own pants were wrinkled and his orange Sheriff's Youth Athletic League sweatshirt looked like it had been salvaged from his dirty clothes hamper. He must have snatched whatever he could find in the dark. Even the band of his black eye patch cut an irregular furrow through his salt and pepper hair.

With my jeans on, I picked up my socks. "You stop at the funeral home?" I asked.

"Yes. The ambulance had just left." His one eye studied my forehead. "Must have been a nasty cut. Bled enough to paint the floor."

I sat in a chair and uncurled the socks. "Who else came with you?"

"Wakefield. He's new, but he can keep his mouth shut. And a friend flew in last night from Boston. He's staying at our house. We were in Nam together and he knew Y'Grok better than I did. Kevin Malone. He's Boston Police. Won detective of the year some time back."

"Is he in the lobby?"

"No. I left him with your mom. Figured we'd head back. I'd like you to take a look at the scene before the crime lab arrives. Reconstruct what happened."

"Sure. What about outside?"

"Reece will keep the scene secure till we've got enough daylight for a decent search. I told him to go easy on the tape."

"Thanks. Mom'll have a fit if the house looks like an Easter basket." I laced my shoes and carefully got to my feet. "Let's go."

"Need a wheelchair?"

"Not with you pushing."

The stars were still visible in the pre-dawn sky. Tommy Lee eased his cruiser through the gate of the emergency room parking lot and turned onto Blair Street. "I'll take you home the back route. Don't want the good citizens thinking I worked you over."

"I didn't know they thought you worked at all."

"Glad to see they didn't knock loose your sense of humor. So, how many jumped you?"

I thought about those harrowing few minutes in the embalming room. "I don't know. I hate to admit this, but I think it was only one guy."

The illumination from the dashboard revealed enough of Tommy Lee's face to show his surprise, but he had the courtesy not to make a joke at my expense.

"And I didn't get in a punch," I confessed. "The guy was fast and experienced. Reminded me of training sessions back at the Charlotte Police Academy."

"Well, give me the story as best you remember."

I took a deep breath. The stitched gash in my forehead began to throb. "I heard a noise in the embalming room. I wasn't sure it was a person. We have a vent in there and occasionally a bird or squirrel has fallen inside."

"What time was this?"

"Around three."

"Birds and squirrels are asleep."

"Fine. Remind me to watch more Animal Planet."

He laughed. "Don't get sore. I'm just trying to prepare you for the next time."

"The next time I'll stay in bed and phone you."

"Did you get a look at him?"

"I saw part of a face behind a ski mask. He's white, about my height, and he came dressed to be invisible."

"Did he say anything?"

"No. He just dispensed with me and went on with his business."

Tommy Lee mulled something for a few seconds. "Just because you faced one attacker doesn't mean someone else wasn't there."

A shudder ran through me. "I stepped on Y'Grok's body."

"You what?"

"In the outside doorway. I remember stumbling over his body like it was an old welcome mat. I think if there'd been more than one, they'd have already loaded the body into their vehicle."

"What vehicle?"

The scene came back to me. A moonlit fender outside the door, higher than a regular car. "He had an SUV, either black or something so dark it didn't reflect color. That's why I think he was by himself. He must have been dragging the body when he heard me coming."

Tommy Lee turned and grinned at me. "Man, you're a magnet for the bizarre. I've had plenty of cases where I've found bodies but never one where the corpse disappeared."

"Tell me. In my business, it's not the sort of thing that endears you to your customers. 'Sorry, we seem to have misplaced Uncle Henry, so we'll shave a little off the bill.' After seventy-five years, I'll be damned if I'm going to let this body snatcher destroy the good name of Clayton and Clayton."

Tommy Lee slowed the car as we approached our driveway. "You're not alone in this, Barry. When he tangled with you, he tangled with me. And when he stole Y'Grok Eban's body, he stirred up a hornet's nest that may unleash more reprisals than our little town of Gainesboro has ever seen."

"Meaning what?"

"Meaning I don't have a clue what the hell's going on, but I do know a lot of vets owe their lives to the Montagnards. They'll explode when they learn someone stole Y'Grok's body." Tommy Lee turned toward me and looked as grim as I'd ever seen him. "And you and I don't want to be caught in the middle of that firefight."

Chapter Three

In the funeral home, a man sat at the kitchen table with Mom and a pot of coffee. Like Tommy Lee, he was in his mid-fifties. He wore a green Irish-knit sweater that hung over black corduroys. Strands of gray hair curled from beneath a Boston Red Sox cap that had seen more than a few extra innings.

Mom jumped up and hurried to me. "My goodness, Barry. Do you want to lie down?" Her eyes never left my forehead.

"No. Susan said the cut's not as bad as it looks. And I should stay awake." I gestured to the clock. It was only a quarter to six. "Why don't you go back to bed? Dad will be up soon enough, and we've got a long day ahead of us." I gave a nod, prompting her to say yes.

Mom understood I wanted to talk to Tommy Lee and his friend alone. "If you're sure you're all right."

"If he starts to misbehave, I'll cuff him to the chair," Tommy Lee said.

I doubted my mother was actually comforted by Tommy Lee's assurances. Working with the sheriff had gotten me shot at more than once.

"I'm counting on Detective Malone to keep both of you out of trouble." She was only half kidding.

"That's right." Kevin Malone rose from his chair and winked at Mom. "Madam, you can depend on the Irish." His Boston accent infused each syllable, and he swept the cap from his head in a grand gesture until it rested over his heart. "At least until the bars open."

My mother looked at us and laughed. The three stooges, alive in her kitchen.

As soon as she was out the door, the smile left Kevin's face. "Can we get to it?"

"Need to sit first?" Tommy Lee asked me.

"No. I need to find Y'Grok Eban's body." I headed for the operating room with the two men close behind.

As I stepped inside the door, Kevin stopped me. "Stand where you were attacked."

"About here. I entered the room, flipped on the light, and saw the empty table."

The detective gently parted the hair on the back of my head. "Someone zapped you on the left side. Nicely done. Not what we call a blackjack shampoo where they just beat the hell out of you."

"Barry thinks there was only one guy." Tommy Lee stood beside Kevin, scanning the operating room.

I repeated the description of the early morning events. Kevin listened carefully without interrupting, and then stepped behind the door to the hall. "Y'Grok's body was only halfway outside and he knew he couldn't get away in time. You opened the door, and he hid behind it between you and the body. He wasted no energy when he attacked you. Very efficient. I'd say he could have killed you if he wanted. Any idea about the vehicle?"

"No. I'd guess an SUV, but it could have been a dark cargo van."

"They're usually light colored," Tommy Lee said.

I walked past Kevin. The outside door was still open. Splinter fragments showed how the lock had been jimmied. I stepped through the rear door onto our small loading dock. The world was cast in pre-dawn shadows of blue and gray. In the murky light, I saw no sign that anything had been left behind. The cement parking area provided no tire tracks.

I turned to Tommy Lee. "It's bright enough now. Let's check around the house."

Outside, we discovered where the security system had been breached. Somebody knew what he was doing. The phone line was arced to bypass the alarm junction so that cutting the wire didn't trigger a call to the monitoring service.

Kevin examined the neatly spliced wires. "Nice work. He must have cased the house."

"Or came well prepared," Tommy Lee added.

We walked completely around the funeral home, scouring the ground for any clues.

"Now he's done it." I led them to the edge of the driveway by the loading ramp. The freshly planted petunias were crushed and mangled. "If Uncle Wayne gets his hands on this guy, he'll choke him for sure."

Kevin stared down at the trampled flowers. "My gram would've claimed justifiable homicide. When I was a kid, I made the mistake of pouring a Guinness in her window box when I heard her coming up the stairs. Killed her petunias and I couldn't sit down for a week."

Tommy Lee examined the petunia stems. "From the way they're bent, looks like the body lay on them."

"But I'm sure I stepped on the body in the room."

"Maybe that's where the guy left Y'Grok while he opened the rear of the SUV," Kevin said.

Tommy Lee shook his head. "But why Y'Grok?"

Kevin gave Tommy Lee a look of disgust. "God damned politics is what I think. Somebody for or against the Montagnards is trying for publicity."

"This isn't Boston," Tommy Lee said. "Everything's not politics."

Kevin chuckled. "Got that right, buddy. This ain't Boston. Drove my rental car all the way from your so-called airport and not one driver flipped me the finger."

"So what am I supposed to do?" I wasn't in the mood for Bean Town humor.

Tommy Lee stepped closer. "Let's go in the house. The crime lab will be here soon. Barry, you need to just lie low and let us handle this."

"No," I said sharply. "Y'Grok's visitation and funeral are scheduled for two. I'm not telling his son over the phone that I lost his father's body."

"And you're in no condition to drive," Tommy Lee shot back. "I'm telling you we'll handle the situation. I need to talk to Y'Suom anyway to see if he's got any ideas about why somebody would do this."

I grabbed Tommy Lee's arm. "The man's father was stolen from my funeral home. I'm telling Y'Suom in person and I'm telling him now."

"Bless me, my lad, I hear some Irish blood bubbling in your voice." Kevin put his arm on my shoulder. "I'll take you to Y'Suom if you'll show me how to get there. Tommy Lee doesn't want me correcting his mistakes in front of his men anyway."

The Boston detective and southern sheriff stared at each other. I knew the look of policemen who'd been through stressful situations together. This look was different—these men had been through a war together.

"All right," Tommy Lee finally said. "Change clothes, Barry, and then you two go ahead. I'll finish processing the scene and talk to Y'Suom later." He shook his head and spoke to no one in particular. "Just doesn't make any sense. Why steal a body?"

I left them pondering the question.

Upstairs, I dressed as quietly as I could and washed my face with lukewarm water, avoiding the swollen, tender spot where Susan had stitched my forehead. I tried wearing a hat to conceal the damage, but the band cut painfully into the raw skin because the lump on the back of my head must have added at least two sizes. One look at my face would settle any doubt whether the body had been forcibly taken from me.

As I came down the stairs to the kitchen, I heard a rapping on the back porch door. Through the window, I saw a uniformed deputy standing with Archie Donovan Junior peering over his shoulder. I glanced at the red clock on the wall. Ten after seven.

"Sorry to bother you, Mr. Clayton." Deputy Wakefield touched the brim of his cap in an informal salute. "This man says it's urgent he speak with you."

Archie Junior looked like he was ready to crawl over the man's back. Then he saw my battered face. "Good God, Barry. What happened?"

"We had a break-in. I got in the way as the culprit made his escape."

"Are your mom and dad okay?"

"Yes. Sheriff Wadkins is investigating."

Archie turned to the deputy. "Meth labs. That's where y'all should look. I've read they steal embalming fluid to make that stuff. Isn't that right, Barry? They took your embalming fluid."

"No. But maybe that's what they were after. I'll mention it to Tommy Lee. Thanks for your concern. Now I'd better let you get to the office." I didn't want Archie delaying me a second longer.

Archie bit his lip, pausing before deciding to continue. "Listen, I know this isn't a good time, but I've got to talk to you about this Y'Grok Eban fellow."

He said the magic words and my heart beat faster. "Do you want to talk to Tommy Lee?" I opened the door wider and Archie stepped around Wakefield.

Archie shook his head. "What for? Is he involved in the funeral?"

I realized Archie knew nothing about the body's disappearance, but I'd made the mistake of letting him in. "Well, he knew Y'Grok from Vietnam." I pulled out a chair from the kitchen table. "I've only got a few minutes. They're waiting on my statement."

I shot a look at Wakefield, hoping he wouldn't contradict me. The deputy closed the door and returned to his post outside.

Archie sat down and I took the chair across the table.

"So what's up?"

"Barry, we've been friends how long? Twenty-six, twenty-seven years?"

"Since kindergarten." I leaned back and folded my arms across my chest, readying my defenses for what sounded like a touch for money.

"Then nearly twenty-eight years. And Barry, I really admire you. What you've done coming back here when your dad got sick."

I didn't say anything. My father wasn't going to be a ploy to soften me up.

"Barry, I've got two words for you. Just two words that can be the key to a golden opportunity."

"If you're pitching some investment, please don't say the deal's so good it's a no brainer. Those two words only mean someone doesn't have a brain."

"Good one, Barry, but you're wrong." Archie leaned forward and whispered, "Daniel Boone."

"Daniel Boone?"

"Yep."

"The TV show?"

"No, man, the man. The pioneer."

I was so astonished I uncrossed my arms and held out my hands trying to pull some sense out of Archie. "Daniel Boone is a golden opportunity?"

He grinned. "A celebrity plot. Just like Mr. Y'Grok Eban."

"I hear your two words, Archie, but you're speaking a foreign language."

He slid back his chair and stood up, too excited to stay at the table. "I went to this insurance conference last February in Frankfort, Kentucky. You know who's buried in Frankfort?"

"Daniel Boone."

"Right. But he didn't die there. I think he died out in Missouri. But after he'd been buried a good while, a cemetery in Frankfort got his kids to ship back his bones. You see, these investors had a cemetery that wasn't selling for squat, so they brought in a celebrity. Had a big festival about Daniel being planted in his native soil."

"If I remember my high school history, Daniel Boone grew up in Pennsylvania and North Carolina, Archie."

"Whatever. That's not important. What's important is the day after Daniel Boone's bones went into that floundering graveyard, plots started selling like hotcakes. People wanted to be buried in the same cemetery as Daniel Boone."

"What's that have to do with Y'Grok Eban?"

Archie walked to my chair and stood over me like a teacher lecturing a slow learner. "Y'Grok Eban's a hero. I read Melissa Bigham's article in the *Vista*. And a bunch of celebrities are coming to Gainesboro for this afternoon's funeral. This is big. I've talked to the mayor and he agrees it would be great if we could have the burial up at Heaven's Gate Gardens."

I couldn't take Archie leaning over me so I stood up and put a little distance between us. "That cemetery up on Bell Ridge? It's not even finished."

"But we'll give him a free plot. We have a section ready enough. We can get some publicity shots of the celebrities standing around his final resting place."

The light went on. "Who besides you has a financial stake in this venture? The mayor?"

"Yes. And his brother-in-law. We've told you all about it. You agreed to help."

I felt my anger boil to the surface. "I agreed to take a look at the cemetery when you had something to show. I agreed to mention the cemetery as an option to families who need a burial plot. But I'm not hawking graves and burying Y'Grok Eban in a god-damned coonskin hat."

I heard a sound behind me and turned to discover Mom standing in the doorway from the stairs. She looked like she wanted to retreat, but couldn't with both Archie and me staring at her. "Sorry. I heard Archie's voice and was checking to see if you wanted me to fix something."

"No, he wants me to fix something, but he's not going to get it. We were just going to finish our conversation outside."

I opened the door, crossed the back porch and headed down the driveway. Deputy Wakefield sat in his car at the entrance.

Archie's BMW was parked alongside. I figured the only way to get rid of my unwanted guest was to lead him to his car.

He jogged up beside me. "Look, Barry. I hate to spring this on you at the last minute. The mayor and I met last night and decided the town could really benefit from the publicity. The cemetery could become a major tourist attraction."

I stopped and stared at him. "It's out of the question. First of all, Y'Grok wanted his remains returned to Vietnam. His son has made that clear. Second, the memorial service isn't going to be attended by as many celebrities as you think. Some of them aren't going to make it in time for the funeral. Your big star-studded event isn't even going to happen."

Archie took a few short gasping breaths like the oxygen had just been sucked from his lungs. "But why don't they wait? Let everybody get here?"

"Because we're doing what's best for Y'Grok's son, Y'Suom, and the resettled Montagnards who'll drive here for the service. Senator Millen is trying to get permission from the Vietnamese government for the return of Y'Grok's remains. Until his remains are returned to Vietnam, he'll be buried at Grace Lutheran. Sheriff Wadkins got him a plot there."

"What if his remains aren't returned?"

I knew Archie meant returned to Vietnam, but I was so concerned about Y'Grok's body being returned to the funeral home that his question caught me off guard. After an awkward moment, I stepped closer and tried to appear sympathetic. "Look, Archie, I'll mention your offer to Y'Suom this morning, but that's it. Frankly, I think you'll have better luck convincing Frankfort to dig up Daniel Boone."

Chapter Four

Kevin Malone opened the passenger door to my jeep and helped me into the seat. I welcomed his assistance. The determination to see Y'Grok's son was fading as the pain in my head increased. I'd popped a couple Tylenol and hoped they'd kick in before I had to face the music.

For the first few minutes, I spoke only to give directions. Y'Suom had been invited by Senator Ryan Millen to stay with him at Asheville's legendary Grove Park Inn. We had a thirty minute drive. Tommy Lee said he'd call the senator to let him know we were on the way and ask Millen to make sure Y'Suom was there. Breaking the news would be my responsibility.

As we merged onto I-26, I reclined my seatback to a more comfortable position. At seven-thirty, traffic was light, the few cars scattered among the eighteen-wheelers bound for Tennessee. "Follow the signs for I-240. Then we'll take exit 5B. It's about fifteen miles."

Kevin looked out his side window. "Pretty."

A touch of gold brushed the tops of the mountain ridges. Although the days were growing longer, the time between first light and the sun's actual appearance would be more than an hour. The Appalachians threw up several thousand feet of extra barrier to scale.

"Must be a great place to grow up." Kevin's gaze returned to the road.

"Yeah. Even though we lived in town, my buddies and I could ride our bikes to ponds and creeks in less than fifteen minutes. I was always bringing home snakes and turtles."

"I grew up in Dorchester. That's a section of Boston where the only snakes I saw were hanging out on the street corners, running numbers or pushing dope."

"We've got our share. Meth labs have replaced moon shiners, and Tommy Lee's busted some Christmas tree growers for squeezing in a little marijuana between the rows."

"So that's why Santa smokes a pipe." Kevin laughed. "I tease Tommy Lee about policing Mayberry, but he's been shot at more times than I have."

"You never know what you're going to walk up on. Some of the wildlife totes AK-47s."

"Tommy Lee says if people ever stop dying, he'd like to get you in the department. Maybe even get you to run for sheriff when he hangs up his badge."

"Sheriff?" The idea startled me.

"Yeah. He's never mentioned the possibility?" Kevin gunned the jeep and zipped around a UPS truck struggling up the grade. "Peppy. I could use one of these to climb over Boston potholes."

"I can't see Tommy Lee ever retiring."

Kevin looked at me and shrugged. "We all lose our edge. That's when the job really gets dangerous. Tommy Lee doesn't talk much, but he's always thinking. Me, I'm just the opposite. Ted Williams, the greatest ballplayer the Red Sox ever had, said 'If you don't think too good, don't think too much.' He could've been talking to me."

"The detective of the year?"

"Lucky break. On patrol in Nam, Tommy Lee used to say even a blind hog finds an acorn now and then. That's me. Root around long enough and I'm bound to find something." Kevin glanced at me. "Don't tell Tommy Lee I mentioned you running for sheriff." He paused. "You know it's not a bad deal. You could shoot them and then bury them. The ones you only wing, your girlfriend could patch up."

I wondered how much of my life quiet Tommy Lee had told this guy. "So, you've known the sheriff a long time." I was anxious to change the subject.

"Not sure of the exact years, but Lieutenant Tommy Lee Wadkins had two eyes."

His reference to Tommy Lee's war injury piqued my curiosity. Vietnam was one subject Tommy Lee rarely mentioned. "Were you there?"

"Oh, yeah. He was my platoon leader. As a matter of fact, he lost his eye on a mission trying to make contact with Montagnards. They were our best source of reconnaissance."

"What happened?"

"Somebody told the VC we were in the area. Our Special Forces unit was in the central highlands working with the Montagnards to break the Ho Chi Minh trail. I mean the trail wasn't an expressway like this, but Charlie had definite routes for his supplies and we wanted to know when and where movement occurred. We moved from village to village picking up information."

"The Montagnards were your eyes and ears?"

"A helluva lot more. Arms and legs and brains as well. They're the indigenous people of the highlands. Like them." He pointed to a billboard for Harrad's Casino on the nearby Cherokee Indian reservation. "They were the Cherokees and the Vietnamese were the white settlers. Montagnards. Means mountain people. That's what the French called them. We called them Yards. They call themselves Degas."

"So the Viet Cong were their enemy as well?"

"And we were their hope, just like the French had been before us. They got screwed over twice, and now they're still paying the price."

"Did one of them tell the North Vietnamese where you were?"

"Only if he was tortured. Or about to see his wife and kids executed." Kevin took his eyes off the road to look at me. "No, these people would never have betrayed us. It's just not part of their culture. Would that we'd been as loyal to them."

I didn't say anything. The vision of an empty embalming table filled my mind. I'd been entrusted with the responsibility for a loved one and I'd failed that trust.

"It was probably a Viet Cong scout who saw us in the area," Kevin continued. "Our platoon walked into an ambush of North Vietnamese regulars. First man killed was the radio op. Hell of a firefight. Y'Grok was our guide. He crawled through the storm of bullets to get to the radio. Called in our position to our choppers."

"He knew how to work your radio?"

"Work it? Hell, the man could have built it. Y'Grok's father had been a radio op with the French before us. Y'Grok grew up in the resistance. He was the most seasoned fighter in the bunch."

"Could the choppers get to you?" The pain in my head was forgotten as Kevin's account pulled me into the action.

"No. Y'Grok gave the coordinates for a clearing a quarter mile away. Yards are slash and burn farmers and he knew all the fields in the area."

I noticed we were passing everything on the highway. Kevin was so caught up in his story that he was driving like we were escaping the enemy. "State troopers patrol this section pretty heavily," I warned.

"Sorry." Kevin eased off the accelerator. "And they might not give a Boston cop a courtesy pass. State boys usually eat and sleep by the book."

"They'll give you five over the limit." I pointed to the cruise control button. "You're safe at seventy."

Kevin made the adjustment and continued his story. "Tommy Lee knew we had to break through and reach the evacuation point. But a spot clear enough for the pickup would be clear enough for shooting us. We had to stay pinned down until we could make a run and reach the pickup spot just as the choppers arrived."

"Y'Grok had to guide you."

"And tote the radio. What was left of the platoon made a concentrated charge, the point men firing, then dropping back as their magazines emptied and others took the lead. No one dared stop to reload. Tommy Lee and Pete Slavinsky stayed back and protected our rear. I climbed on a chopper and looked back to see Tommy Lee and Pete as they broke for the hovering birds. Then Pete went down. Tommy Lee wouldn't leave him. As he threw Pete over his shoulder, a chunk of grenade shrapnel took off half his face. The stubborn son of a bitch still held onto Pete and staggered toward me. I jumped down and helped lift Pete aboard and then tried to push Tommy Lee ahead of me. 'You get in,' he gurgled through blood and mangled flesh. Hands of my buddies hoisted me up. Then every man on the bird reached down to grab our Tommy Lee. He was still firing as the chopper rose and we pulled him in."

"That's why he says Y'Grok saved his sorry ass."

"If not for Y'Grok and Tommy Lee, our whole platoon would have been wiped out."

"And Slavinsky?"

Kevin shook his head. "Died in the air. Tommy Lee crawled back beside him. Pete's last words were 'you damn fool.' He was right. If Tommy Lee hadn't stopped for a dying man, he wouldn't be wearing that eye patch today. But, men do foolish things in war. Guess there's a thin line separates a fool from a hero."

"Tommy Lee said you knew Y'Grok better than he did."

"I returned to the central hills with him. We set up a network with the Yards to get downed pilots out. Eventually the operation was taken over by military intelligence. That's how Franklin Talbert got involved."

"And now he's a big movie star."

"That's what his press clippings say. Action hero. Well, he was pretty damn skittish when I knew him."

"How'd the network operate?"

"I could tell you, Barry. But then I'd have to kill you."

Kevin held back his laugh just long enough to make me nervous.

The Grove Park Inn sat on the side of Sunset Mountain over-looking a golf course. In the distance, the skyline of Asheville rose above the trees.

The huge, rambling stone structure had originally been built in the early 1900s as a grand resort hotel for the rich and famous. The likes of Harry Houdini, Will Rogers, and F. Scott Fitzgerald once graced its halls. Today it enjoyed a renaissance with a new multimillion dollar spa and a manmade waterfall that tumbled down between stone garden terraces.

Kevin pulled the jeep up to the main entrance. "Not too shabby. I'll let you out and save you the walk. Looks like I'll have to park down the hill."

Even though it was only eight o'clock, the guest parking lot offered no spaces. A ground crew bustled around flowerbeds, setting out spring plants that dwarfed Uncle Wayne's puny petunias. I stepped out of the jeep. "See you inside."

A doorman smiled, and then tried to suppress the panic flood-ing his face. My fresh stitches and bruises were not the sort of look that appeared on their brochure: The Grove Park Inn—visited by eight presidents since Woodrow Wilson, and the Frankenstein monster.

"Can I help you, sir?" The doorman looked worried about me and the guests I might scare.

I glanced at his name tag. "Thank you, Craig. I'm expected by Senator Millen. My colleague is parking our car, and then we'll check with the front desk."

"I'll be glad to take care of it. Why don't you sit by the fire? What name should I announce?"

"Barry Clayton and Kevin Malone."

"Very good, sir. Please follow me."

The young man escorted me into the mammoth lobby. At each end, massive stone fireplaces towered to the ceiling three stories overhead. The scent of wood smoke hung in the air. The doorman led me through the maze of small tables to one near the hearth on the right.

"This should be comfortable," he said. "The fire takes the edge off the morning chill. In the spring, it's cooler in here than outside."

And darker too. The better to keep me unobserved. "I'm not sure my friend will see me."

"I'll direct him, sir. And I'll notify Senator Millen's staff you're here."

His staff? My tax dollars at work. I wondered what federal budget this little excursion was coming out of.

For a few minutes, I watched the guests queue to be seated on the breakfast patio. Their attire ranged from designer to designless. At least the hotel was exclusive enough that it didn't need to post a notice, "No Shoes, No Service."

"Jesus, Mary, and Joseph."

I turned to find Kevin gazing at the sheer size of the lobby.

"If Patsy's cooking weren't so damn good, I'd dump Tommy Lee and try to ride on Ryan Millen's nickel."

"Quite a place," I agreed. "There're even guest elevators inside the two fireplaces."

"That's some bar." Kevin gestured to the fine wood piece in front of the hearth across the lobby. He sat down in the chair beside me. "I could get use to this."

"Who's the senator got with him?" I asked. "The doorman said he'd notify his staff."

"Probably an aide. I spoke to Ryan last night after he got in. Stormy's aide is here as well."

"Stormy?"

"General Harold Weathers. He was Captain Weathers in Nam, but everybody just called him Stormy."

"I thought he couldn't get out of Iraq."

Kevin shook his head. "He got delayed and can't make this afternoon's service. His aide came ahead to represent him. Stormy's due in tonight. I'm told he'll probably fly into Fort Jackson in Columbia."

"That's a couple hours away."

"What's he care? His aide will probably meet him. I bet it's been so long since Stormy's been behind the wheel of a car, he'd have to get someone to show him how to start the engine."

"Excuse me." Craig the doorman walked to our table. "The senator is ready to receive you."

"You hear that?" Kevin looked at me. "Receive us." He turned to the doorman. "Well, la de da. Can you whisk us up the chimney to him?"

Craig looked to me for help.

"He wants to ride in the fireplace elevator."

"Yeah. I'm from that backwoods town of Boston. Only smoke and Santa Claus go up our chimney."

"Of course," Craig said. "But I thought the Red Sox season also goes up in smoke every year."

Kevin grinned. "I like this guy. Not enough to tip him, but I like this guy."

Craig led us around the hearth where an elevator door was embedded in the stone. "The senator's rooms are in the Vanderbilt wing."

Kevin winked at me. "Rooms no less."

We rode to the top floor and followed the doorman to the end of the hall.

"This is the senator's suite. Would you like me to wait and see if anyone would like breakfast?"

Kevin dug deep in the front pocket of his corduroy pants and extracted a money clip. "No thanks." He peeled off a five. "And I was just kidding about the tip."

Craig took the money with a nod. "I wasn't kidding about the Red Sox."

"Yeah? Good, cause I was gonna give you a ten."

They both laughed and the doorman left.

"Nothing like a smartass to make me feel at home." Kevin gave two solid raps on the door. "None of that groveling southern hospitality for me."

Senator Ryan Millen opened the door. I recognized him from TV and the picture that accompanied Melissa Bigham's article in the previous day's *Gainesboro Vista*.

"Kevin, you old Irish windbag, it's good to see you." Millen grabbed the detective in a bear hug, pounding him enthusiastically on the back.

"Careful. These days I break easy."

The men stepped apart and Kevin turned to me. "This is Barry Clayton from the funeral home in Gainesboro."

"Ryan Millen." The senator shook my hand. "Thank you for all you've done."

Wait till he heard what I'd done. The senator must have been over six feet two inches tall. His thick gray hair was razor cut and well combed. He wore a blue oxford shirt with the sleeves rolled up and looked like he'd been awake for hours. We walked into the suite and I saw a laptop and scattered folders on a desk in the corner. Maybe tax dollars were at work, at least for his constituents in Idaho.

Senator Millen enjoyed the reputation of being a no-nonsense, non-ideological Republican. He was someone liberal Democrats found hard to hate and conservative Republicans hard to embrace. The pundits occasionally mentioned his name as presidential material, but he disavowed any interest in such aspirations.

The senator also had a potential problem. When his jet fighter had gone down in Vietnam, he had sustained a head injury that permanently damaged the muscles of one eye. Unlike Tommy Lee, he hadn't lost his sight, but his left eye turned inward and didn't align properly. While his natural charisma carried him through his personal appearances and dealings in the senate, television magnified this physical anomaly, making him look odd at best and shifty at worse. In an election age where image is everything and substance is secondary to the packaging, Ryan Millen was a mass marketing challenge.

"Sit down." Millen swept his hand to the sofa. "Would you like some coffee?"

"Black," Kevin said.

"No thanks." I didn't want anything to take the edge off the Tylenol.

Millen's gaze fixed on me. "What happened to you?"

"That's why we're here. I need to talk to Y'Suom."

"If you've had an accident and require some extra help, just say the word."

"Nothing like that, sir." I sat on the sofa and said nothing further.

Millen hesitated, like he wanted to pursue the matter and then decided not to. He walked to his desk and picked up the telephone. "Bruce, bring Y'Suom to my suite." He replaced the receiver on the cradle and walked to the kitchenette in the back of the room. He poured coffee from an ivory carafe into a china cup. No Styrofoam in the Grove Park.

"So, how you been, Kev? Heard you're the Sherlock Holmes of Boston." Millen handed Kevin the cup and pulled up a chair.

"I got lucky on a couple cases. Then you get so old they feel obliged to give you something just for breathing."

"You guys had any anti-terrorism training?"

"Some coordinated exercises with the fire department, and I get copied on all the Homeland Security suspect sheets."

"Hell of a mess. It's like we've got the Viet Cong living in our own neighborhoods. No battle front."

"About the size of it," Kevin agreed. "And it doesn't help when we betray our friends."

The statement brought a flush of color to the senator's face. Before he could reply, a knock came from the door.

"Come in," he said.

The electronic key clicked and a man stepped inside. He wore a dark blue suit with a pale blue shirt and burgundy tie. Seven-thirty in the morning and he looked ready to face network cameras. I pegged him at close to my own age—thirty-two or thirty-three at the most. Immediately behind him came a younger, shorter man. His dark brown skin and ink black hair were a stark contrast to the first man's pale complexion and blond curls. Whether it was simply ethnic traits or a strong family resemblance, Y'Suom bore the visage of the father. The tightening in my stomach caught me off guard. I dreaded what was about to happen.

Senator Millen rose to his feet, and Kevin and I followed.

"Good morning, Y'Suom," Millen said. "This is Kevin Malone. He served with your father in the resistance."

I noticed Millen didn't say Vietnam War. Kevin's eyebrows arced slightly at the phrase and he smiled at the senator. Then he walked over and vigorously shook the Montagnard's hand.

"Y'Suom. You're the image of your father and that's a comfort. He was a great man."

Y'Suom nodded. He was obviously struggling to keep his composure. His military fatigues were wrinkle free and his black boots spit shined for inspection.

Millen nodded toward the man in the suit. "And my communications director, Bruce Nickles."

The impeccably dressed staffer extended his hand. "A pleasure to meet you, Mr. Malone."

"Kevin, please."

"And this is Barry Clayton, the funeral director." Millen turned to the young Montagnard. "Y'Suom, I believe you've talked with Barry on the phone."

We had spoken a few days before through a military communications patch. Y'Suom was in the army stationed in South Korea. The Specialist Five had received humanitarian leave to return for his father's service. He had asked me to coordinate arrangements through the Lutheran social worker who had resettled many of the Montagnards.

"Thank you for your help." His voice was a mixture of southern and Asian accents.

The door to the hallway hadn't closed and a second military man slipped inside. He wore a more formal uniform. Having never served in the military, I had no idea of his rank other than that the numerous ribbons and insignias adorning his chest and sleeves signified officer status.

"And here's Captain J.R. Randall. He's a personal aide to General Weathers and plans to represent him at this afternoon's service. It's a shame Stormy got delayed after the Montagnard community made such elaborate plans."

Our own introductions were repeated, and then Millen turned to me. "I understand from Tommy Lee you've information that you wanted to bring in person."

Instead of talking with Y'Suom alone, I faced an audience of five. I would have to make the best of the situation. "Would everyone please take a seat?"

Kevin steered Y'Suom to the sofa and sat beside him. The other men settled into chairs. I decided to remain standing.

"Around three this morning, we had a break-in at the funeral home. As you can see, I had a personal encounter with the intruder and came out second best."

"Is the burglar in custody?" Captain Randall asked.

"No. I was jumped and knocked unconscious. The man got away. Our sheriff, Tommy Lee Wadkins, is investigating." I paused and took a breath.

"Do we need to move the visitation?" Senator Millen asked. "Perhaps there's a room at the church."

I shook my head, and then focused on Y'Suom. The soldier stared at me with dawning comprehension.

"It's my father," Y'Suom whispered.

"Yes. Your father's body was stolen. I'm so sorry."

"Stolen," Millen shouted. "How could that happen?"

Kevin jumped in. "Ryan, I personally investigated the scene. The guy knew what he was doing. He disarmed the security system including the monitoring relay. And Barry's lucky he wasn't killed."

Captain Randall quickly rose from his chair. "I guess we know who the hell's behind this."

"The Vietnamese." Y'Suom's voice remained low. "They did this thing."

"We don't know that." Nickles got up and placed his hand on Y'Suom's shoulder.

"The hell we don't." Randall glowered at Millen. "General Weathers will blow sky high when I tell him. This is where your coddling has gotten us. I hope you're satisfied."

"Now hold on," Nickles said. "The senator—"

"The senator can speak for himself," interrupted Millen.

"But can he think for himself," Randall snapped.

I'd been worried about the son's reaction. I never dreamed an angry shouting match would ensue among the others.

"Wait. Wait." The sudden power in Y'Suom's voice got everyone's attention. "My father would not want you fighting. You are his friends."

His words sobered them.

"You're right." Randall sat back down. "I shouldn't have flown off the handle."

"Why do you think it's the Vietnamese?" I asked.

"They don't want to accept my father's remains. And they don't want to have to refuse Senator Millen's request that my father be returned to his land. But no body, no problem."

"Y'Suom," Millen said softly. "I'm very upset this has happened and I'll do whatever I can to help. But I don't believe the Vietnamese are behind this. Believe me, they want as little attention drawn to your father as possible. Even a suspicion of their involvement would be politically embarrassing. They would never risk it. There must be another reason."

Y'Suom looked at Randall. "Raven."

Randall shook his head. "Like I said last night, that was a long time ago."

"Right," Millen agreed.

"Raven?" I didn't know what they were talking about.

Millen looked at Kevin.

Kevin got off the sofa and walked over to me. "Just a code name. One of our old missions."

"The one Tommy Lee got wounded on?"

Before he could answer, Millen interrupted, "So, Kevin, what do you think we should do?"

"Nothing. Whoever took the body wants us to send up a hue and cry."

"We say nothing?" Nickles fidgeted in his chair. "What do I tell the press on behalf of the senator?"

"This isn't about me," Millen chided. "It's about Y'Suom and his father."

Y'Suom looked at me. For the first time I saw the tears in his eyes.

"You have taken wounds for my family, Mr. Clayton. What do you think I should do?"

No less than a U.S senator, an aide to a three-star general, and Boston's detective of the year looked at me for an answer.

Chapter Five

My phone doesn't actually ring. I leave the setting on vibrate to avoid embarrassing interruptions in the middle of eulogies. But standing in front of the five men, I felt like the phone's flashing screen was a searchlight. I snatched the instrument from my belt and checked the incoming number. Tommy Lee.

Kevin saw the number. "Better answer."

Tommy Lee's question was short. "Any decisions?"

"We're just starting to talk. Any leads?"

"The state mobile crime lab won't be here for another hour. I wanted you to know a caravan has arrived at the funeral home."

I looked at my watch. Fifteen minutes after eight. "Caravan of what?"

"Montagnards mostly. I guess over twenty cars. Those from the eastern part of the state drove all night. There's some vets as well. One guy's out in your front yard waving a Rolling Thunder banner."

"Rolling Thunder?"

Kevin and Millen exchanged a glance.

"Special Forces unit. Some vets retired around Fort Bragg and are active with the Yards. I'll talk to them as soon as you've made a plan." Tommy Lee paused. "Your mother's a little bewildered by everything."

Poor Mom. She'd feel like she had to feed them. And Dad. What would go through his shattered mind when he looked out the window and saw a convoy of Asians camped on the lawn with battle flags flying? Fortunately Mom had gotten all of the guns out of the house soon after his diagnosis.

"Hang on the line. You might as well be part of this discussion." I placed the phone on the coffee table where Tommy Lee could hear the conversation.

I briefed the others.

"They came?" Y'Suom asked. "They came for my father?"

"Yes, but that doesn't change the fact that your father's body is missing and these people will want to pay their respects." I'd heard enough about Montagnards to know they were primarily Christian, but I wondered if some of the rituals I'd observed while conducting a Cambodian Buddhist funeral were part of a broader Asian culture. That visitation had included taking pictures of the deceased in the casket.

I turned to Captain Randall. "When is General Weathers scheduled to arrive?"

"About eight tonight. I've got a military vehicle from Fort Jackson, and I'm going back to meet him. He planned to have breakfast tomorrow with Y'Suom and then we're scheduled to take a commercial flight to Dulles to brief a congressional committee."

"I'm the chair of that committee," Millen said.

"And Franklin Talbert?"

"His publicist called me." Bruce Nickles made no effort to hide his disdain. "Talbert's scheduled to get into the Asheville airport tomorrow afternoon. That's the quickest he can be here from his shoot in Australia. The publicist wanted me to give Talbert's regards to the senator and the general."

"I can tell you what General Weathers will do with his regards." Randall's tone was sarcastic.

"He's coming to see Y'Suom." Millen glared at Randall. "Not me or Stormy."

"He's coming late so he doesn't have to share the stage," Randall grumbled. "That's what he's doing."

I saw the opportunity. "Senator Millen, can you possibly slide back your hearing two days?"

"Well, we were working around Stormy's schedule."

"Now you and the general both have a compelling reason to postpone," I said. "We could reschedule Y'Grok's service for Thursday. I can announce that Y'Suom has decided to delay the service because a number of his father's friends aren't able to arrive in time."

"We really can't sit here for three days," Nickles said. "The senator has a very busy schedule."

I put the phone to my ear. "What do you think, Tommy Lee?"

"I think Ryan should remember what Y'Grok did for him. The lives that man saved are worth him sitting on his fat ass for a few days, and I expect him to assist my investigation any way he can. Tell him that."

Kevin was grinning at me. He had a good idea of Tommy Lee's opinion.

I looked squarely at Senator Millen. "The sheriff might need your help. He thinks what Y'Grok did for you merits a couple days of your time."

Bruce Nickles looked at his boss, waiting for a cue.

"And he's absolutely right," Millen replied. "Although I expect you cleaned him up a bit."

I stepped closer to Y'Suom. "Is that okay with you?"

"What about the people who have come? The ones who drove all night? They're why I scheduled the funeral for today."

"Tommy Lee and I'll work something out."

"If the senator is delaying the briefing, then General Weathers should be fine, especially when he hears the real reason." Captain Randall cleared his throat. "I'd like to make one suggestion. I don't think Bruce should notify Talbert's publicist. If Talbert does have a personal agenda, I don't think we should give him another reason to delay his arrival."

"A good point," Nickles agreed. "But he could hear some other way."

Randall shook his head. "I doubt it. He's on a movie set and then he'll be on a plane. Once he's in the air, he can't turn back."

"What about the media?" Kevin asked.

Millen turned to Nickles. "Bruce, you can help."

Nickles smiled. "Let's play it like Barry suggests. I'll add the delay will also allow General Weathers and you to jointly prepare for the briefing. That's a little unorthodox, but we're at war with terrorists and it'll reinforce that you and the general are on the same side."

"I'll need to clear that with General Weathers," Randall said.

Millen smiled at the captain. "And if Stormy says no, that's okay."

I took a deep breath and relaxed. Pieces of a plan were falling into place. Except for one minor detail. Where the hell was Y'Grok's body?

The unspoken question wasn't lost on Nickles. "And if we haven't retrieved Mr. Eban's body by Thursday?"

"Then I suggest you and Tommy Lee hold a joint press conference, Mr. Nickles. You can say the senator was cooperating with the authorities who requested silence while they tracked fresh leads, and Tommy Lee can make an appeal to the public for new information. Then we'll have a memorial service without the body."

Kevin patted Y'Suom's knee. "Don't worry. Tommy Lee and I'll work round the clock. And Barry used to be a damned good policeman himself."

The men looked at me with new respect.

"I can make some confidential inquiries and see if this merits FBI involvement," Millen said.

"Military police as well," Randall offered.

"Thanks." Kevin gave Randall an appreciative look. "But let's see what we can turn up first. If the bastard makes a political ultimatum, then we might deal ourselves some extra cards."

I turned to Nickles. "Don't bother with the *Gainesboro Vista*. I'll talk to the reporter." I hoped I could count on Melissa Bigham's cooperation.

Nickles eyed my cell phone. "Both of you give me the fastest way to reach you."

"Reach me through Barry or Tommy Lee," said Kevin.

"What's the fastest way to him?"

I was hesitant to give out Tommy Lee's private cell. I raised my phone. "Let me step out in the hall and go over some things with Tommy Lee."

I closed the door behind me and walked twenty feet toward the elevator. "You hear all that?"

"Yeah." Tommy Lee's voice crackled in the weakened reception. "Go ahead and give them this number." He paused. "You bought us the extra days, but I wish I knew what the hell to do with them."

I moved to a hall window hoping to increase the signal strength. The mountain across the valley had a distinct band of light green running from the base to a third of the way to the ridge crest. In the Appalachians, altitude corresponded to latitude and the growing season near the peaks was closer to New England's. Each day spring crept higher up the slopes as new leaves appeared. "Maybe the crime lab will turn something up."

"Maybe," he grunted. "I asked your mother not to feed or water Democrat this morning."

"Why?"

"On the off chance the little booger got a piece of the guy or at least some of his clothing. He doesn't floss, does he?"

"Not yet. We're still working on gargling." My police pride smarted that I hadn't thought about that evidence possibility.

"Good. You and Kevin heading back?"

I looked at my watch. "We'll be there around nine."

"I'll cover the people here on the delay. You said we'd work out what to do with them. Any ideas?"

I was glad Tommy Lee couldn't see my grin. "Yeah. Ever heard of Daniel Boone?"

As Kevin drove down the interstate, I swallowed two more Tylenol without water. The pain in my head had returned as a dull ache.

Kevin cut his eyes to me. "You're thinking pretty clear for a guy who took a hard zap. Want me to stop at a drugstore for anything?"

"No. Let's just get back."

Kevin set the cruise control and settled into his seat. "I've been thinking. Did you have any personal belongings of Y'Grok at the funeral home?"

"Harvey Collins brought by the burial clothes."

"Who's he?"

"The Lutheran social worker from Hickory. Y'Suom spoke with him from Korea. His father didn't bring much from Vietnam."

"I bet Y'Grok got out by the skin of his teeth."

"Why'd he wait so long? Y'Suom arrived in '86."

"Y'Suom was only eight then. A new round of persecutions had started and Y'Grok and his wife wanted the boy safe. He trusted we'd look after him."

"We?"

"Those vets who haven't forgotten the Montagnards."

I remembered the tension back in the hotel room. "Is that what was going on between Senator Millen and Captain Randall?"

"Partly. You see Ryan's been critical of the way his own administration has been prosecuting the war on terrorism. He's had some sharp exchanges with Stormy, and Captain Randall's thin skinned about it."

"So Randall wasn't angry about the Montagnards?"

"I'm just saying that's extra fuel for Randall's fire. Some of us are pissed at Ryan because he bottled up a human rights resolution condemning Vietnamese persecution and the confiscation of Montagnard tribal lands. The bill would have imposed sanctions."

"Why'd he do that?"

"He claimed the sanctions wouldn't work and would only make the Vietnamese more determined to show they wouldn't cave under U.S. pressure. They consider the Montagnards an internal affair."

"How do the Montagnards feel?"

"Betrayed."

"How do you feel?"

"How do I feel?" Kevin drummed his fingers on the steering wheel. "It's more how I believe. I like to think loyalty and honor still mean something."

"And you believe the senator doesn't?"

"I'm not saying that. Our late congressman Tip O'Neill used to claim all politics is local. If Ryan were a North Carolina senator with the largest constituency of Montagnards outside Vietnam, he might have acted differently. And he's not alone. John McCain and John Kerry share his views." Kevin shook his head. "Me. After thirty years on the Boston police force, and seeing my fellow citizens abuse and murder each other in more ways than imaginable, I guess I like to hold onto whatever ideals I can still find. Loyalty and honor are more than words to the Yards."

I gazed out at the surrounding hills and wondered if they were anything like the central highlands of Vietnam. Were they what brought Y'Grok to our area to die? Alone, away from even his own people?

"But Ryan came here for the funeral," Kevin continued. "I'll give the senator credit for that."

We rode along in silence for a few miles. Then I remembered Kevin's original question.

"Why are you interested in Y'Grok's belongings?"

He hesitated a few seconds. "Just a thought. Someone broke into your funeral home because of Y'Grok. The guy may have been looking for more than a body."

"All the hospital sent over was a bag of clothes. They must have been what he was wearing when he died."

Kevin glanced at me. "I didn't realize he died in the hospital."

"He didn't. Harvey Collins told me Y'Grok had refused to go to the hospital. He stayed on a piece of land up here owned by some guys in the Hickory VFW. A hunt club. When Collins drove up to check on him last Friday, he found the body. He'd been dead about a day."

"Tough old bird," Kevin said. "I think he finally came out of Vietnam because he knew he was dying. Hoped to see Y'Suom again."

I'd performed enough funerals to know the ravages of lung cancer. "I'd say it came quick at the end. He could have been walking around in the morning and dead by dusk."

"I know. Lung cancer killed my father."

I didn't ask for details. Kevin knew well enough how desperate Y'Grok's last breaths would have been. "When Collins found the body, he called Tommy Lee. They'd been expecting it. They brought Y'Grok down to be officially pronounced dead. No autopsy required."

"Then his stuff's still up there."

"I suppose. We'll need to make arrangements to have Y'Suom go through them."

"Might be good for me to go with him."

The forced nonchalance in his voice caught my attention. "You're looking for something, aren't you? Either with his clothes or at the place where he died."

He laughed. "Tommy Lee told me you were sharp. I should have remembered that."

I took a shot in the dark. "The theft of Y'Grok's body's about Raven, isn't it?"

My statement choked off his laughter. A hard glint flashed in his eyes and a tough cop broke through the congenial surface. "If you're sharp, you'll be careful where you say that word."

"It was obvious that Senator Millen didn't want me asking about it. What's Raven got to do with Y'Grok?"

Kevin didn't speak.

Frustration drove my voice higher. "I'm the one who was knocked senseless this morning. I'm the one who has to conduct a funeral without a body. If you know something, tell me. Otherwise, I'm having a much different conversation with the reporter at the *Vista*."

Kevin's knuckles whitened on the steering wheel. "And you'll screw everything up. You don't know what you're dealing with."

"Then enlighten me."

He looked in the rearview mirror like someone could be eavesdropping in the backseat. "All right. But it's my call who else gets this information."

I pointed to the upcoming exit ramp. "Here's I-26."

Kevin had pulled into the passing lane and was about to blow right past our exit. He slowed and cut in front of a mini-van to make the turn. When he'd regained cruising speed, he started talking. "Last week I received a letter at my district from Y'Grok. I'd learned he'd arrived in North Carolina and I sent word through some vets for him to contact me. I'd expected him to phone, but I guess he wasn't comfortable doing that. In his world, staying secretive meant staying alive."

"Even here?"

"Somehow Y'Grok escaped through Cambodia. It's the only way the Yards can get out. Now, those refugee camps are closed and they've been forced back into Vietnam. He'd only been here a few months and wasn't sure who to trust. His son was stationed in Korea."

"What was in the letter?"

"A few words. He said he was dying. He'd found Tommy Lee and he had a place to meet me."

"You were coming here anyway?"

"Yeah. I got Tommy Lee's call about Y'Grok's death on Saturday. I already had my ticket."

"What's all that have to do with Raven?"

"His last line of the letter. 'Raven come home' and 'you see.'"

I thought of Poe's poem and the bird that wouldn't leave.

"Raven was the network," Kevin explained. "The one I told you about. A sort of underground railroad that got downed pilots and isolated infantry grunts out of enemy territory. Raven became the code name for the operation."

"Why didn't Y'Grok tell Tommy Lee?"

"Tommy Lee was never part of Raven. He'd already been wounded and shipped home. Ryan Millen was one of the pilots smuggled out, Talbert was a military intelligence operative on the ground, and Stormy Weathers had oversight."

"But you're the one Y'Grok turned to."

"That's right. And I'm not going to screw this up."

I didn't understand. Why would Kevin and Y'Grok be playing war games? What difference did it make now? "And you're still trying to protect the operation?"

"Raven was blown as an operation years ago. After the war, most of the Montagnards who helped us were caught and either executed or imprisoned."

"So what's come home?"

"Money."

I stared at Kevin, waiting for an explanation. His smile returned.

"The Yards were fighting with us. It was their war of resistance, of independence. Understand, they weren't mercenaries."

"Okay."

"But we provided funds to bribe officials and pay others to help. Some of the cash was funneled through Y'Grok, but I doubt he ever used much, if any. The money might be thirty-five years old, but it's still very spendable."

"How much?"

Kevin made a short clicking sound with his tongue. "Military intelligence liked round numbers. I know of at least a hundred thousand dollars delivered to Y'Grok. More would have gone to other operatives. I figure close to a million dollars was circulated to fund Raven. That's a nice ransom figure, don't you think?"

Chapter Six

Small clusters of people milled around the front lawn of the funeral home. Most were dark-skinned Montagnards. Several children appeared to be playing tag. A few men in camo fatigues were standing beside a flag hoisted on a pole they'd stuck in the ground. Flapping in the breeze was the emblem of an eagle soaring down on Southeast Asia. The words "Rolling Thunder" were stitched above it.

Cars lined the side street and the shoulder of the main road. A man and woman wearing dark clothes with thin rows of colorful embroidered patterns stood close to the highway. They held a white banner unfurled between them. Across the top in bold letters read "United Dega People." Beneath the phrase was a flag with three stripes of green, white, and red. A bull elephant was in its center. Beside the flag were written the words, "We want to be free to live in peace in Vietnam."

"Looks like they're creating a political rally," Kevin said.

As we approached our driveway, a deputy stepped from behind a patrol car and signaled us to stop.

"Reece Hutchins," I whispered to Kevin.

He rolled down the window. "Deputy Hutchins."

Reece was surprised to be addressed by someone he didn't know. He peered past Kevin to me. "You okay, Barry?"

"Yes. This is Kevin Malone. Old friend of the sheriff."

Kevin stuck his hand out the window. "Tommy Lee's told me a lot about you."

Reece took Kevin's words as a compliment. "Boston detective, right?"

"You pegged me. Where's Tommy Lee?"

"With the crime lab. We put them around the other side of the garage near the scene."

"Good," I said. "What's the official word?"

Reece puffed himself up. "Break-in. Least that's what we told those people out front. Sheriff gave me the scoop on the body, but no one's getting that out of me."

"Good job." Kevin gave Reece an appreciative nod. "We could use some men like you in Boston."

That flushed Reece's broad ears with pride. "You can pull around my car and park by the garage."

"Anybody else here from town?" I asked.

"Not yet. Sheriff told me to keep a lookout for the mayor."

Kevin saluted and closed the window. "Now there's a guy who sleeps in his uniform."

"How long would he last in Boston?"

"On the street? Probably a minute and a half."

"Well, I know he can keep a secret if he thinks it's privileged information. And with the mayor on his way, we might get some help for these people."

Kevin parked the jeep in front of the garage. We found Tommy Lee talking to a crime lab technician outside the embalming room. He gave us a nod, said a few final words to the techie, and walked over. "Quite a party out front."

"Reece says the mayor's on his way."

Tommy Lee laughed. "I told Archie Junior that Daniel Boone had arrived at the funeral home and he telephoned the mayor before I could."

Kevin gave Tommy Lee a quizzical look. "What's the deal about Daniel Boone?"

"Barry's idea."

I told Kevin the story, realizing the Yankee would think we were all a bunch of yahoos.

Kevin gazed into the distance. "Not a bad idea. The Irish in Boston love wakes and cemeteries. Gram would drag us to funerals for people we didn't know just because she thought someone from our family should be there. When she passed, her procession moved unimpeded from Murphy's Funeral Parlor to the graveyard. My fellow officers from Dorchester closed off the streets." He shrugged. "Not for me. For Gram. She'd attended at least one family funeral for each of them." He looked back toward the front yard. "And that's the kind of community the Yards have."

I turned to Tommy Lee. "Is there someone I should talk to?"

"There's a preacher. I guess he's a preacher. He's with a Lutheran congregation in Charlotte."

"What's his name?"

"Earl Hucksley. I told him the schedule had changed. He saw you had a break-in, but he doesn't know about the body."

"Maybe I should wait a bit. See what the mayor says."

Tommy Lee bent down and broke off a stem of straw grass growing next to Uncle Wayne's crushed petunias. He stuck the stem in his mouth like a toothpick. "Yeah. That's what I'd do. Mind if I sit in on your conversation with the mayor?"

"No. You got any ideas, speak up."

Tommy Lee chewed on the grass and said nothing.

"They find anything in there?" Kevin nodded toward the embalming room.

"A few things. A smear of blood for one."

"Mine?" I asked.

"Possibly, but they don't think so. It's on the back of the doorknob to the storage closet. There also seems to be a residue of powder."

"Talc?" Kevin asked.

"We'll have to wait for the lab report."

"Latex gloves." Kevin stared into the empty embalming room. "The guy came prepared to leave no prints." He turned to me. "I'd say your dog nipped him as he got tossed in the closet."

I felt a sense of pride that Democrat had tried to defend me.

Tommy Lee kept chewing on the stem. "Not enough blood that we should be looking for a suspect with a missing hand, but enough that we could pull a DNA match if we have to."

"Yeah, but you've got to have a suspect to match," I said.

"We'll get there. I have to rule people out first. Who goes in that room besides you and your uncle Wayne?"

"Occasionally Mom will sweep the floor. She doesn't handle the supplies. And Freddy Mott assists us." I knew where the sheriff was headed. "Are you talking prints?"

"Yeah. Kevin's right, the guy probably wore latex gloves. But we don't know for sure."

The Sheriff's Department already had my prints on file. Mom, Uncle Wayne, and Freddy would have to be inked. My uncle would see it as one step away from a mug shot. "Can you do them here?"

Tommy Lee nodded. "I'll tell Reece to go easy. You'll need to get Wayne and Freddy by later."

"Find anything else?" Kevin asked.

"Not sure. There's something caught on the nails of the threshold and porch. The old wood has spit the heads up a bit and traces of black rubber are on them."

Kevin looked at me. "You slide anything in and out of that room?"

"No. Deliveries come on a rolling gurney."

"Maybe he dragged Y'Grok's body on a mat," Kevin said.

"Maybe," agreed Tommy Lee. "Or maybe he came with his own hearse and body bag. At this point anything's possible."

"Sheriff. The mayor's here." Reece Hutchins made the announcement as he rounded the corner of the funeral home. Behind him walked Mayor Sammy Whitlock and Archie Junior.

Archie's eyes were wide and he glanced back over his shoulder at the crowd on the front lawn.

The mayor wore a yellow sport coat over an open-neck, tangerine shirt and lime slacks. He looked like a squat glass of rainbow sherbet. Whitlock had been mayor for the past six years and carried the officiousness of the mostly symbolic office with him at all times. He went straight for Tommy Lee.

Although the morning air was cool, he pulled a handkerchief from his hip pocket and wiped the perspiration off his bald head. "What happened? These people try to break in?"

"No," Tommy Lee said. "They're here for Y'Grok Eban. We're investigating a burglary that happened during the night."

The mayor nodded, and then saw my damaged forehead. "Good gracious, Barry. Did you fall down the stairs?"

"I danced a little tango with our unwanted guest."

"Good for you. Bet he got the worse end of the deal. Get a description?"

Tommy Lee jumped in. "Too dark. But we've got some things to go on. Even a big city detective." He introduced Kevin.

"And this Montagnard saved your life too?" Mayor Whitlock asked.

"More than once," Kevin said.

"Must have been quite a fellow, pulling in so many people from so far away." The mayor stared at Archie Junior, signaling for him to pick up the cue.

"Oh, yeah, and people will want to pay proper respects in a proper cemetery."

"I can't promise anything." I rubbed the knot on my head. For some reason the pain had gotten worse. "I haven't talked to his son yet."

Archie's face flushed. "Well, why'd you bring us down here then?"

I looked toward the front yard. "For those people. To give your Honor the chance to welcome them to Gainesboro. And I'll be glad to carry that message to Y'Grok's son as well." I turned back to the mayor. "And Senator Millen, General Weathers, and Franklin Talbert. They'll probably want to meet you."

Sammy Whitlock's jaw dropped. "The movie star?"

"You haven't heard? Y'Grok's son is delaying the service till Thursday. That is if we can do something to help his fellow Montagnards till then." I looked beyond the mayor to a circle of kids playing some version of Duck Duck Goose. "Otherwise, I guess Y'Suom will want to go ahead this afternoon."

"He can't do that." Archie looked from me to Tommy Lee.

The sheriff shrugged. "I reckon he can do anything he wants. Not against the law to bury your daddy."

"It's not even against the law in Massachusetts," Kevin said.

"Surely we can do something." The mayor appealed to each of us, his pudgy hands raised prayerfully to his chest.

"You're the mayor," I said. "You could mobilize support. That's what the general and senator would do."

My statement had the desired effect. Mayor Whitlock's eyes lost focus. I knew he was searching for a way to stand shoulder to shoulder between a general and senator—for a photograph of course.

"And a movie star is impressed with someone who acts decisively," Kevin added.

The mayor reached a decision. "It's not these people's fault that the service has to be delayed. And it's important to have General Weathers and Franklin Talbert able to attend if they're coming halfway round the world."

"Yes," Archie echoed.

We stood in awkward silence. The mayor had no clue how to act decisively.

I broke the silence with a suggestion. "You could make an appeal to the town churches. Mobilize a casserole brigade."

Kevin picked up on the idea. "Do you have a discretionary fund? Maybe get some motels to give or discount some rooms that you could supplement."

"Spend money?" The mayor looked horrified.

"Yes," Kevin said. "I thought you were a politician."

"I have an idea." Tommy Lee hooked his thumbs in his belt and waited for our full attention. "Why not let them use Carson Park? It's city property with picnic shelters, and there's a safe area for the kids to play. You could sanction that, Mayor."

"We could feed them through the churches," I added. "But what about sleeping? It's chilly at night and could rain."

Tommy Lee smiled. "No problem. The VFW post is adjacent to the park. There's enough space in the activity room and we keep a supply of cots and mats for emergency shelter needs."

"Who would authorize that?" asked the Mayor.

"I'll poll the board," Tommy Lee said. "Who'd want to tell General Weathers we refused the Montagnards and those Rolling Thunder vets traveling with them?"

"That's a good plan. Who do I tell?" The mayor saw the successful parade forming and wanted to be leading it.

"Barry's going to talk to the Lutheran Family Services social worker." Tommy Lee had the mayor hooked. "You can make the official offer."

"I'm ready." The mayor rocked back and forth on his white buck shoes. "Just say the word."

"All right." Tommy Lee nodded to Reece. "Stay with the lab boys. And let Kevin ask any questions he wants."

As we walked across the front lawn, the sheriff whispered, "Barry, we might need Y'Suom at the park sometime this afternoon. The senator too. I'm sure not all of these people can stay till Thursday and they'll want to pay their respects. If they're away from the funeral home, then the absence of the body won't be questioned."

"Maybe the minister can make a few remarks. Do you have a PA at the VFW?"

"If the bingo callers haven't worn it out. Now there's an idea for you. A funeral service followed by bingo. Winner gets the flowers."

A little girl squealed with delight as she slid down the sliding board into the arms of her father. He set the bundle of energy on the ground and she sped off to the swings, her thick black hair bouncing with each stride.

A mix of laughter and foreign syllables filled the warm air. Under the picnic shelters, women began setting out food for lunch. The Montagnards had traveled with enough supplies to get them through the day. Those families choosing to remain would be served by the Gainesboro Interfaith Coalition, an association of the town's churches and synagogue that cooperated on community issues.

I sat on a park bench beneath a stately white pine because the hardwoods had yet to develop enough foliage to provide shade. Although the spring equinox had occurred only a few weeks ago, the sun's direct rays made my wool shirt hot and itchy. The ache in my head added to my misery and I scanned the parking lot for the person I needed to see before I could return to the funeral home for a rest.

"Waiting on a bus?" Melissa Bigham stood behind me. Her impish grin vanished as she saw my stitched forehead. "Barry?"

"Sit down. You shouldn't sneak up on an old guy like me."

Melissa was in her late twenties, a crackerjack reporter with too much talent to be biding her time on Gainesboro's small daily. She had the lithe body of a dancer, the freshly scrubbed face of the girl next door, and a carefree attitude that used to be called perky. In a journalist, those traits were a dangerous combination that let her ask hard questions of people who thought she was cute and didn't recognize her killer instincts until too late. I wanted to talk to her because I knew she was one person I couldn't fool.

"I'm all right. Where'd you park?"

"In the VFW lot. I got wind of the request to shelter the Montagnards and thought I'd check it out. Picked up your voicemail from my cell phone."

I shifted on the bench so I could look directly at her. She had yet to bring out her notepad. "I need you to trust me for a little while."

"Oh, shit," she muttered. "A delayed funeral, a battered undertaker, and an off-the-record request. What are you into this time?"

Melissa had been my ally on two previous occasions that had given her national bylines. She stayed in Gainesboro for the mountain lifestyle, but, like any good reporter, she couldn't resist the inside track on a major story.

"The scary part is I don't know, and I can't bring you into my confidence if you have any qualms about sitting on the information until I say okay."

"And if the information leaks elsewhere?"

I shrugged. "Then the rules change, but I'd still want you to clear how much you need to make public."

She laughed. "Come on, Barry, you're killing me. How much is much? Should we meet in an underground parking garage?"

"Maybe," I said flatly. "Maybe we should. Somebody plays rough."

Her eyes narrowed. "You talking to anyone else?"

"No. It's you or nobody." I paused for a second. "Of course, when the story breaks, it'll be every man for himself."

It took her all of two seconds to weigh the pros and cons. "I'm in. Tell it the way you want."

I began the story I'd rehearsed in my mind. "Last night we had a break-in at the funeral home. That's on the Sheriff Department's overnight sheet. What we've withheld, and this is putting Tommy Lee in an awkward position, is that Y'Grok Eban's body was stolen."

"Stolen?" Melissa's hand made a sudden move for the purse beside her, an involuntary reaction for her notepad. She caught herself and stopped. "So this delay on the funeral isn't for the convenience of General Weathers and Franklin Talbert?"

"No. We're buying time. We think a single intruder took the body. He knocked me unconscious and whisked it away. We don't know why."

"Why the cover-up?"

"I wouldn't call it a cover-up. The theft might be some political publicity stunt. If so, we don't want to give them what they want. Or it could be something entirely different."

"Senator Millen knows this?"

"Yes, he's particularly sensitive to the political implications for the Montagnard and Vietnamese issue. We'd just like to be on firmer ground before accusations are made."

Melissa bit her lower lip and thought a moment. "Who else knows?"

"I had to tell Y'Grok's son. He gave us permission to delay the service. General Weathers' advance man knows. We'll tell Talbert when he flies in tomorrow afternoon."

"What happens if you don't find the body?"

"Then we'll have to go public. Tommy Lee's doing everything he can, and Senator Millen and General Weathers' aide have offered extra resources. But Thursday's as long as we dare delay. I hope maybe the general and even Talbert might have some ideas as to who would do this and why."

She looked at me suspiciously. "Why are you telling me?"

"Because you're smart. I'd rather have you know than digging around. And like it or not, I'm in this mess up to my neck. The body was under my care. Whatever's going on, I want to know. Tommy Lee's got his resources and you've got yours. Tommy Lee has certain rules he has to follow. You, on the other hand, are a reporter." I stopped and smiled. "You don't follow any rules."

Melissa reached over and playfully put her hand on my arm. "Thank you. That's the nicest thing you've ever said to me."

I saw more than sunlight in her eyes and felt a little nervous.

"What can I do?" she asked.

I looked around the park. A makeshift stage was being set up at the far end. Senator Millen, Y'Suom, and the Charlotte minister, Earl Hucksley, would be making remarks at two. "There seems to be another dimension here. Some undercurrent among the people who knew Y'Grok the best."

"Undercurrent?"

"I don't know. Something I feel but can't see. Maybe you could look into the backgrounds of some of our esteemed guests, particularly how they relate to Y'Grok and each other."

"Anything else?"

I decided it was worth a shot. "And a military operation in Vietnam called Raven."

"Barry, where are we headed?" Her playful tone was gone. "In the movies that's the kind of request that always gets people shot."

"I know."

Chapter Seven

Mom had a bowl of chicken noodle soup waiting for me back at the funeral home. The lunch guaranteed to cure all ills.

The lab team had gone, taking the yellow tape and the fingerprints of Mom, Uncle Wayne, and Freddy Mott with them. I sat at the kitchen table, spooning up a soup refill under the watchful eye of my uncle. He nursed a cup of coffee while my mother puttered at the sink.

"Is there going to be enough food for them?" Mom asked.

"The mayor said First Methodist and Grace Lutheran will cover tonight, Clearview Baptist and Memorial Presbyterian are set for tomorrow, and St. Anne's and Temple Beth El will provide lunch on Thursday and a meal after the memorial service."

"Who's going to provide the body if we ain't got one?" Uncle Wayne said. "That's what I want to know."

"Tommy Lee's doing everything he can," I snapped. "That's all you need to know."

Uncle Wayne paled. I heard Mom gasp behind me. Even Democrat looked up from where he lay in the corner.

I dropped my spoon in the bowl. "I'm sorry. I'm—"

"You don't need to apologize." Uncle Wayne stood up from the table. "Should have kept my fool tongue quiet. You're the one who got his head stove in."

Mom laid her hand on my shoulder. "Why don't you rest? It's almost two."

"And don't worry about the petunias," Wayne added. "I'm going for another flat."

I almost laughed out loud. The petunias had certainly not been on my list of priorities. "All right, but if Tommy Lee calls, I'll want to talk to him."

I rose from the table and headed for the back stairs. A rap on the kitchen door stopped me. Kevin Malone stood on the back porch, grinning through the small panes.

"See if he wants coffee or tea," Mom said.

Kevin wanted neither. "Sorry to bother you. Patsy let me borrow her car. I just have a question or two for Barry."

Wayne started to leave.

I waved him to stay. "That's all right. We can talk in the parlor." I led Kevin down the hall toward the front rooms.

"Actually I wanted to look through Y'Grok's things."

I stopped and turned around. "Do you want to take them back to the department?"

"No. Examining them here is fine."

We went through the viewing room and its connecting door to the operating wing. A smaller room was across the hall. That room contained lockers and drawers where the personal items of the deceased could be stored. Y'Grok's belongings had come in a plastic bag from Laurel County Hospital. I handed the bag to Kevin. He took it to a counter under the window and carefully extricated the contents.

A pair of dirty gray workpants had been tightly rolled up. Instead of unrolling them, Kevin first checked the cuff of each leg, sliding his finger around the circumference in search of anything that could be tucked inside. Finding nothing, he rolled out the garment until he reached the waist band.

A worn brown leather belt fit loosely through the loops. Kevin pulled the belt free and examined the inner side.

"What are you looking for?"

"Anything. A note. A sign. Y'Grok's letter said 'come see' so that meant he had something to show me."

He curled the belt, set it aside, and then went through the waist band as carefully as the cuffs. When that yielded nothing, he turned the pockets inside out. Finally he completely reversed the pants, checking the pocket pouches and inner seams meticulously.

Finding nothing, Kevin unfolded a ratty green sweatshirt. The cuffs were frayed and elbows threadbare. Cracked remnants of a logo for the University of North Carolina at Charlotte showed the shirt had been through multiple owners. At the bottom of the hospital bag, he found a wadded pair of boxer underwear. The elastic band had lost all tension. He began putting the clothes back in the bag. "No shoes or socks."

"I guess Harvey Collins found him dead in bed."

"Who?"

"The social worker from Lutheran Family Services."

"Guess we should talk to him. Is he in town?"

I started putting the clothes back in the bag. "He was with Pastor Hucksley. They're both staying at the VFW with the Montagnards."

Kevin stared out the window for a few seconds. Then he leaned against the counter and looked at me. "You know where this place is? Where Y'Grok had been living?"

"Not exactly. Somewhere in the northern part of the county. Near Winkler Creek."

"That means nothing to me. Can you find it?"

"I'd want to get specific directions from Tommy Lee. Otherwise we could wander over a hundred miles of back roads."

"How about this Collins guy? He knows."

A prickle of suspicion tingled down my neck. "Why are you going around Tommy Lee?"

"I'm not going around him. He's got his hands full. The lab report's on fast-track, he's got deputies checking vans and SUVs for a body, and he's in constant contact with Ryan and Randall back at the hotel."

I refused to give ground. "Tommy Lee's heading the investigation, Kevin. I'm not going to a key scene without telling him."

"Don't worry. He'll appreciate it."

"Then he won't hesitate to give me directions, will he?"

Kevin couldn't keep his annoyance from showing, but he had no choice. "All right, all right. We'll do this however you want." He straightened up and gave me a mischievous grin. "Guess I'm just used to working things my way."

"My office is down the hall."

Kevin sat in the red leather chair beside my desk. I dialed Tommy Lee's direct number from memory. He answered on the first ring.

"Kevin's at the funeral home with me. He wanted to look through Y'Grok's clothes."

"Find anything?"

"No. But he thinks there's a chance Y'Grok might have left some information at his place and he wants me to take him there."

"Why didn't he ask me?"

I didn't answer. Kevin frowned. He knew what the sheriff was saying.

Tommy Lee let us sweat a few moments before speaking. "Well, I had the same idea. I'm heading out now. Have Kevin sit tight and I'll pick him up."

"No. You'll pick us up."

"And when are you supposed to be recovering from that blow to the head?"

"When we've recovered Y'Grok." I looked at Kevin and made my next statement for his benefit. "Meanwhile, neither one of you is going to leave me in the dark."

Tommy Lee laughed. "In the dark? Buddy, you're not alone."

It was nearly three thirty when Tommy Lee's patrol car turned onto the dirt road by Winkler's Creek. Although the sky was clear, the sun had fallen behind the steep western ridge of Redman Gorge, leaving us in the cool shadows of the gorge's depth. Occasionally a driveway branched off to one side, marked only by a cluster of mailboxes. The farther we traveled up the gorge, the fewer the turnoffs and the number of mailboxes at each junction.

Finally, the clusters dwindled to single boxes. There were no names, only rural route and box numbers.

"Should be the next one," Tommy Lee said. He pointed to a mailbox with a hand-written number forty one. "Less than a quarter mile."

The route number had long ago faded off the mailbox. The road forked to the left, crossing the rushing stream over a wooden slatted bridge of questionable strength. This section of the gorge bulged into a wider diameter as the steep ridges on either side curved away from each other. If Redman Gorge were a long python, we were in the globular lump that was swallowed prey.

Tommy Lee braked the car at the edge of the bridge.

"Are we crossing that thing?" Kevin asked.

"The ambulance made it." Tommy Lee looked over his shoulder at his friend in the backseat. "You can get out and walk across."

"No thanks, Lieutenant. You know I'll follow you anywhere."

The timbers creaked and buckled under the car's weight, but the old bridge held. We rounded a bend and came to a dead end in front of a rundown house. A bold feeder stream flowed between the shack and a weathered building on the other side.

Tommy Lee opened the car door. "I haven't been up here in years."

Kevin didn't take his eyes off the moaning bridge. "I thought you said you'd seen him before he died."

"In town. The social worker brought him into the hospital. We both tried to get him to stay, but he refused. That was less than two weeks ago." Tommy Lee shook his head. "I meant to get up here."

We followed Tommy Lee up a dirt path to the front door. Cement and stone created the single step to the threshold. Tommy Lee jiggled the doorknob. "Locked. Hate to break in."

The three of us walked into an overgrown flower bed and looked through the gap in the dingy sheer curtains that years ago might have been white. Tommy Lee used his flashlight to pierce the gloom of the interior. The beam played across a table, and I thought of my high school English teacher, Miss Stephenson. She had read aloud the scene from *Great Expectations* where the banquet hall is discovered, readied for the wedding reception which never occurred, and left undisturbed for years except for the rats and flies who dined on the rotting feast.

Although there was no food to be seen, the place settings, serving bowls, and drinking glasses were set for the next meal. The homey scene lay smothered under a layer of dust, and spiders had spun a gossamer shroud from the wrought-iron chandelier to the natural wood planking of the table surface. A chipmunk, aroused by the pounding on the door and the invasive beam of the flashlight, scurried across the floor. The chipmunk was nothing more than a Dickens' rat with a cuter wardrobe.

"Doesn't look like anyone's lived here in years," I said.

Tommy Lee stepped away from the window. "This was the old Woosley place. They were killed in a car wreck about five years ago. The guys from Hickory bought the property from the estate. They only use the land for hunting."

Kevin and I followed him around to the rear of the house. He stopped at each window, but every room appeared coated in dust.

"He couldn't have stayed here." Kevin looked across the stream to the structure on the other side. "What about that building?"

The late afternoon shadows had not yet grown dark enough to hide the round paddle wheel hanging off the stone side of a building's wall. It was a gristmill shut down long ago when the family and their neighbors no longer needed to grind their own corn. The old waterwheel remained a testimony to the isolation of the gorge in those bygone days when the first settlers scratched out their homesteads.

We walked down to where the ground became rocky and flaked with mica. The sounds of our footsteps were swallowed by the steady roar of the strong current that once powered the mill. Tommy Lee stopped at the lip of the steep bank and looked for the best way across. We trailed him along the edge until he came to a fallen oak that stretched to the far bank. Limbs were cleared from the top side and the bark had been worn down from countless journeys over it.

"Somebody's been using this footbridge." Tommy Lee started across. "Just be careful. It's slippery. I didn't plan on going swimming."

I followed his lead with Kevin behind me.

"When I was a kid, we dared each other to walk the seawall at Boston Harbor. You never forget how. Just like riding a bicy—" Kevin's word was choked off as he tumbled into the stream.

The backsplash soaked my shoes. I watched the swift current bounce the detective over the slick rocks until he grabbed onto the overhanging branch of a rhododendron. He stood up, spewing water like a surfacing whale.

We hurried across and stood on the bank above him.

"You were saying." Tommy Lee couldn't hide his grin.

"Come on in. The water's fine."

I found a long willow limb and we pulled the soaked Irishman up.

Tommy Lee held Kevin by the back of his sweater. "He's kinda small. Maybe we should throw him back."

Kevin pulled off his sweater and wrung it out. As he turned around to spread it on a rock, I noticed the thirty-eight revolver holstered in the small of his back. A Smith & Wesson Special, the same pistol I owned. "I've got a handkerchief if you want to dry your gun."

"Thanks. Glad the damn thing didn't go off. I always keep the hammer on an empty chamber." He wiped down the weapon, released the cylinder, and swabbed the barrel.

Tommy Lee looked to the meadow beyond the mill. "Afraid I don't see a sunny spot. If you're chilly, you can run the heater in the car."

Kevin holstered his pistol and squeezed his hands down his pant legs. Water poured over his feet. "I'm fine. I'll try not to drip on the evidence."

Tommy Lee led the way to the other side of the mill, where we found a door unlocked. Inside, a large room had been swept clean. The old axle shafts of the mill's inner workings were still in place. The circular grindstone held a variety of tins and utensils and served as an open pantry.

"Here's where Y'Grok must have stayed." Tommy Lee walked around the room. He lit the kerosene lamps hanging from vertical beams in the stone walls. As each flickering flame intensified, an illumined portion of the room revealed something of the final days of the Montagnard.

An army cot was set up along one wall and an olive drab blanket lay folded across its foot. A small keg, which had once held penny nails, served as a night stand. In the middle of the keg, as if centered upon an altar, lay an old Bible. The gilt edges of its open pages worn by the years. In another corner of the room, a wooden dowel rod was fastened catty-cornered between two walls. Along it, a few coats, shirts, and pants hung from hangers. Adjacent to this makeshift closet was a three-drawer bureau whose stripped surface was bare of any photographs or keepsakes.

The only other furniture was a small eating table and a single straight-back chair. Tommy Lee lit the kerosene lamp on top of the table. The glow showed the black wood-burning stove behind it. The sheer size of the cast iron monstrosity indicated it worked for both cooking and heating.

Here existed a one-room universe that sufficed for the needs of body and soul. An empty copper basin beside the stove suggested a lack of running water. I walked over to the Bible open on the keg. The Twenty-third Psalm: "The Lord Is My Shepherd." Perhaps, for Y'Grok, it was as simple as that. The Lord was all he had left. When I picked the Bible up, I made a discovery.

Three Bic ballpoints had been snapped in the middle. Blue ink stained the rough wood beneath them. An open pocket knife and a large needle lay alongside, their tips coated with thick ink. Smudges of fingerprints dirtied the red plastic casing of the knife.

"Look at this."

Tommy Lee and Kevin came over.

"Prison tattoos?" Tommy Lee took a handkerchief and picked up one of the pens by the end. "Looks like he extracted the ink from the broken barrels."

Kevin bent closer. "Traces of dried blood on the blade and needle." He looked up at me. "He left the message on himself."

"What message?" Tommy Lee stared at Kevin, his one eye unblinking.

Kevin looked surprised. "Didn't Barry tell you?"

I bristled. "It's not my story."

Tommy Lee set the broken pen back on the keg. "I'll get some evidence bags later, but first we're all going to have a little chat. Unless both of you prefer to find your way out of these hills on foot?"

"Until now I didn't have anything to tell." Kevin looked at me for support. "I told you Y'Grok had something to show me. I'm not hiding anything."

I was in no mood for semantics. "Then tell Tommy Lee about Raven and about the ransom possibility."

"That's the second time today I've heard that word." Tommy Lee pointed to the chair. "Have a seat, Kevin. I'm sure your wet pants won't do any damage."

Kevin repeated what he'd told me about Operation Raven. He said he hadn't told Tommy Lee because Y'Grok's secretive note implied the information was only for him. Y'Grok had had opportunity before he died to tell Tommy Lee, if Raven was something he had wanted him to know.

Tommy Lee paced the room. "So you think stealing Y'Grok's body is about money, not politics. That's your story now?"

Kevin's face turned red. "God damn it, I'm not making up stories. I'm trying to deal with the facts. You know the drill as well as I do. Facts first, theories second. I got the letter, Y'Grok said 'Raven's come home,' then his body's stolen and now I learn he might have left me a tattooed message. I don't know what else it could be. Y'Grok must have found a way to get the money out of Nam."

I followed Kevin's sequence of events but they didn't make sense. "So someone steals a body and plans on ransoming it back?"

"And exactly who does this body snatcher think has the money now?" Tommy Lee asked.

"Either someone who was involved in Raven or his son, Y'Suom."

I still didn't get it. "Who's going to give up a million dollars for a dead body?"

Tommy Lee fixed his eye on me. "Someone who owes his life to Y'Grok and doesn't want to see him humiliated, even in death."

"Amen," Kevin said.

I stood outside the bonds forged in battle and felt about two inches tall. "All right. I understand." I turned to Kevin. "Why would Y'Grok want you to have the money?"

"Because he knew what I'd do with it." He smiled at Tommy Lee. "No offense, but you weren't part of Raven. Y'Grok knew he could trust me to put the money to good use."

"Doing what?" Tommy Lee asked. "Earning interest?"

Kevin jumped to his feet. "To keep their resistance alive. These people never got out of the god-damned war, Lieutenant. Their families are persecuted. Their young men are taken away to be re-educated, and then never return. Y'Grok knew I hadn't forgotten them."

Tommy Lee remained calm. "And the rest of us?"

Kevin looked back and forth between us. "You tell me. He sent me the letter."

Tommy Lee said nothing

Kevin walked back to the keg. "What better way to make sure a message isn't lost?" He turned toward me. "Did you see anything?"

"My uncle prepared the body." I wasn't ready to tell him about the tattoos, not until I talked to Tommy Lee alone.

"Did your uncle say anything?" Kevin's eyes were hopeful.

"He said Y'Grok had ink under his nails and he had to use Soft Scrub to get them clean."

"Well, then we need to talk to him. Right, Tommy Lee?"

"We need to know what he saw."

"The idea of a ransom might be a moot point," I said. "If there was a message explaining where the money is, the guy might have already found it. Then he'll just dump the body."

"Maybe," Kevin replied. "But if I know Y'Grok, the message will be in code. Only somebody familiar with Raven will be able to figure it out. Damn, I hope your uncle can remember."

"We'd better get back." Tommy Lee looked at the needle and pens. "First I'll get some evidence bags and take this stuff."

I forced a laugh. "I'll help you across the log, ol' timer."

Kevin stayed to nose around the room some more.

As Tommy Lee and I walked along the stream, I whispered, "I saw the tattoos."

Tommy Lee stopped. "You did?" He looked back at the mill. "I admit he's acting strange, but I'd still trust Kevin with my life."

"Even with a million dollars at stake?"

"Yes." He paused. "Well, what were the tattoos?"

"I remember part of them." My mind replayed the scene in the embalming room. "They were upside down on his thighs."

"Upside down?"

"Facing the torso."

"That fits. If he made them sitting down, that's the way they'd appear."

I started walking again, anxious to put some distance between us and Kevin. "Viet was on one thigh, Nam on the other. Over Viet was the number 2000. I thought maybe that was when he fled the country."

Tommy Lee shook his head. "No. He came out of Nam last fall and finally made it here a few months ago. You're sure about the number?"

"Positive. And the words Viet and Nam. There was another design, but I didn't get a chance to examine it."

"Can you remember anything?"

I reached the footbridge and stopped. "It was like a compass. The letter V was in the center and four points like north, south, east, and west. But something was wrong. The letters weren't right."

"What were they?" Tommy Lee prompted.

"I don't know. I remember thinking something was odd about them. I'd just started to look closer when Mom called me out of the room."

"Maybe your uncle will remember." He swept his hand to the log. "You first. Watch your step. I'm not going in after you."

We crossed without mishap.

As we approached the patrol car, Tommy Lee said, "Let me get a phone patch through to your uncle. I'll go back to the mill and you can talk to him without Kevin listening. Mix your memories with his and Kevin won't know you held out on him."

"Okay." I laughed. "And if Uncle Wayne draws a blank, you can always hypnotize me."

"Don't tempt me. I'd love to make you cluck like a chicken."

Mom said Uncle Wayne had replanted his petunias and left about thirty minutes before I called. He'd mentioned something about swinging by the VFW to see what all the fuss was about. I tried his house but got no answer. As possibly the last person in Laurel County to own a rotary phone, my uncle had no use for the cellular age. Our inquiries would have to wait.

When Tommy Lee and Kevin returned to the car, Kevin couldn't hide his disappointment. "Can we go straight to your uncle's house?"

"I guess so, but I can't say when he'll show up."

Tommy Lee laughed. "I can count the places Wayne goes on one hand—funeral home, barbershop, grocery store, Harold's Texaco, and church. Any place else is a special occasion."

"Then let's go," Kevin insisted. "He'll be there when we arrive."

Tommy Lee eyed his friend's wet clothes. "Fine. I'll drop you at the funeral home to get Patsy's car. You can go to my house, change into something dry, and meet Barry at his uncle's."

Kevin seemed unconcerned about his soaked condition. "Aren't you coming?"

Tommy Lee looked at his watch. "General Weathers is on the way from Fort Jackson. I plan to be at the Grove Park when he gets there." He opened the car door. "We'd better get a move on."

Kevin stopped. His jaw muscles flexed as he ground his teeth. "Damn. I can't be in two places at once."

"That's your problem," Tommy Lee said.

"All right. I'm going with you. We'll see Wayne later." He grabbed the handle of the rear door and yanked it open.

Tommy Lee winked at me over the car roof. "What about you? You look like you're having trouble being in one place at once."

"You're not getting shed of me." I slid in and buckled the seat belt.

Kevin's laugh turned into a high-pitched giggle. "Aren't we a sight? A one-eyed sheriff, a beat-up undertaker, and a half-drowned Irishman. I can't wait to see Stormy's face when this trio of trouble shows up."

Chapter Eight

General Weathers quickly rose to his feet as we entered his suite. He rushed to greet Kevin and pumped his hand vigorously. "You look pretty good for an old blowhard. Want a police job in Iraq?"

"Hell no. You've got enough of a mess as it is." Kevin turned to Tommy Lee. "But here's the guy for you, General. Hand him a scimitar and turn him loose."

"I don't doubt it." The general surprised Tommy Lee by giving him a salute. "I've read your record, Lieutenant. It's my honor to meet you."

For once I saw my friend blush.

"Thank you, sir. All in the line of duty."

"Duty." Weathers looked back at Senator Millen standing by the sofa. "That seems harder to determine every day. Are we soldiers or are we policemen? At least you two gentlemen got to make a choice."

He turned to me and the creases in his leathered face softened. "Looks like you've seen action, young man."

"I felt more action than I saw, sir."

He nodded, and then gestured to the sitting area. "Anybody want a drink? The mini-bar is well stocked."

Tommy Lee and I declined.

Kevin headed for the bar. "I claim the best whiskey, and I'll drink it standing."

For the first time, Weathers and Millen noticed Kevin's damp clothes.

"What happened?" Millen asked.

"I fell in the drink, and after the drink's in me, I'll tell you the story."

Weathers followed Kevin to the bar. A tanned bald spot on the back of his head broke through his buzz cut. He wore khaki pants and a maroon golf shirt, but he carried himself as if he were in full uniform.

Millen winked at me and then called after Weathers, "And I'll take a light scotch."

"Sorry, Ryan. Didn't mean to slight you. I'm always willing to buy a drink for a guy who sits on the Appropriations Committee."

Over the sound of ice and clinking glasses, Kevin asked, "Have you seen Y'Suom?"

"Yes," Weathers said. "I gave the boy my condolences. Ryan and I sent him to eat with—" He snapped his fingers trying to recall the name.

"Nickles," Millen said.

Kevin took a slow sip of the whiskey. "And Captain Randall?"

"No. J.R. drove me from Fort Jackson. Damn army vehicles guzzle fuel like a jet fighter. I told him to gas up the car and get some shuteye. We may need an early start on the morning." Weathers brought Kevin a double and handed the scotch to Millen. Then he sat down. "So what've you got? Bring Ryan and me up to date."

Kevin and I looked to Tommy Lee.

"At first we thought the theft was a political publicity stunt to draw attention to the Montagnards. Then Y'Suom said the Vietnamese wanted the body to disappear so that they wouldn't have to honor a request for Y'Grok's remains to be returned to the highlands."

Millen sat on the sofa across from Weathers. "I briefed Stormy on that."

Weathers leaned forward in his chair. "And the situation could be just the opposite. The Vietnamese stole the body to take back to Vietnam as a warning that the Montagnards can't outrun them. They could hold Y'Grok's body up for public ridicule."

"Sounds a bit over the top," Millen said.

"God damn it." Weathers slapped his thigh in frustration. "Nothing's over the top these days. Can't you and your senate cronies understand that? Who thought we'd have beheadings on the internet?"

Millen sipped his drink and held his tongue.

"We have a new theory," Tommy Lee said. "Not politics but old-fashioned greed."

"A ransom?" Millen asked.

"Maybe. But so far no one has contacted us. We think the motive's money from Raven."

Weathers looked at Millen. "Raven? There's a name I haven't heard in a long time. How's that play in this?"

Tommy Lee raised his hand to Kevin. "The floor's all yours."

Kevin stepped to the center of the room where he could face all of us. He began his story with the letter he received from Y'Grok.

Millen interrupted. "Why didn't you say something this morning?"

"This morning I thought the theft was a publicity stunt by some political group just like everybody else."

"But not anymore?" Weathers asked.

Kevin walked them through the discovery of the needle and ink at the mill.

General Weathers stared at me. "Did you see these tattoos?"

Before I could answer, Tommy Lee spoke up. "His uncle embalmed the body. We're going to see him when we leave here."

"Maybe we should all go," Weathers said.

My stomach tightened. Uncle Wayne wouldn't be pleased with an entourage arriving on his doorstep after nine at night. "My uncle's in his seventies. I think a calm conversation with just a few people is the best way to get any information."

"All right," Weathers agreed. "So we have to hope this message is something only Kevin would understand. A code to the money. We find the money and get Y'Grok's body back for the honorable burial he deserves."

Kevin rubbed his hand across his chin. "Be damned if I can think of anything else. What's got me puzzled is who else could have known about the money? We need to find out from Y'Suom who his father might have spoken to about Raven."

The room fell silent. A disturbing thought crept from the back of my mind. "It still concerns me that whoever has the body will try to decipher the tattoos and get the money without the danger of a ransom exchange. What's going to happen when they fail to break the code?"

"They'll find someone who can," Weathers growled.

We all looked at Kevin.

He grinned mischievously. "Bring them on. People say I've never met a stranger."

Weathers' face stayed fixed as granite. "And if they think someone else saw the tattoos and could give you a description?"

All eyes now turned on me.

I wasn't worried about myself. "We'd better get to my uncle."

Weathers nodded. I saw the anger flash in his eyes and knew "Stormy Weathers" was more than just a play on words.

His voice turned brittle. "Y'Grok Eban was one of the finest allies this country ever had. And I'm going to find his body if I have to turn over every stone on this god damned mountain."

When we returned to the car, I called Wayne on my cell phone.

He answered on the sixth ring. "The body show up?"

"Don't ask that first thing," I said in exasperation. "What if it wasn't me?"

"Who else could it be? Good thing you gave up detective work."

I fought the urge to remind him I'd been a patrolman, not a detective, but police were all the same to Uncle Wayne. "I'm with the sheriff and Kevin Malone. We'd like to stop by and talk."

"Don't know what I can tell y'all, but come on. Your mom gave me half a rhubarb pie."

Dusk had turned the white exterior of my uncle's farmhouse into a bluish gray silhouette. We stood on the front porch and heard the bell ring on the other side of the door. No footsteps followed.

"How's his hearing?" Kevin asked.

"Not as good as he thinks it is."

Tommy Lee rapped on the door as only a sheriff can do. No one answered but the yard crickets.

"He must have migrated." I headed around the house.

Kevin looked confused. "Migrated?"

"My uncle's like a goose, except his seasonal migration is from the kitchen to the back porch. From now till fall, he'll spend most of his free time sitting in his wicker rocker behind the safety of his screen walls."

We found Wayne as I'd predicted, sitting in his rocker and reading his latest copy of *GRIT* magazine, the homespun publication he'd sold door-to-door in his youth. Although he wore a checked wool shirt to combat the chill, in his mind spring had arrived.

"Evening, Wayne." Tommy Lee stood at the door and looked out at the back hillside. The gnarled shapes of a small apple orchard receded into the gloom. "Going to be a nice night."

Wayne set his magazine aside and rose to unlock the screen door. "My time of year. Not too hot, not too cold, and no bugs."

"Getting much off your trees?" Tommy Lee wiped his feet on the hemp mat and stepped up on the gray floorboards.

"I just look at the blossoms. Be out soon. Tyler Nolan picks whatever fruit comes along. Hardly enough to make it worth his while." Wayne led us to a table in the corner beneath a porch light. "Speaking of apples, have some rhubarb pie."

Four plates were set out and each held a healthy slice. I wasn't sure how speaking of apples got us to rhubarb, but my uncle had his own way of making connections and they usually made sense, eventually. All I knew was the chicken soup from lunch had abandoned my stomach long ago.

I slid into the chair next to the wall and picked up my fork. "You don't have to eat yours, Tommy Lee. It could spoil your supper."

"If your mom made this pie, it's history." He maneuvered his holster out of the way, and pulled the chair close to the table.

"I can make a pot of coffee." Uncle Wayne stood over us, ready to head to the kitchen.

"Sit down and eat your pie before we fight over it." Tommy Lee loaded his fork and a quarter of the slice disappeared.

Uncle Wayne sat down and picked at his crust. He wasn't good at chitchat. "Barry said you wanted to talk about that body."

For a moment all we heard were crickets and a hoot owl. Tommy Lee swallowed his pie and took a breath. "We found some things up where Y'Grok died."

"Things?" Wayne echoed.

"Ink coated needles and broken ballpoint pens. Looked like he'd made some homemade tattoos. You see them?"

"See them. I had to work around them." He studied his fingertips. "So that's where that ink came from."

"Work around them?" Tommy Lee asked.

"Ran into some clot problems and had to inject embalming fluid in the femoral artery. The man had tattoos near his groin. The skin was still irritated and I didn't want to—" He stopped, as if no further explanation was necessary.

I completed his thought. "Have the surgical procedure damage them."

"That's right. Though it beats me how anyone would ever see them. Must be something those people like to look at while they're on the john."

"We don't think the tattoos are a cultural thing," I said. "We think they're a special case."

Tommy Lee pointed his empty fork at Wayne. "So what'd they look like?"

Wayne held up his hands in protest. "I don't read other people's mail."

The bizarre statement left Tommy Lee's mouth hanging open and Kevin looking at me for a translation.

I didn't have a clue. "What are you talking about?"

"What do you think I'm talking about? Nobody would put tattoos down there to be gawked at." He cut off a chunk of pie with his fork and jammed it in his mouth.

Tommy Lee eased back in his chair like he had all night. "I know how you feel, Wayne. I'm not one to pry myself. But sometimes I have to. Those tattoos might help us recover the body. That's the only reason I'm asking."

Uncle Wayne relaxed. "Well, I did notice some letters in a circle. Near, as I recall."

Tommy Lee pressed on. "What were they?"

"Like I said, near. N, E, A, R."

Tommy Lee glanced at me and then back to Wayne. "Could they have been points on a compass?"

"Maybe. Don't know what A and R would stand for. I thought it looked more like a clock face."

"Why's that?" the sheriff asked.

"Because there were two hands in the center, but I don't know what time it was. Could've been pointing at ten and two."

Maybe Uncle Wayne was onto something. I hadn't thought about a clock. "Any numbers?"

"Not on the clock, but there was a 2000. That was over Viet." Wayne paused. "Almost forgot about those words. Viet on the right thigh and Nam on the left. Guess they write backwards."

Then I remembered the words were written right to left. In my mind, I'd transposed them.

"And there's the four," Wayne added. "That's the one gave me the dickens of a time working around."

"Four?" I hadn't seen a four.

"Yeah. The number four and the letters K M. Right down where I needed to make my incision. Damnedest thing."

Kevin, Tommy Lee, and I looked at one another. I knew they understood. Y'Grok had coded the tattoo "For Kevin Malone."

"You've got a good memory." Tommy Lee winked at me. "Better than your nephew by a long shot."

"Nobody conked me on the noggin."

"That's true, even as hardheaded as Barry is, I've got to cut him some slack this time." Tommy Lee reached out and laid his hand on my uncle's bony wrist. "But that also means we're dealing with some desperate people."

"They got the body and those tattoos. What else do they want?"

"We don't know," Tommy Lee said. "Maybe nothing. But if they can't figure out what the tattoos mean, they might not want anybody else to have the chance."

"Nobody else has seen 'em."

Tommy Lee just nodded and let Wayne draw his own conclusions.

"You think they'll come back to the funeral home?"

Tommy Lee shrugged. "Maybe. Maybe even out here. I'd keep an eye out if I were you."

Uncle Wayne laughed. "As if they could find this place."

"Somebody might have tracked Y'Grok Eban from halfway around the world," Tommy Lee said. "I don't think a few twisting turns through a mountain cove will pose much of a problem."

As we drove away, Uncle Wayne waved from his front porch. I didn't know how seriously he had taken our warning. I hoped he'd at least lock his doors.

"Damn, damn, damn." Kevin spoke the words in huffs of exasperation. "What a crafty old devil. But Y'Grok gave me too much credit for being able to figure out he'd leave the message on his body."

"He probably expected you to find those broken pens and needle," I said.

"Maybe. Who else has been up there?"

"That social service worker," Tommy Lee said. "And the EMTs. I can get their names. But since Y'Grok died a natural death, the scene wasn't secured. Anybody could have gone up there the last few days."

"The EMTs might have seen something when they transported the body, and this Lutheran guy might have learned something from the other Montagnards." Kevin leaned forward until he was right behind my ear. "We've got to decipher what those tattoos mean. We've got to find that money or we've got nothing to trade for the body. If it was a clock face, then your uncle said the hands were pointing at ten and two. Must be significant."

I thought about my original impression of a compass. "Or northwest and northeast."

Kevin grunted. "Doesn't take us anywhere I know of. Has to be something I'd understand. We should have had your uncle write it down."

I looked at the clipboard mounted on the dash. "Mind if I use this?"

"Go ahead," Tommy Lee said.

I turned on the courtesy light, flipped to a clean sheet of paper, and used the ballpoint attached to the clip. Uncle Wayne had given me the correct letters at the four points of the compass, but I drew his clock hands as the "V" I remembered.

Kevin peered over my shoulder. "V for Victory, maybe? If you read the letters as a circle, Near Victory or Near Vietnam?"

"Could it mean near victory for the resistance?" Tommy Lee suggested.

"Could be," I said. "I don't think the V stands for Vietnam. He'd already written that word."

Kevin reached for my drawing. "No, he'd written it as two words."

I pulled the clipboard away from him. "But in reverse order. Nam Viet." I stared at the circle, and then I saw it. "Reverse order. Counter clockwise."

"Raen?" Kevin asked.

"Yes." I jabbed the pen into the V. "But with this letter in the middle. RAVEN."

Chapter Nine

As we headed back to the funeral home, jagged streaks of lightning revealed the thunderheads building in the night sky. Between their bursts of brilliance only the car's headlights pierced the darkness.

"Oh, Christ," Kevin said. "Just what we need. A double shot of stormy weather tonight."

Tommy Lee turned on the wipers as a few splats hit the windshield. "Part of spring down here. Gulf air slams into the last of the arctic air mass and a storm front can last for days. We get some real gulley washers."

"Tornados?"

"No, the mountains break them up, but flashfloods can do as much damage."

I watched the first streaks of rain turn into a silver curtain. "I'm glad we got the Montagnards bedded down at the VFW."

"Me too," Tommy Lee agreed. "One good thing about this mess, Barry. You won't be conducting the funeral in tomorrow's rain."

On cue, the sky opened up and the car slowed to a crawl.

Kevin shouted above the pounding on the sheet metal roof. "I hope Talbert can fly in all right. Maybe the tattoos will mean something to him. Stormy won't sit still when he learns what your uncle saw."

I turned around in the seat until I could see the vague shape of Kevin's face. "You don't want Weathers' help?"

"Help's one thing, red tape's another. Stormy Weathers is too far up the chain of command to call in resources without every bureaucrat in Washington shitting on himself afraid that some other agency will get the credit. They'll spend as much time covering their asses as investigating."

"And you think Franklin Talbert will know something you don't?"

"No, but that asshole's about the only card that hasn't been dealt."

"Why's nobody like Talbert?" I asked.

"Why bother to like someone who loves himself so much he bottles his farts and sells them as air freshener?"

I didn't have an answer to that question.

When we got to the funeral home, Tommy Lee pulled the patrol car beneath the overhang by the operating room. The shattered lock and splintered frame of the door reminded me that I should have arranged for repairs. Now I'd need to wedge the door shut to keep the wind gusts from blowing it open.

I cracked the car door enough to trigger the interior lights and looked at Tommy Lee. "What's the schedule tomorrow?"

"You got me. I'll talk to Y'Suom about his father's tattoos. My recommendation to Weathers and Millen will be to talk with Talbert before we go public."

"What about that Lutheran social worker?" Kevin asked. "He was the last person to see Y'Grok alive."

"Harvey Collins," I said. "He'll probably be at the VFW."

"Why don't you and Kevin go see him in the morning. I'll go back to the Grove Park."

"Sounds like a plan." Kevin motioned for me to get out of the car. "Get some sleep. You're making me hurt just looking at you."

I waved goodnight and closed the damaged door behind me. A straight-back chair provided a brace under the knob and I left the room reasonably secured against the elements. Our part-time assistant Freddy Mott was also a skilled carpenter and I'd have him repair the damage the next day.

An indistinct murmur of voices came from the parlor and at first I was concerned we had a death to deal with. I heard Mom say, "That must be him now."

Seated on the sofa, as far away from each other as possible, were Susan Miller and Melissa Bigham. My mother was perched on the edge of a chair on the other side of the coffee table. Three cups of cold and neglected black coffee sat on a silver tray.

"Are you all right?" Mom rose to greet me. "We tried to call."

"I turned my phone off to save the battery. I was out at Uncle Wayne's where there's no reception." I smiled at Susan and Melissa. "We may have gotten a break in the case."

Melissa's eyebrows arched.

Susan's descended into a scowl. "The only break you've got might be in your head. You were supposed to rest."

"I'm sorry. But I've felt fine all day."

"Give me enough credit as a doctor to know that's a lie. Sit down and let me look at you."

Susan directed me to the chair Mom had vacated. With a gentle touch, she probed the stitches on my forehead. "The incision's redder than it should be. No wonder. You've gotten the wound wet and dirty." She ran her hand over the knot behind my ear. "At least this swelling's gone down."

Susan pulled the table lamp closer. "Tilt your head back."

I did as I was ordered. She brought her face within inches of mine. She covered, and then uncovered each of my eyes, checking the consistency of the pupil dilation.

She stood up, shaking her head. "Well, I guess there's one advantage to being so hardheaded." She returned to the sofa where her purse lay on the floor. "I suspected your antics would expose you to infection." She fumbled through her bag and retrieved a bottle of pills and a small elongated box. "I brought some antibiotic samples. Take one tablet tonight and one with each meal for the next three days. And here's a tube of antiseptic cream. Put it on the incision twice a day." She handed the medicine to my mother. "Now you need to get to bed." She stared at Melissa. "And we need to leave."

Lightning flashed through the front window and the thunderclap hit as our house lights flickered.

"Sit down, Susan," I said softly. "Melissa's helping me and I need to talk with her. I want you to stay because you'd be as foolish as me to go out in the height of the storm."

Susan retreated to her end of the sofa, her lips drawn tight and her arms folded across her chest.

"Mom, would you put that medicine in my room. I'll lock up down here."

My mother glanced at the cups on the table. "Would anyone like fresh coffee or something to eat?"

"No thank you, Connie," Susan said.

Melissa stood up and offered Mom her hand. "I'm sure the storm will break soon, Mrs. Clayton. Thank you for your hospitality."

My mother hesitated, sensing a tension boiling below the surface. But she didn't know what to do. "Democrat's in the kitchen. Y'all drive carefully." She disappeared down the hall.

Melissa returned to the sofa and we sat quietly till Mom's footsteps faded. Thunder rolled and rain beat against the windowpanes. But the atmosphere outside wasn't as electrically charged as the atmosphere inside.

I felt exhausted. Whatever had created the hostility between Susan and Melissa was beyond my energy to placate. I just wanted to cover Melissa on the day's events and go to bed.

I pulled my drawing from my pocket. "What I say here stays here."

"All right," Melissa agreed.

Susan said nothing.

I handed the paper to Melissa. "Y'Grok Eban tattooed himself a short time before he died. Here's what I've reconstructed from Uncle Wayne's memory."

While Melissa studied the sketch, I reviewed the meeting with General Weathers and Senator Millen and explained the shift in the suspected motive from political publicity to money.

Melissa gave the paper to Susan. "And Kevin Malone was the only person Y'Grok contacted?"

"As far as we know. Tomorrow we'll backtrack the people he might have talked to locally."

"Who was his doctor?" Susan asked.

"His doctor?"

"Yes. If the man was diagnosed with lung cancer, somebody must have examined him. Fresh tattoos would be a red flag to a doctor or nurse."

Melissa nodded in agreement. "And if they didn't see the tattoos, you'll know more precisely when they were made."

They both raised good points. "Tommy Lee told me he saw Y'Grok when he came to the hospital about two weeks ago. Susan, do you think you could get some information?"

Melissa jumped in. "What about patient privacy rights?"

"The patient's deceased," Susan snapped. "Besides, you're the only one in a position to blab medical information to the world."

Melissa reddened. "I've never betrayed Barry."

The challenge in her voice surprised me. "I trust you both. But we'll let Susan decide what's appropriate to share."

"You'll let me?"

I was glad I had only two feet because I seemed to be putting them in my mouth each time I opened it. "You had a good idea. I'd appreciate if you'd follow up."

Susan shrugged. "I'll see what I can do." She stood up. "We should be leaving. You need to get to bed."

Melissa started to say something, and then thought better of it.

I followed them to the front door. A stand in the corner of the foyer held several black umbrellas we kept on hand in case the weather turned nasty during a visitation. I gave one to each, and then took one myself. Opening the door, I found the rain had slackened. "I'll walk you to your cars."

I had the good sense to go first to Melissa's Ford Focus. She clicked her security key and the interior lights came on. She handed me the umbrella as she slipped under the steering wheel. I thought I heard her whisper, "I'll be back." I walked over to Susan and we watched Melissa drive away in the light rain.

"I'm sorry I kept you waiting. I should have phoned."

Susan unlocked the door of her Subaru. "Yes, you should have."

"I had no idea Melissa would be here." The words sounded defensive, and I was angry with myself for feeling I had to give an explanation.

"She's a reporter. She's competitive." Susan leaned under my umbrella and kissed me. "And she's a woman, and she's very competitive."

With that cryptic pronouncement, Susan gave me her umbrella, closed her door, and drove off. I stood in the rain looking like a very confused umbrella salesman.

Democrat lay across the bottom step to the upstairs. He was ready to go to bed. He watched me bring the tray and coffee cups to the kitchen sink and rinse them out. I heard his tags jingle as he got to his feet and moved toward the back door. Rain never discouraged the lab from going outside, but ten at night seemed late for nature's call. He gave a low whine. Then I heard pounding on the back porch.

I unlocked the kitchen door and flipped on the exterior light. Melissa stood at the back porch's screen door, her wet face glistening in the harsh glare of the overhead bulb.

"Did you forget something?" I unlatched the hook and helped her up the step.

"I've got some news I didn't want to mention in front of Susan in case there's nothing to it." She caught my arm. "We can talk out here. No sense dripping through the house."

"Don't be silly. We'll sit in the kitchen." I nudged Democrat away before he could embarrass both of us with a curious and extremely personal sniff of her wet jeans.

I handed her a dry dish towel and she patted her face and hair.

"Thanks." The cold water had brought a surge of color to her cheeks and curled her hair in dark ringlets. Her long-sleeved rust turtleneck that had been merely fashionable in the parlor now clung to her body like paint. The only thing left to the imagination was a possible tan line.

I forced my eyes to remain locked on hers. "You can trust Susan."

She sat down at the table. "So, everything's all right between you two?"

The question surprised me. "You've heard differently?"

The red in her cheeks darkened and she fidgeted with the towel. She forced a laugh. "Oh, you know, in my business I can't assume anything."

"Susan and I are all right." Then I added, "As far as I know." The words were only half facetious. My ex-wife, Rachel, said I was clueless when it came to women. Otherwise, how could I have expected her to follow me from Charlotte to Gainesboro when my father got ill? Rachel now lived in D.C. and the woman I lost as a wife I cherished as a friend.

"I called in a favor at the *Washington Post*. Their database is a little more sophisticated than the *Gainesboro Vista*."

"How'd you set that up?"

"I told my friend I was profiling a local vet for a feature that would run Memorial Day weekend. My subject had been involved in an operation called Raven and he was too modest to talk about it."

"Sounds plausible." I sat down at the table opposite her. Democrat gave up and went back to the stairs, anxious to go to bed.

"Give me some credit for creative storytelling. Anyway, my contact called back late this afternoon. He'd found Raven in a set of documents released a few years ago under the Freedom of Information Act. Senator Millen had convened a hearing on efforts to pursue leads on MIA and POW sightings. Raven was one of the topics."

"That makes sense. When Millen was shot down, he escaped through the Raven network. Why had it been classified?"

"Because names were discussed. Montagnards who had aided U.S. Special Forces were considered possible sources of information on which missing men were known by them to be dead. And the Montagnards might guide investigators to identifiable remains."

I knew Millen had made several trips to Vietnam in the late eighties. About the time Y'Grok's son came out. "So the committee was afraid the Vietnamese would take reprisals on these men?"

"Evidently." She pursed her lips. "And they were right. After the fact-finding trips to Vietnam, the summary of the final Millen report concluded that the majority of Raven's members had been eliminated by 1980. Those left alive were afraid to assist Millen and his Vietnamese hosts in their efforts."

"Was Y'Grok one of them?"

"Don't know. The names of the living Montagnards were deleted. Only those confirmed dead went into the report."

I sat quietly for a few moments. Y'Grok had been kept out of a hearing's documentation which limited the dissemination of his ties to Raven. But, congressional hearings were notorious for leaking like a rusty bucket. Someone in Washington could have speculated on a connection between missing money and Y'Grok. I wondered how long Nickles had worked for Millen. "Did your contact say who had access to the uncensored report?"

"Barry, that was nearly ten years ago, right after Clinton normalized relations with Vietnam. You want Tommy Lee to post pictures of every congressional aide?"

"No. I'm interested in people we know are here. What's Nickles' story?"

Melissa rolled her eyes. "He wasn't on my A-list."

"He might be worth checking out. Anything else?"

She flashed a smile that told me she'd uncovered a morsel. "Archie Donovan called earlier this evening with a tip that Franklin Talbert won't be staying at the Grove Park Inn. Archie and the mayor arranged for him to use one of the condos up at Crystal Cascades. They thought he needed a gated community."

"They would. They get him a tee time as well?"

"I asked that. I guess my sarcasm went over Archie's head. He said there wasn't time because he and Mayor Whitlock will be personally driving Talbert to meet the Montagnards at the VFW and then give him a private tour of the Heaven's Gate Gardens Cemetery."

"Tomorrow?"

"Yes. They worked through Talbert's publicist and are meeting him at the airport in the afternoon. Archie's hoping Talbert will be joined by Senator Millen and General Weathers at a reception the mayor's trying to arrange at the Gainesboro Country Club."

"When's that?"

Melissa laughed. "Archie told me twenty hundred hours. Can you believe it? He's adopted military time. I guess because Talbert and the others have been in the service, he thinks military time will impress them."

I could see Archie worrying whether to shake hands or salute. The closest he'd come to military service was wearing his Good Humor uniform during his summer job in college. "Makes you wonder if Archie didn't steal the body just to get his celebrities together."

Melissa's eyes instantly narrowed. "You think so?"

"Of course not. Archie's not that foolish." I could tell Melissa wasn't convinced. "And what's he going to do, have the body reappear as if this never happened?"

"I guess you're right, but I might just check his alibi."

"Be my guest. Kevin and I have other leads to follow."

"Kevin Malone," she repeated. "What do you know about him?"

"Just what I've told you. He's Tommy Lee's war buddy and Y'Grok's closest confidante, if we're to believe he got that letter from Y'Grok."

Melissa leaned forward over the table, placing her palms face down. "Kevin Malone's not on the Boston police force."

"What? Who told you that?"

"A lieutenant at his district."

"District?"

"They don't call them precincts in Boston. The lieutenant first said Kevin was on administrative leave. When I pressed him, he admitted Kevin's on suspension without pay—six months."

"What'd he do?"

"He wouldn't go into any details, but he did say it involved the death of his partner. Happened last November. Disciplinary action came down in February. He'll be reinstated in July, unless he opts for early retirement. He hasn't been into his district for eight weeks."

"But that's where he got Y'Grok's letter."

"So he says." Melissa rose from the table. "That's the main thing I wanted to tell you. Check it out however you want, but I didn't think it smart to spring the news in front of your mom or Susan."

I got to my feet. "Thanks. I'll let you know what I find out."

She took a step closer. "Be careful. I don't want to lose you. You're too much fun to work with." Before I could answer, she kissed me on the cheek. "Good night, Barry."

I managed a faint "good night" as she closed the kitchen door.

Chapter Ten

Around eight the next morning, Tommy Lee dropped Kevin at the funeral home. No developments had occurred overnight so while Kevin and I tracked down Harvey Collins at the VFW, Tommy Lee planned to share my sketch of the tattoos with Millen and Weathers. We'd check in with each other later in the morning and decide when to bring Franklin Talbert into the picture. I warned Tommy Lee that Archie and the mayor had their own plans for the movie star.

I didn't mention Melissa's revelation about Kevin's status with the Boston Police Department. Its relevancy to our investigation might only be how Kevin received Y'Grok's letter and I didn't want Kevin thinking I was spying on him.

The gray morning sky hung low on the ridges. The forecast called for scattered showers, but a classic spring conflict of cold dry air slamming into warm moist air threatened to create a major storm front that could send bands of violent thunderstorms through the mountains the next day. Perhaps that would work in our favor. The Thursday memorial service could be inside the Lutheran church without a casket, and then there'd be no graveside ritual because of the downpour. I'd discuss that possible schedule with Y'Suom.

The jeep's wipers swept on intermittent, providing a constant smear on the windshield. The VFW was at the opposite end of town.

As we drove down Main Street, Kevin peered out the side window at the assortment of shops and galleries that comprised our small business district. "What time's this place wake up?"

"Between nine and ten. Other than the barbershop and the Cardinal Café, most of the early morning action's out near the interstate exit. Bojangle's and Hardee's."

"How about Krispy Kreme? That's a North Carolina export us Yankees have taken to."

"Afraid Gainesboro finds their doughnuts only in grocery stores. Asheville's got a couple locations, one with a drive-thru."

Kevin laughed. "Must be a pileup of police cars. There's a detective back in Boston who vacations in North Carolina. He always returns with cartons of Krispy Kreme doughnuts and cartons of Winston cigarettes. A guy could make a pretty good living smuggling both."

"You been to the North Carolina mountains before?"

"Nah. Whenever I took off, I'd head for the cape. My wife and I'd rent a place in the fall, after the rates dropped. I'd fish and drink beer. She'd read and drink wine. We'd go for days without talking." He paused. "Just like at home. Guess that's why I'm not still married."

"Any kids?"

He shook his head. "Wanted them. Thought about adopting. I tried to get Carolyn to consider a Vietnamese or Montagnard child, but she thought the race difference would be too hard. I thought kids are kids." He leaned back against the headrest.

After a minute of silence, I pressed an innocent question. "Will you retire to Cape Cod?"

"Can't afford it. Carolyn gets half my pension and property's zoomed so sky high I couldn't buy a Port-a-John." He looked at the deserted sidewalks. "Town like this might be nice."

"We get a good share of retirees. Most of them keep summer homes here and winter in Florida. They've driven up our land prices."

"Maybe I could live in Y'Grok's old mill."

"Maybe. But you'd better put a hand railing on that log over your swimming hole."

I braked at a stoplight up the hill from the VFW. A gaggle of children in yellow raincoats trekked to the elementary school on the other side of the street. A female crossing guard wearing an orange poncho and toting a portable stop sign shooed along a straggler. The little boy went out of his way to stomp in every puddle.

Kevin chuckled. "A lad after my own heart. Looking for trouble."

"A rebel in training."

"So, why's this wicked Melissa Bigham interested in me?"

His question came from nowhere. The child, the rain, and the traffic light blurred out of existence. Suddenly the universe shrank to the interior of the jeep. Sound collapsed to Kevin's breathing as he waited for my answer. I suspected he had intentionally caught me off guard, watching for my reaction.

I smiled as innocently as I could. "Did she ask you for a date?"

"Not yet. Maybe she's shy. Maybe that's why she checked with my lou first."

"Lou?"

"What we call our lieutenants. Lieutenant Stone was on the stick when she called."

"The stick?"

He shook his head impatiently. "The shift. The woman tracked me down to district eleven in Dorchester and interrogated my lou. What the hell for?"

I decided there wasn't much percentage in playing cute or deceptive with him. "Melissa knows about the missing body. I told her because she's too good a reporter not to have figured out something was wrong."

"Okay. Why me?"

"You're not an exclusive club. She's doing background on everyone who knew Y'Grok."

A horn honked behind me. I looked in the rearview mirror and saw I'd created a two-car traffic jam. I waved an apology and drove through the green light.

"Tommy Lee know about this?" Kevin asked.

"That Melissa's aware of what's really going on? No. And she won't be telling him."

Kevin seemed to relax. "My suspension's bullshit. That's why I got the courtesy call last night from my Deputy Superintendent. The department's just playing tough for the media. Not have it look like I'm getting special treatment."

I was tempted to ask "Are you?" but drove down the hill without speaking.

Kevin lowered his voice. "I told Mike to stay with the car. Wait for backup. We'd spotted a guy who'd been on the morning sheet at roll call. There were warrants out on him for a string of armed robberies in the area."

"But you're a detective." Be-on-the-lookouts, or BOLOs as police call them, were normally handled by the uniforms.

"The sucker stepped out of a car right in front of us. We're in an unmarked and I said, 'Jesus, Mike, that's Riley Conner.' I stopped the car and Conner gave us a look back over his shoulder. He acted cool, but I knew he'd made us. He cut down between some triple deckers. I hopped out to tail him. I lost him for a moment, and then caught a glimpse of his jacket as he ducked through a side alley. An eight-foot chain link construction fence crossed the far end. I couldn't tell whether the fence blocked the exit or allowed a squeeze-through around the buildings. If it was sealed, I didn't think Conner had had time to scale it."

Kevin paused as I turned into the VFW lot. I found a parking space at the far end and left the motor running as a cue for him to continue his story.

"I'll admit walking down a possible dead end alley isn't the smartest move in the book. There were a few cellar doors on either side, so I took out my piece and stepped as quietly as I could over the broken bottles and trash decorating the cracked pavement, checking the doors as I went. I'd nearly reached the fence when I heard wood scraping behind me. I wheeled around just as Conner sprang out of a doorway. He'd apparently found a door open and then locked it until I went by. He had a pistol in his right hand. When he saw my gun, he popped a shot that zinged past my ear. I fired once down the alley, but missed. We both fired a second shot. He fell back into a trashcan, tried to get up, and I emptied my clip at him."

"He missed you?"

"Yeah. The autopsy showed my first hit was enough to burn him, but the M.E. wasn't there handing me his report at the time."

"And your partner?"

"Mike had come around the corner of the alley just as I fired the first shot."

Jesus. Melissa's source in Boston had sugarcoated the incident. Kevin had killed his own partner.

"I told him to stay with the god damned car." Kevin yanked open the door, and then slammed it shut again. He turned to me and his voice shook. "You want to hear the crazy part. The community and media didn't have much to say about Mike's death, but they raised holy hell about how many times I'd shot Conner. Finally the mayor and commissioner caved under the pressure and did the politically correct thing. They couldn't nail me on Conner, even Internal Affairs ruled that a good shooting, so they went through our policy and procedure manual and came up with a charge of not exercising due diligence in the interest and pursuit of my duties. In other words, they blamed me for Mike's death. Gave me a six month suspension. How's that for justice?"

We walked in silence through the gentle rain.

The smell of pancakes met us at the front door. Families sat on blankets spread on the floor of the VFW's main room. Behind a long table near a side wall, volunteers tended electric griddles. Bowls of batter replenished their supply as the breakfast treats went like, well, hotcakes. I looked around for Harvey Collins.

"Mr. Clayton. Mr. Malone."

We turned to face Captain Randall. Beside him stood Y'Suom. Randall's impeccable uniform was in sharp contrast to Y'Suom's ill-fitting tweed sport coat with the sleeves too short and the shirt collar too large. His wardrobe must have come from a church's donation closet. The young man's wide, brown eyes asked the question he didn't need to speak.

"Nothing's come up," I said.

"But the sheriff's running down some leads with the senator and general this morning," Kevin added. "And Talbert gets in this afternoon."

Randall looked around the room. "What do we tell these people?"

Most of the Montagnards were still eating from paper plates. Several men began collecting trash in plastic bags. Near the rear exit, four kids kicked a pillow in a makeshift soccer game. I saw a nearby group of women glance at us and then turn away as if they didn't want to pry.

I stepped into the hall. "Let's find a place to talk."

Randall shook his head. "If the sheriff's with General Weathers, I'd better get back. Y'Suom, we'll talk later." He executed a snappy pivot and left.

Y'Suom and Kevin followed me to a closed door at the other end of the hall. I listened at the frosted pane and then tried the knob. We found a small empty conference room whose walls were decorated with scores of military banners and insignias. I took a seat at the single round table and indicated for the others to join me.

"I have a suggestion for you to consider. Regardless of what happens today, we'll go through with the service tomorrow. If your father's body hasn't been recovered, an announcement will be made at the beginning and then prayers can be offered for the return of your father's body."

"Will people accept that?" Y'Suom asked.

"You know their customs better than I do. We can tell them as much or as little as you want, but we have to say something."

"Barry's right," Kevin said. "Till tomorrow we could always explain we didn't want to compromise our investigation with media coverage, but concealing the facts by pretending every-thing's normal for the service would turn into a cover-up."

Kevin's point wasn't lost on Y'Suom, and I thought how Melissa Bigham would surely balk at withholding the truth while reporting on the funeral.

"Who would make this announcement?" Y'Suom asked.

"The minister."

"Or maybe the sheriff," Kevin said. "Makes it more official."

Y'Suom shook his head. "You, Mr. Clayton. You can tell what happened because it happened to you. They'll know it's true."

His demand hadn't been part of my plan. I flashed forward to the proposed scene. "Hi, I'm Barry Clayton. A funny thing happened on the way to the funeral." Or, "I'm Barry Clayton, here to tell you why the word funeral begins with fun." My only way out was to find Y'Grok's body before then.

"All right. I'll talk to the minister. Anything else you want to change in the service?"

"We're adding remarks by Senator Millen, General Weathers, and Mr. Talbert since now they'll all be here."

"Good. Will you be speaking to Talbert? He doesn't know the situation."

"No." Y'Suom shifted his gaze to Kevin. "Captain Randall and I were just talking about Talbert. He'll take care of him. I'll spend my time with my people."

Kevin reached out and laid his hand on Y'Suom's. "Son, we need you to spend some time with us."

Y'Suom flinched at the touch, but didn't withdraw his hand from the table top. "What can I do?"

"You can tell us about Raven, and what your father told you. You know why he sent for me."

For an instant, I saw a flicker of fear in the young man's brown eyes. Then he shook his head, as much to erase the expression as to signify he had nothing to say.

"Give me something," Kevin insisted. "He carved a message for me into his own flesh. Is this how you would honor him?"

"In his flesh?" Y'Suom's startled face revealed genuine shock.

"Yes. And we don't know what the tattoos mean. The sheriff is talking to the senator and general now. But it's about Raven."

Y'Suom's voice dropped to a hoarse whisper. "He wanted justice."

"Who for?" Kevin asked.

"He told me for Raven."

"Did your father have money? Money from Raven?"

Y'Suom hesitated, looked at me, and then he seemed to relax. "Yes. He said he had money that didn't belong to him and that you'd find a better use for it."

Kevin pulled his hand away. "How was I supposed to find this money?"

Y'Suom shrugged. "He would leave you a message. That's all he said."

"And you have no message for me?"

The trace of a smile graced his lips. "No. Not for you."

"Damn. Barry, describe the tattoos for him. Maybe they'll mean something."

If the crude drawings had any significance for Y'Suom, he kept his knowledge well hidden. I was about to ask who else his father might have spoken with when the door opened.

"Oh, we're sorry. We didn't mean to interrupt." The man making the apology started to back out.

I recognized him as Earl Hucksley, the minister from Charlotte who'd be conducting tomorrow's service and the person I'd have to tell why Y'Grok didn't show up for his own funeral. A second man had followed behind and now tried to get out of the way of the back-pedaling preacher.

I spoke up before they closed the door. "We're finished if you need the room."

"No, it's okay," Hucksley said. "We were looking for Y'Suom." He smiled at the Montagnard. "Some of the families are asking for you."

I stood up. "Why don't you go? Kevin and I'll catch up with you later."

Y'Suom nodded.

As he and Kevin rose, I spoke to Collins. "Can we have a word with you? Just take a moment."

Harvey Collins stepped from behind Hucksley. Collins was younger, about thirty-five, with short-cut brown hair and a goatee. He wore jeans and a UVA sweatshirt. He'd probably slept on the floor in them. I'd only met him a few days ago, but he seemed genuine enough and the Montagnards held him in high regard.

"Sure." He turned to Kevin. "Harvey Collins. Lutheran Social Services."

Kevin shook his hand and motioned for him to take Y'Suom's seat. I walked over and closed the door. As I returned, Kevin gave me a tilt of his head before he sat down. My show.

"Harvey, Kevin's a friend of Sheriff Tommy Lee Wadkins and Y'Grok. The three of them served together in Vietnam."

"Boy, that must have been some team."

Kevin leaned forward and smiled. "I was the weak link. Of course, so was Tommy Lee compared to Y'Grok."

Harvey returned Kevin's smile. "It was a privilege to know him these last few months."

"Kevin's here from Boston," I said. "Y'Grok sent him a letter that he wanted to see him."

"I know," Harvey said. "I posted it for him."

"So, he told you what the letter was about?"

"No. He'd asked me for some stationery and an envelope. The next time I returned, he had the letter ready to mail." He turned to Kevin. "You're with the police, aren't you?"

"Yes." Kevin took the opportunity to ask a question. "And he didn't mention anything about me? Why he wanted to see me?"

"I didn't ask. Y'Grok was a private person."

I picked up the questioning again. "Is that why he wanted to live in the old mill?"

Harvey sighed. "God only knows. That was a terrible place for a sick man, but what else could I do? He'd wanted to see the mountains and I brought him up for a day trip. He fell in love with the spot."

"Anybody else come see him?"

"We had some volunteers from Grace Lutheran in town who checked on him. He didn't want company, but I made the arrangements. I couldn't leave him up there for days on end."

"How many different people?"

"Six or seven. They worked out a rotation schedule." Harvey stroked his goatee with his left hand and eyed me cautiously. "Is there some problem? Believe me, he didn't want to stay in a hospital. He must have failed rapidly because we would have taken him if we'd found him in the final stages."

"No, no problem," Kevin said. "We're not second guessing anyone's decisions. It's just that Y'Grok said he brought something back from Vietnam for me. And now that he's gone, it's even more important to me, but Y'Grok didn't tell me what he brought. Guess he wanted it to be a surprise."

"Probably in that ammo case," Harvey said.

I caught my breath and locked eyes with Kevin. His jaw trembled, but he waited for me to speak. "Could be," I agreed. "Was it an old one, like from the war?"

"Yeah. Those things are indestructible. This one was pretty beat up. I never served so I don't know what caliber." He moved his hands to show the size of a small suitcase. "I can take you up there."

"Thanks," I said. "We went with Tommy Lee yesterday, but didn't see an ammo case."

Harvey tucked his bottom lip under his upper teeth and gnawed on his whiskers. "That's right. Last time I saw Y'Grok the case wasn't in the room. He usually kept it beside a nail keg he used as a nightstand."

"We saw the keg," I said. "You ever ask him about the case?"

"He had it when I first took him up there. I teased him. Asked if it was his wardrobe chest. He said something about the case was really a circle, coming round to where it began."

"Could someone have stolen it from him?" Kevin asked.

"I don't see how. I think he would have told me. Like I said, the case wasn't there last time I visited. I noticed it was gone, but didn't ask him about it. I thought he'd just moved it someplace."

He looked at Kevin. "You think that's what he wanted you to have? The ammo case?"

Kevin didn't answer. He stared at the wall of insignias as if neither Harvey nor I were in the room.

Chapter Eleven

"We need to get to that mill." Kevin spoke the words as an order and then jogged for the jeep.

I ran behind, knowing that if I didn't drive him, he'd try to find his own way up there. The rain had picked up and navigating through the fog and muddy roads would be a challenge, probably an impossibility for the Boston native.

I climbed in the driver's seat and ran both hands through my wet hair, matting it flat to my scalp. "Shouldn't we check in with Tommy Lee? Maybe Millen or Weathers deciphered the tattoos."

Kevin snapped his seatbelt. "Call him now. If he doesn't answer, we go and keep calling as long as you have a signal."

I unclipped my phone from my waist. "You dial. I'll have enough trouble driving in this soup." I told him Tommy Lee's cell number as I pulled out of the parking lot.

"Hi, pal, any luck?" Kevin listened and then shook his head to share Tommy Lee's answer. "So what do they suggest?"

I continued out of town accompanied by an occasional grunt from my passenger.

After a few minutes, Kevin said, "I don't know, let me ask him."

I risked a quick glance from the road to see Kevin take the phone from his ear.

"Everyone's in the dark about what the tattoos mean. Maybe Franklin will have a clue. He's coming in at two, but this Archie

Donovan and the mayor have him tied up as soon as he lands. There's evidently some reception tonight and Stormy and Ryan are attending. Tommy Lee says we're all supposed to go."

"Twenty hundred hours."

"What?"

I decided not to get into my late night meeting with Melissa Bigham. "I had a message last night from Archie. Didn't think about it till now. The mayor's throwing a cocktail party at the Gainesboro Country Club under the guise of honoring Y'Grok, but it's really to get his picture made with our dignitaries."

"Dignitaries. No one's ever applied that word to me." Kevin spoke into the phone. "Can we get Talbert between this afternoon's bullshit and the reception?"

I didn't wait for Tommy Lee's answer. "We need to get Talbert away from his self-appointed handlers. Surely they're going to give him some time alone at the condo."

"But I don't want an entourage going there or to the Grove Park. Franklin will treat it like a damn movie junket." Kevin listened a few seconds to whatever Tommy Lee offered and then answered, "I haven't asked him yet."

"What?" I prompted.

"Tommy Lee thinks we should get with Franklin, Stormy, and Ryan at the funeral home on the quiet. Maybe you could pick Franklin up, bring him there, and then take him to the reception. We could say we needed to go over things for tomorrow's service."

I thought about how the mayor and Archie could still tag along, and how Mom would feel responsible to host everyone. "I've got a better idea. Get word to Franklin Talbert we're going to meet about the funeral, but I'll take him to my cabin instead. Tommy Lee can bring the others. Any onlookers will assume we're going to the funeral home."

"I like it." Kevin repeated the plan to Tommy Lee, who agreed. "They'll shoot for six," he told me. "And they'll arrange for Franklin to be ready at five-thirty."

"Tell Tommy Lee what we're doing now, and that I'll drop you at his house when we're finished."

Kevin filled Tommy Lee in on our conversation with Harvey Collins and our effort to find the missing ammo case.

When he finished, he handed me back my phone. "He says to keep an eye on the weather and to remind you the creeks can rise fast."

"That's for your benefit. Don't get any ideas about body surfing again."

We stood across the stream from the mill. The level was up a couple inches from yesterday and whitewater gurgled around the broken spokes of the wheel. I could see from the brush trapped between them that the stream frequently flooded its banks. I didn't want to get stranded on the other side.

I'd brought a compass from the jeep's glove box and umbrellas from the cargo space. Kevin leaned on one as if it were a cane, content to let the fine rain fall on his uncovered head. At this elevation, the clouds enveloped us like a soggy linen sheet and we could hardly see ten feet in front of us.

"What now?" Kevin asked.

"I vote we go inside. This time we know what we're looking for and maybe something from the tattoos will make sense when we see it." I lifted the open umbrella over my head and slowly crossed the foot-log like a tightrope walker high above a circus crowd. When I safely stepped on the far bank, Kevin mimicked my performance without any comment on how he'd done it back in Boston.

We spent thirty minutes thoroughly examining every inch of the room. Over the years, the wood had been scarred by insects, animals, and humans. Initials of long forgotten lovers decorated the rough planking. Numbers carved into beams near the millstone bore witness to an operator's need for an impromptu ledger. None of the figures contained 2000, nor was there a circular drawing like the possible compass. We checked for loose floorboards and shined our flashlights through gaps in the stone foundation in an effort to determine what lay beneath the mill. Nothing.

"What do you think two thousand represents?" I asked. "We're talking a lot more money, right?"

"If we're talking Raven, we are." Kevin slammed the flat of his palm against the millstone. "I'm missing something. Y'Grok counted on me thinking like he thought."

"How did he use numbers?"

"Like we all did. Coordinates for longitude and latitude. Distance. Radio frequencies."

"What was the common measurement for distance? Yards?"

"Meters. Y'Grok grew up under French colonialism."

I didn't need a calculator to know 2000 meters equaled more than a mile. "He couldn't have lugged the ammo case that far."

"Then maybe it's feet. He was in America."

"That's still over a third of a mile. And which direction? I think the lines of the V pointed northwest and northeast."

Kevin paced to the far corner of the room. "For all I know he could've been drawing a god-damned piece of pie."

I looked down at the keg Y'Grok had improvised as a nightstand. We had turned it over once to make sure nothing had been hidden inside it. Its round top matched the circular shape of the tattoo and the rim of the metal hoop had a coat of rust. "Not a slice of pie," I said, "but a slice of a circle. The V defines an arc with the N point in the middle."

"A triangle? You think Y'Grok was using some sort of triangulation?"

"You tell me. Maybe he got double duty out of his letters to spell Raven and got the N to stand for north."

Kevin walked back with renewed energy. "That'd be like him. Make the tattoos work on multiple levels. Triangulation with N at the center of the third side. And he gave us the distance."

I shook my head. "Two thousand feet? Two thousand meters? That's a long way."

"But what if two thousand is the combined length of all three sides. We're looking at a third. That's—"

"Six-six-six. A little ominous, don't you think? Did Y'Grok read Stephen King?"

"No, but he knew how lousy I was at math. And if N is on an arc of the circle, then the radius will be the same. I'd say his ammo case is buried a little over six hundred and sixty feet from here. Roughly two hundred meters."

"North." I pulled out my compass and took a bearing. The direction went parallel to the stream. "At least we don't have to cross the log."

"Unless that stream turns."

"It turns, but away from us. That's the rickety bridge we drove across coming in."

Kevin picked up his umbrella. "Then let's get moving."

We stood with our backs against the mill and I sighted the compass due north. On a clear day, I could have used a distant pine or rock outcropping as a landmark. Today, the fog limited my line of vision to a scrub patch of rhododendron about thirty yards away. I'd have to take frequent bearings or risk zig-zagging off course. Otherwise we could miss the spot by fifty yards.

"I'll lead and you count the paces." I set off at a brisk walk, watching the ground for stones and roots.

With Kevin muttering his numbers behind me, we crossed a depression in the weedy pasture. At some point in the past, this spot of ground had been the basin of a millpond that controlled the water flow for the wheel. Its simple earthen dam was probably washed out years ago.

I stopped at the thicket. "Look at this."

Kevin held his count and reached out for the broken ends of rhododendron. He looked beneath the plant. "Somebody snapped off some branches. You can see where the bark's been stripped."

I scraped an exposed end with my fingernail. "Not in the past day or two, but I'd say within the past week."

"We're on to something. Y'Grok knew we couldn't go through the thicket so he left us a sign."

His deduction made sense. We'd have to walk around the small cluster and pick up the trail on the other side. I took another compass reading and selected the trunk of a large white pine just beyond the rhododendron. "You'll have to estimate the distance." I looked again at the broken branch ends. "I wonder why he carried the limbs away."

"Maybe some animal took them."

I'd been reared in the mountains, but I wasn't an expert on wildlife. Still, I'd never heard of animals using rhododendron branches for nesting, and there were no teeth marks of a beaver or signs of a rutting buck.

We looped around the thicket and checked the plants on the other side. None of them had been broken. We headed for my marked tree and Kevin resumed counting. I felt confident that even with limited sight I'd been able to keep an accurate bearing. My confidence evaporated when the fog dissipated enough to reveal a problem. As Kevin mechanically droned from one hundred thirty three to one hundred thirty four, we walked into a sheer wall of granite.

"How'd this get here?" Kevin touched the wet rock to make sure the stone bluff wasn't an illusion.

"I'd guess something to do with plate tectonics and incredible geo-pressure."

He wasn't amused. "God damn it, didn't you know it was here?"

"No, I didn't. I saw this land for the first time yesterday. And I was concentrating on the mill, not the countryside."

"I'm sorry. You're right." He paced along the base of the bluff, searching for a way up. "Maybe there's a cave or a crevice."

I looked up and saw only gray rock merging into gray clouds. As if to add insult to injury, the heavens opened with a deluge that would have forced Noah to batten down his hatches.

We huddled under our umbrellas and assessed the miserable state of affairs.

"Maybe we veered off when we came around the rhododendron," Kevin said.

"I don't see how. The pine stood right on the compass line. We can walk the edge of the rock face and see if there's a break. But from the condition of his body, I can tell you Y'Grok didn't have the stamina to do any climbing."

We spent another thirty minutes examining impenetrable granite for signs of a crevice or overhang that might yield a possibility. Water poured down the bluff like an overflowing pot. I hung in as long as I could, waiting for Kevin to quit. At last, after having trudged along the same muddy path for the sixth time, I'd had enough. "This is nuts. We don't even know if we're interpreting the tattoos correctly."

"But the broken rhododendron."

"That could have been a hiker. Maybe Y'Grok wanted the branches for something else." I looked at my wet wristwatch. "It's one-thirty. We need to get back. There's no cell coverage here and who knows what's happened in town. Franklin Talbert lands in half an hour and I want to make sure we're set for the meeting."

Kevin didn't argue. He turned without a word and headed back to the mill.

The stream now boiled a foot higher than when we'd arrived. The foot-log had plenty of clearance, but I wouldn't have wanted to tumble into the rushing current underneath. Wind gusts blew from the south, slamming the heavy raindrops into us like buckshot. We didn't dare cross holding the open umbrellas for fear of being yanked off our feet. Kevin went first, as fast as he dared, while I stood on the bank ready to fish him out if he fell. Then he took the post on the opposite side. I held the closed umbrella like a balancing pole and stepped onto the log. To hesitate would expose me to the full force of the storm. I was a yard from safety when a sudden shift of the wind caught me. I desperately struggled to regain my footing.

Kevin scrambled up the bank crying, "Jump!"

I sprang from the log at the angle of my momentum. With only inches to spare, I reached the side. The steep incline provided no handhold and I started sliding backwards. Kevin reached down and snatched me by the collar of my jacket. He hauled me up like a half-drowned puppy, and we both fell on the muddy ground.

"I haven't had so much fun since I sprawled headlong into a Vietnamese rice paddy." Kevin got to his knees and turned his face to the sky. "Might as well let Mother Nature hose me clean."

"At least here no one's shooting at you."

"Not yet, anyway." He stood up and looked at his mud-streaked clothes. "Well, I'm wetter than a duck's butt and not nearly as warm."

"I'll run the heater on high all the way back. You can tell Patsy this time you dove in the water to save me."

Three miles later, the rain had turned to a slow drizzle and the interior of the jeep had turned into a sauna. Kevin took my phone and reached Tommy Lee. "No luck here. What's the status on Franklin?" He listened a moment. "I'll tell him. See you at the house. Oh, and I might need to borrow some dry clothes." Kevin hung up before Tommy Lee could ask any more questions.

"What's up?" I asked.

"Everything's go. Tommy Lee told your mayor to have Franklin at the condo at five-thirty or he'd have to answer to the general and the senator."

"That would scare him."

"He said your name will be left at the guard gate with directions. One good thing about this rain, Franklin won't be in the mood to tour some half-finished cemetery."

"Not even if he could be the next Daniel Boone?"

Kevin laughed. "I forgot about that. Franklin's someone who should definitely have his head jammed up a coon's ass."

Now I had another problem. How could I meet movie star Franklin Talbert and keep a straight face?

Chapter Twelve

Democrat whined as I approached my driveway. Two nights away from his beloved woods had made him homesick. As much as he liked the attention from Mom and Dad, nothing beat patrolling his world of squirrels, quail, and raccoons.

My cabin sat in the middle of five acres of hardwoods, plenty of room for Democrat to roam. He wasn't a runner like a beagle who'd follow a scent for miles till he dropped. The lab stayed within a safe distance of a quick retreat and never wandered farther than the sound of my whistle. His only major sin was one he'd never repent. The sin had been bred into his DNA. Democrat loved water, and I knew as soon as I opened the jeep's door, he'd leap for the freedom of the open woods and remain outside until he was joyfully drenched to the skin. I had the option of either letting him roam free while I cleaned the cabin for the evening meeting or carrying him inside. If I let him loose, I'd pay later when I'd have to dry the squirming puppy so that he wouldn't trash my place with muddy paws and rain-soaked fur.

I drove the hundred yards down the gravel lane and was surprised to find Susan's Subaru parked in the turnaround. Although she had a key to my cabin, she sat behind her steering wheel. I lifted Democrat in my arms and ran to the cabin's porch as she dashed ahead of me.

"Hi. This is a nice surprise." I fumbled for my door key as the dog struggled to greet Susan.

"I just pulled up. Here, I've got my key handy."

As she opened the door, I glanced back at the two vehicles. Wisps of steam rose from my hood where the cool rain hit the warm metal. Susan's had distinct puddles of standing water and no steam.

As we walked in the living room, squeals penetrated through the closed door to the guest bedroom. My organic security system was functioning flawlessly. George the guinea pig made her presence known.

"Your mother said you'd gone out with Tommy Lee's friend early this morning and she hadn't heard from you. I was afraid you might not have time to check on George."

I set Democrat down and he ran to the bedroom door. George Eliot had been my companion as I transitioned from marriage to repeat bachelorhood. The lab had adopted her as a litter mate, and the affection was reciprocated, especially since Democrat didn't eat lettuce.

I started to ask Susan why she hadn't called me on my cell, but I sensed some other agenda at play. "Thanks. I left her food dispenser filled with pellets and hung three water bottles, but you never know."

Susan turned away, went to the kitchen, and opened the fridge. George's squeals intensified. I let Democrat in to see his pal. The black and white, long-haired Peruvian guinea pig stood up on her hind legs, scratching the glass side of her terrarium. Democrat gave a sniff to assure himself everything was in order and then ran back to the kitchen in case Susan had found more than lettuce in the refrigerator. I lifted two empty water bottles and followed him.

Susan held the lettuce under the spigot, and then patted the leaves dry with a paper towel. "How's your head?"

"It's okay. I put my medicine on this morning, but then we got caught in the downpour."

"I noticed."

I looked down at my mud-streaked pants. Mother had wanted me to change when I picked up Democrat. I wondered if she'd put in a call to Susan, alerting her that I was flagrantly disobeying my doctor's orders. But how could Susan have beaten me up here? "I've just got to get through tomorrow. After that, things will be out of my hands."

"There's not much in your hands now. Let Tommy Lee and the professionals take care of it." She gathered up the lettuce and headed for the bedroom.

"I used to be a professional too." I heard the bitter twist in my words and wished I could call them back.

The only sounds in the cabin were Democrat's nails clicking on the hardwood floor and George's peals of hunger. Then her squeals abruptly ceased as she devoured her leafy feast.

Susan returned and leaned against the counter. She studied me for a few seconds without any hint of anger. "A professional knows his limitations."

"Look, I'm not driving this thing. Tommy Lee's been telling Kevin and me what to do. Kevin's a good cop but he's a fish out of water down here."

"So you're both working for Tommy Lee?"

"Right."

Susan bit her lower lip and studied her fingertips. Then she gave me a cold stare. "How does Melissa Bigham fit into this?"

My throat went dry. The unexpected question hinted at why Susan had been sitting in front of my cabin, waiting for my return. "You knew I'd taken her into my confidence about the body, and you heard our conversation last night."

"I heard one of your conversations. Or did Melissa return simply to watch you sleep?"

The cut on my forehead burned as blood rushed to my face. I knew I looked guilty and the more I'd protest, the worse I'd appear. "She had information she didn't want to share in front of you. Her idea, not mine."

"About the body?"

"About Kevin Malone."

That answer softened her indignation. "Oh." She faltered, unsure whether to press a confidential matter.

I remembered Melissa's kiss and knew some of my guilt was deserved. "She found out Kevin's been suspended from the Boston police force. He accidentally shot his partner."

"My God. Does that have something to do with Y'Grok Eban?"

"No. But Melissa figured since I'm working with him, I ought to know his past history."

"Does Tommy Lee know?"

"No."

"Are you sure?"

"I heard it from Kevin."

Susan's eyes widened. "You asked him about the shooting?"

"The officer in Boston who spoke to Melissa phoned Kevin and warned him a reporter was snooping into his background."

Democrat nudged his nose into the back of Susan's knee. She crouched down and stroked his neck. "I'm sure that put her in an awkward position."

"She doesn't know. I haven't told her yet. Despite what some people think, Melissa Bigham's not at the top of my to-do list."

I should have left well enough alone. Instead, with that one sarcastic phrase, I snatched defeat from the jaws of victory.

Susan got to her feet. "I don't care whether she's at the top of your to-do list or not. And I'm not going around spying on you, if that's what you think. I saw her car last night because I came back to apologize for being bitchy. Now I'm glad I didn't have the chance." She started for the door.

"Look, Susan."

"Just forget it. We can talk about this after tomorrow." She was out the door before I could say another word.

"Mr. Clayton. Remember me? Edith Delaney." The woman leaned out the small window of the guardhouse so that I could see her face.

The pale skin, straw-blonde hair, pointed chin, and deep-set brown eyes were as common in the mountains as honeysuckle on a fence post. The only thing distinctive about her was the rent-a-cop security hat.

"You buried my grandmother last month. Miss Ida Mae Hyder."

"Of course. I remember you," I lied. "Must be the uniform."

Edith Delaney beamed. "That's right. My husband didn't want me to wear it, but I thought Grammy'd like the official air I could give to the service."

Now I did remember her. As a self-appointed traffic cop, she'd tried to direct the funeral procession out of the church parking lot and caused a fender bender.

The sudden pink tinge in her cheeks showed she'd recalled the incident as well. "Your name's on the admittance list, Mr. Clayton." She reverted to her official tone. "Go ahead."

The gate bar to Crystal Cascades lifted and Edith waved me through. She hadn't bothered to ask me who I planned to see.

Tommy Lee had called me at the cabin with the condo's address. He said Franklin Talbert had wanted a description of me and my vehicle and the assurance that I'd be coming alone. I guess he thought I'd bring a carload of star struck mountaineers to gawk at him. He'd be disappointed to learn I didn't know anyone other than Archie Donovan and the mayor who wanted to meet him.

If the cliff dwellers of the Southwest had half a million dollars to spend on each dwelling, they'd have created Crystal Cascades. The luxurious condos clung to the side of a mountain. The architect had designed floor to ceiling windows to insure each residence offered a spectacular view. On a sunny day, the lowly peons in the valley like me saw the prismatic effect of the glass turn the mountainside into a massive wall of jutting diamonds.

The road carved the exclusive development into terraces as it snaked up the slope. Small parking areas shared the ledges and I never understood how so many retirees could get so many Buicks so high without tumbling over the edge. Of course, no one lived here during the winter, and very few homes were occupied this early in the season, which is why the mayor was able to arrange accommodations for Franklin Talbert on such short notice.

Talbert's condo was about halfway up. A black mailbox atop a wrought-iron post marked the entrance down a short, steep driveway. A double garage formed the base of the unit and a brick-paved ramp curved up through shiny galax to the front door. A wheelchair could make the ascent, but too much speed coming down would turn the walkway into a ski jump.

I checked myself in the rearview mirror. The fresh application of ointment glistened over my stitches and the bruised skin now had a purple tinge. I wore a rain slicker and pulled the hood over my head. The front edge just covered my battle scar.

I had to admit I felt a twinge of excitement at meeting Franklin Talbert. Although I wasn't a big fan of his films, I'd seen a few and couldn't help but be a little awed by someone whose twenty-foot image on the silver screen played to millions of moviegoers. I wanted to make a good first impression.

I pulled an umbrella from the backseat, but didn't bother to open it. It would be for Talbert's use if he needed protection from the light drizzle. As I stepped onto the walk, I looked up at the wall of windows. The dull sky made them less reflective and I could see the interior of the condo. Franklin Talbert stood looking across the valley. He must not have heard me drive up because as he caught sight of me, a flash of surprise crossed his face. Immediately, he disappeared into the shadows.

I rang the bell. After a few minutes, the door opened and Talbert held up a hand that first stopped me and then beckoned me in. He had a cell phone pressed against his ear.

"Well, you tell them to Fed-Ex the script revisions to me tomorrow or I'm out of the deal." He swept his conducting hand to indicate I should take a seat. "And I won't just be backing out as the star, but the producer as well." He turned his back to me as he closed the door. "See what that does to their completion bond."

Funny thing. He hadn't been on the phone while standing at the window. And he must have had a terrific service since no cellular tower I knew of covered this side of the ridge.

Franklin Talbert was at least three inches shorter than me— all of it in his legs. At five-six, many of his leading ladies and certainly his cinematic archenemies must have towered over him. But, a long waist and rugged face made perfect camera fodder. Put him on a box or stand his true love in a hole and the illusion of John Wayne for the 21st century would be complete.

He faced me as he listened, or pretended to listen, to the recipient of his anger. He gave me a nod of greeting, and then pointed to the phone as if it were some inoperable growth he could do nothing about. "No. That's not acceptable. I wrap in two weeks, and if they're not ready to start mid-May, there are three other projects waiting in line. The revisions tomorrow, Allan, or send me another deal. No excuses."

He snapped the phone away from his ear and tossed it on a leather sofa. "Enough of that." His short legs took a mighty stride toward me. "Sorry. My agent's on the verge of botching my next picture, and it's either a new script or a new agent." His broad hand reached out. "Franklin Talbert. Thank you for getting me."

Whether his phone conversation had all been an act or not was immaterial. The guy was good and now I had become the center of his universe.

I shook his hand and met him eye-to-eye. "Barry Clayton. I'm handling the funeral arrangements for Y'Grok."

"Yes, Y'Grok Eban. A real hero. I owe my life to that guy. And my career."

"Your career?"

"My first film. It was based on our mission in Vietnam. I was on the ground in the central highlands. Y'Grok was one of my contacts. *Operation Falcon.* Jesus. Hard to believe that movie came out nearly twenty-five years ago."

I took a closer look at the actor. Beneath the tan were a few wrinkles, especially around the eyes. His black hair had a slight touch of gray at the temples. He must have been over sixty, but he'd pass for forty-five with good makeup and lighting.

"*Operation Falcon,*" I repeated. "I saw that movie." I had seen the film, but I'd been eight years old. "Was that the name of the real operation?"

"No. And the storyline was fictitious, but the action wasn't. Y'Grok got me out of more than one close call." He looked at his Rolex. "Got time for a drink? The bar's well stocked."

"Thanks, but no. We'd better head on. We're supposed to meet the others at six."

"Okay. But I still don't understand what's happening. Your mayor said the service had been delayed so I could get here. Is this some kind of rehearsal before tonight's party?"

I hadn't realized Talbert would be so clueless. I'd expected Senator Millen's aide to have at least covered him on the basics by now. "No. There's been a complication. I'll give you the background on the way."

"Let me grab a jacket." He disappeared up the stairs and returned five minutes later. He'd quickly changed into a well-tailored cashmere sport coat with a cable-knit sweater underneath. "I assume we'll be going straight to the mayor's schmooze-fest afterwards."

"Yes, then they'll probably bring you back here."

He sighed. "I'd like to avoid that, Barry, if it's not any trouble. They've been very gracious, but I've enjoyed as much as I can stand of Tweedledum and Tweedledee."

I laughed. Franklin Talbert had pegged Mayor Whitlock and Archie Junior perfectly. "Sure. And I'll be the excuse if you want to leave early."

The heavy clouds created an early dusk and I waited until I'd safely negotiated the winding road down before dropping my bombshell. "This meeting is not about tomorrow's service. Last Monday someone broke into our funeral home and stole Y'Grok's body."

"Stole his body?" Talbert's voice trembled. "What for?"

"We don't know."

"But that's crazy. Does some yokel want to get on the front page of the local paper?"

"No." I pulled the hood of my slicker away from my forehead. Even though the daylight was fading, Talbert could see the jagged cut across my forehead.

"Christ. They did that to you? In broad daylight?"

"Actually it was Tuesday at three in the morning. Only one guy. One very efficient guy like someone right out of your movies."

"Umm," he grunted. "That's more than a prank. So what are we supposed to do? Why are we having this meeting?"

"Y'Grok had a message for Kevin Malone."

"Malone?" An edge grew in his voice. "He's mixed up in this?"

"Yeah. Didn't you know he'd be here?"

"My publicist said Stormy and Ryan. I got the news about Y'Grok's death and hopped the first flight out of Sydney, even though I thought I'd miss the funeral. Didn't even bring an assistant." He made his trip sound like he'd crossed the Sahara with one bottle of Evian water.

"Y'Grok wanted to see Kevin before he died," I said. "He had something for him. We think from Vietnam."

"Who's we?"

"Senator Millen, the General, Kevin, and Tommy Lee."

"Who's Tommy Lee?"

"The local sheriff. Tommy Lee Wadkins. He's a vet who knew Y'Grok. I was the only one without a personal stake until I got my head bashed in and a body stolen out from under me. We were hoping you might know why someone would want to steal Y'Grok's body."

I kept my eyes on the road, but heard Talbert shift in his seat. For a few seconds, he said nothing. Then he whispered, "Who knows about this?"

"Nobody outside that circle." I decided to keep Melissa, Susan, and Uncle Wayne out of it for now. "But we're going to have to go public before the service tomorrow."

"And this message for Kevin Malone is tied in somehow?"

"We think the message was tattooed on Y'Grok's body."

"Do you know how outrageous that sounds? It's like a damn movie pitch. A secret message for Kevin. And I suppose Kevin's the one who said Y'Grok wanted to see him."

"He got a letter."

"Did you see the letter?"

"No, but—"

"But Kevin Malone is a loose cannon. Believe me, he worked my operation in Nam and I wouldn't trust the guy to follow an order for a cheeseburger and fries. Always had to do things his own god-damned way and then blame somebody else when he screwed up."

I drove without comment and thought about a dead cop in Boston.

Talbert snorted. "Maybe I can solve this mystery after all. Kevin Malone probably cooked this whole thing up to draw attention to himself. Look important when the story breaks. A secret message just for him. Ten to one he's the guy who whacked you."

I shook my head. "That won't fly. He was at the sheriff's house when I was attacked. And a preacher admits mailing Y'Grok's letter to him, and my uncle saw the tattoos when he embalmed the body."

"Then what's any of this have to do with me?"

"The letter to Kevin made only one statement—Raven's come home."

I heard a sharp intake of breath.

"Raven." He exhaled. "No wonder Kevin came running. You know about Raven?"

"They've given me the background."

"Yeah, but what I bet they didn't say is that somebody blew the lid on that operation. Curious thing. I transferred Malone out for insubordination and then our operatives started disappearing."

"You're saying he betrayed the network?"

"I'm saying he may have a very good reason for not wanting Y'Grok's message to see the light of day. He's no fool and just because he has an alibi doesn't mean he's not behind the theft. He knows the cardinal rule of covert operations—deniability—and believe me, Kevin Malone's the master of keeping his hands squeaky clean when he's up to his elbows in shit."

Chapter Thirteen

As my jeep rounded the final curve of my driveway, its head-lights swept across Tommy Lee's cruiser and a dark blue Mercury Grand Marquis with a Hertz bumper sticker. My guests had arrived ahead of me.

I'd had the foresight to leave an extra key under the mat and to tell Tommy Lee to make himself at home. I stepped into the rain and smelled the welcome aroma of wood smoke.

Talbert followed me to the door. "Someone's got a fire going."

"And I hope a pot of hot coffee." I turned the knob and took a deep breath. Were we about to face a constructive conversation or a confrontation?

Inside, Senator Millen had one foot resting on the stone hearth and prodded the burning logs with the poker. General Weathers sat on the sofa with Democrat nestled against his lower leg. The lab's tail beat a steady rhythm on the wide planked floor as Weathers ran his broad hand through the thick fur on the dog's neck.

Kevin Malone carried a coffee mug from the counter that separated the kitchen from the living room. He raised the cup to Talbert and me as we stepped across the threshold. "Well, look what the cat drug in."

"Hello, Kevin," Talbert said. He looked at the other two men and smiled. "Ryan. Stormy. Good to see you."

Weathers got to his feet and offered his hand. Millen replaced the poker in the rack and did the same. Kevin kept both hands wrapped around his mug.

"You guys don't look any worse for wear," Talbert said. "Especially you, Stormy. Hell of a job you're doing over there."

"Maybe." Weathers scowled at Millen. "If the job didn't keep changing."

"You're training the Iraqis to police themselves, right?" Talbert looked to Millen for confirmation.

Millen laid a hand on Weathers' shoulder. "I think Stormy would trade a hundred Iraqis for one Y'Grok Eban."

"Damn straight. Or any Montagnard. Best allies we ever had."

Kevin lifted his cup higher. "I'll drink to that."

Tommy Lee emerged from the kitchen. "There's more coffee if either of you wants a cup." He approached Talbert. "I'm Tommy Lee Wadkins, sheriff of this bucolic community."

"My pleasure, Sheriff. And I understand you're a vet."

General Weathers gave Tommy Lee a pat on the back. "Nothing less than a silver star."

Kevin pulled a chair from the dining table, turned it around to face us and sat down. "Watch out, Tommy Lee. Franklin will steal your life story and put his own face on the silver screen."

"And then maybe the public would appreciate the sacrifice he and Y'Grok Eban made." Talbert glared at Kevin. "I don't see you doing anything to help the Yards."

"I don't need my face out in front leading the parade."

"And who the hell would follow you?"

Kevin smiled and took a sip of coffee. "You might be surprised."

The fire popped, shooting an ember onto the floor. I grabbed a small shovel from the hearth, tossed the glowing coal back on the logs and replaced the screen.

"Sorry," Millen said. "I shouldn't have left the screen open."

I pointed to the char marks littering the floor at my feet. "Simply adds to the authenticity of the old wood." I glanced at the front door. "Anybody else coming?"

Millen sat down on the sofa. "Nickles is drafting some notes from an informal conversation Stormy and I had this afternoon in preparation for the hearing."

"And Captain Randall's summarizing the day's dispatches from Baghdad." Weathers took the rocker to my right, leaving Talbert to share the sofa with Millen.

All three men cut commanding figures. Weathers wore his dress uniform, Millen sported a crisp blue suit, and Talbert's tailored cashmere jacket shouted casual, but expensive elegance. Tommy Lee sat beside me on the hearth and Democrat curled up on the spiral braided rug as the centerpiece of our council.

"How about Y'Suom?" I asked.

"He's at the VFW," Tommy Lee said. "The mayor will send a car for him and the Lutherans."

"Then why don't we get started. I assume everyone's going straight to the party from here."

They all nodded in agreement.

"On the drive over, I covered Franklin on the theft of the body and the tattoos that might tie in with the letter Y'Grok sent Kevin."

Kevin didn't wait to be questioned. "The letter came last week to my house."

He'd told me the district but this new explanation was in case someone other than me knew he'd been suspended.

"And the note just said Raven's come home?" Talbert asked.

"No, a little more. He said he'd seen Tommy Lee. Y'Grok knew he was dying and he had something to show me. He closed with Raven's come home, come see."

"Raven's come home," Talbert muttered. "What's left to come home?"

"We think it might be the money," Weathers said.

"The money?" Talbert leaned forward and laughed. "After more than thirty years? I made most of the drops myself, starting with Y'Grok. That money's probably crossed so many palms by now you can see through it."

"But what if it hasn't," Millen said. "Franklin, you know most of the Yards weren't helping us for money. What if the resistance leaders used it sparingly if at all? Y'Grok Eban's just noble enough to make the effort to return it."

"Maybe." Talbert seemed to warm to the idea. "He'd at least want to see that the money helped his people." He looked at Kevin. "You do have a parade, don't you?"

"Memorizing those corny scripts has helped your brain," Kevin said. "Y'Grok knew he could trust me to get the money where it would do their cause the most good. What's that say about you?"

"Not a damn thing," Talbert snapped. "Just like it doesn't say anything about Ryan or Stormy. Some of us are harder to reach, that's all. How many layers do you think you have to go through to connect with a general or a senator?"

"Stay focused," Weathers demanded. "Kevin got the letter. Why isn't the issue. But he can't decipher the code. None of us can."

Millen reached into his inside coat pocket and retrieved a folded piece of paper. "Here's what we have to go on. Barry's uncle noticed the tattoos at the funeral home."

Talbert took the sheet and spread the paper out on his thighs. He studied it for a few minutes while the rest of us sat in silence.

"I see the letters for Raven. But the circle. Does it mean things have come full circle?"

"Maybe," Kevin said. "In the abstract. What could a circle mean as a marker?"

"A village," Talbert suggested. "We used to draw circles to represent villages. They were always moving."

"But we're halfway around the world," Weathers said.

"Which means that whoever stole the body could be halfway around the world by now." Talbert held the paper closer to his eyes. "This number two thousand. That's got to be the key."

I spoke up. "Kevin and I went out to the place where Y'Grok died. We used two thousand as feet and yards and the circle as a compass, but we found nothing."

Talbert turned the paper around and held it up like a court-room exhibit for the jury. "What if two thousand is a year?"

"Y'Grok was still in Vietnam," Kevin said.

"Exactly," Talbert replied. "He's written Viet and Nam back-wards. Back to Vietnam. Where was his village in 2000? Their slash and burn farming techniques would hold them for a year or two before they moved on. I think he's telling us to find the site of his home village in 2000."

"No," I said. "That's not it."

The others looked at me with hope I'd discovered the answer.

"Going back to Vietnam doesn't explain the missing ammo case."

"What ammo case?" Talbert asked.

I explained how Harvey Collins had seen the ammo case at the mill and that Y'Grok placed special significance on it.

"I could get some men and some metal detectors," Tommy Lee said. "We can organize a more efficient search when the weather clears."

"No." Kevin and Talbert spoke in unison.

Kevin cut his eyes toward Talbert. "You tell him."

For the first time, Talbert gave Kevin a smile. "Sheriff, if Y'Grok wanted this money to go to the resistance, how do we dig it up in the presence of witnesses and keep control of it?" He looked at Weathers and then Millen. "Am I right to assume we don't want any part of this money? Isn't that really why you're here without the usual entourage? Deniability, gentlemen. We know nothing. I'm willing to let Kevin complete Y'Grok's mission. Are you?"

No one answered. No one had to.

Weathers looked at his watch. "We don't have much time and we're not going to recover the body tonight. How do we handle tomorrow?"

"I'll go public tomorrow," I said. "I can say the body was stolen, but at the request of Y'Grok's son we kept the theft quiet."

Tommy Lee nodded. "That should be enough. Turn any other questions over to me as head of the investigation. I've no need to get into the tattoos or Raven. I suggest the rest of you refrain from comment on the grounds that you're here to pay your respects, not second guess a police investigation."

"The heat will really be on then." Millen shook his head. "When the networks and larger papers get wind of this bizarre twist."

"And you'll be gone," Talbert said.

Weathers got to his feet. "Tommy Lee, you'll keep us posted, unofficially."

"Of course, sir."

"Then I recommend we end this discussion and drop by the party and butter up your mayor. Tomorrow he's going to get more attention than he bargained for."

We all rose and prepared to leave. While Millen and Weathers donned their raincoats, I walked to the door and flipped on the outside floodlight. Rain fell in a steady stream.

Tommy Lee spoke to Millen. "Ryan, since Kevin and Franklin don't have cars, would you mind giving them a ride? I still want to go over a few things with Barry about tomorrow."

Talbert frowned at me. "You're coming, aren't you?"

"Yes, and I can give you a lift to the condo."

The joy of not being left to the mercy of the mayor and Archie radiated from his face. "Then lead on, Senator Millen. I put myself in your competent hands."

"Don't tell me you're a constituent from Idaho." Millen stepped out on the front porch followed by Talbert, Weathers, and Kevin.

Talbert paused to open my umbrella and share it with Kevin.

A rifle cracked and the umbrella flew into the air. Wood splinters exploded from a log inches above my head.

"Down," Tommy Lee cried. "Get down."

The four of us dropped like stones. Tommy Lee jumped across the open doorway and swatted the light switch. The front of the cabin went dark.

"Get out of the spill light," Weathers ordered.

I heard bodies rolling into the shadows, and then footsteps running through the brush up the hill.

"He's getting away," Weathers yelled.

Democrat's tail brushed against me. Whatever game we were playing caught his fancy. He heard the steps move onto the gravel and run up the driveway. With a bark of enthusiasm, the dog leapt in pursuit.

"Democrat, no!"

I'll never know whether he reacted to my command or some warning scent. He stopped about twenty yards up the hill, his bark reduced to a whimper.

Stormy Weathers went into full command mode. "Barry! What weapons have you got?"

"A twelve-gauge, a twenty-two, and a thirty-eight revolver."

"Get them. And kill all the lights inside."

I sprinted to my bedroom closet. You don't question a three-star general.

I was back on the porch in less than thirty seconds. Tommy Lee had given Kevin a pump twelve from his patrol car. I gave Stormy Weathers the shotgun and Talbert the twenty-two. I kept the five-shot Smith & Wesson. Millen said it'd been so long since he'd fired a gun, he'd be a liability.

"I can hold a flashlight," he volunteered.

No one doubted his bravery. A flashlight made the best target.

"Spread out," Weathers ordered. "Ryan, stay in the middle since you're unarmed. None of us should lose sight of the man to either side. There might be more than one shooter and I don't want us killing each other in a crossfire. Now take it slow."

We started forward. Up the hill, a car engine roared to life followed by the squeal of tires as a vehicle lurched from gravel to the blacktop. In a few seconds, the sound vanished into the wind and rain.

Weathers called from off to my left. "That was probably him. But keep alert. We'll sweep the area to the highway."

Fifteen minutes later, we returned to the porch. Our would-be assassin had left no trail. All we found was a piece of a small branch that might have been clipped by the shot.

Kevin held the branch between his fingers. "This could have deflected the bullet just enough to miss."

"What do you think the shooter fired?" Millen asked.

"Sounded like a thirty-aught-six," Tommy Lee said. "Most common deer rifle around."

Millen's wayward eye sparkled in the backwash of his flashlight. "You're saying this guy's a local?"

"I'm saying he fired a thirty-aught-six, but we won't know for sure till we dig the slug out of the side of Barry's cabin."

Weathers took the severed branch from Kevin and twirled it between his fingers. "Might not be a deer rifle. The M1 Garand fires a thirty-aught-six."

"Military," Tommy Lee said. "But not active issue for years."

"Oh, there're plenty to be had," Kevin said. "But that's not the important question, is it, pal?"

"No. The important question is who was the target?" Tommy Lee turned to me. "And the person he came closest to hitting was you, Barry. Pissed anybody off at a funeral lately?"

Chapter Fourteen

While Tommy Lee and I dug the slug out of my cabin wall, the others tried to regain a presentable appearance. Rolling around on the porch and driveway under fire had created an unusual fashion statement. Towels and a hairdryer would fix most of the damage, although General Weathers had gouged his spit-polished shoes and Ryan Millen's solid red tie now featured a permanent water-splotched pattern. I lent Millen a blue replacement from my closet and dug up a bottle of KIWI Scuff Magic for Weathers. Kevin and Talbert had fared better since they were still on the porch when the shot was fired.

The bullet had smashed through the stem of the umbrella before burrowing into the log. I held a flashlight with the beam tightly focused across the entry hole. Tommy Lee dug into the wood with a buck knife while Talbert and Kevin stood watch. We took seriously the possibility that our shooter could return.

"Are you sure you don't want to call this in?" I whispered.

Tommy Lee kept digging. "Why? So Reece can type up a report for me to read in the morning? Neither Millen nor Weathers wants to turn tonight into a circus. That's all that would happen. With the high profile of the possible target, we'd be smothered with press. I'll get some men up here at daylight to look for clues. Maybe we'll get lucky and find a shell casing with prints."

"I doubt it."

"I do too. That's why we'll keep this quiet for now."

"Somebody must have tailed Millen's car." I moved the light more head on. A tip of twisted metal gleamed in the wood.

"Or followed my car from town, or your jeep from Crystal Cascades."

"Maybe the shooter knew we were meeting here."

Tommy Lee stopped digging. "That's what I'm finding out. I used my cell phone to call the department when everyone went back inside."

"So you did report the shooting."

"No. I asked Reece and Wakefield to check on a few people's whereabouts. See if they'd suddenly gone missing."

"Who?"

We heard the creak of a porch board as Kevin walked closer.

Tommy Lee changed the subject. "You have some needle-nose pliers, Barry? I'm ready to pull this sucker out."

A few minutes later, we stood in a circle in front of the fireplace, passing the mangled slug around.

"It's the right size for a thirty-aught-six," Weathers said. "It's a thirty caliber for sure."

"I wonder how long he'd been waiting out there," Millen said. "He must have known we'd be leaving soon."

Franklin Talbert tossed the bullet up and down in one hand. "And we were all in the light when he fired. So, who was he after?"

Tommy Lee snatched the slug out of mid-air. "Since we don't know, I advise each of you to consider yourself the target. I've assigned extra deputies at the country club. Make sure you walk in with one." He pulled his keys from his pocket. "And let's change our ride plans. Kevin, you drive the rental car and Barry can go in his jeep. I'll lead the way with the rest of you. Maybe our shooter will think twice before firing at a sheriff."

I brought up the rear of our little convoy. Tommy Lee turned on his blue flashers, but kept his speed under the limit so Kevin and I had no trouble keeping up. At the main gate to the club,

Tommy Lee stopped to exchange a few words with one of his deputies. The officer stood beside his own car and the blue flashing lights of the two vehicles projected a pulsing psychedelic display over his yellow slicker. Evidently, the deputy was noting down everyone who entered.

The Gainesboro Country Club had been constructed about fifty years ago on the outskirts of town, and its land lay along a narrow valley which once contained a rich deposit of clay. Much of Gainesboro had grown out of that natural resource because, in 1919, dirt-poor Roland Foster began making bricks out of his backyard. His feat of clay made him dirt-rich as the town expanded and the Roland Foster Brick Company flourished. But the excavation left an unsightly blemish of scarred earth in its wake. When the clay petered out and Roland Foster's heirs found other sources for their bricks, the town petitioned the company to do something about the environmental eyesore. One of the grandsons suggested a golf course, and the Midas touch that changed clay into gold transformed eroded gulleys into playable greens.

The clubhouse preserved its brick heritage. Not only was the exterior built of Roland Foster's finest, but the immediate grounds were enclosed by a six-foot-high brick fence with ornate wrought-iron gates that could close off both the roads and the golf cart paths. Whether he realized it or not, the mayor's selection of the site had been a plus for security.

The deputy waved our cars through and I followed the procession to the front entrance of the long building. I wasn't a member, preferring archery to golf, but I had attended numerous functions in the ballroom. I noticed that a red carpet had been rolled down the walkway to the curb. There would be no need for Tommy Lee's passengers to have a deputy escort.

As Tommy Lee braked to a stop, Tweedledum and Tweedledee hurried down to greet the trio of dignitaries. Archie outpaced Mayor Whitlock, who kept waving to someone behind him. A photographer bolted through the massive doors and sprinted after His Honor. I hoped he had a wide-angle lens.

It was nearly eight-forty, but the adjacent parking lot still offered plenty of spaces. Either the rain or a select guest list had kept attendees to a manageable number, and we were able to park our vehicles together.

Tommy Lee got out holding his umbrella. "Do you have one that's not been shot?"

"A good funeral director's always prepared." I grabbed a spare from the backseat.

Tommy Lee walked over to Kevin's car to share his. As the three of us headed toward the clubhouse, he said, "Deputy Beale at the front gate says he knows everybody who's come in. No surprises."

"Y'Suom here?" Kevin asked.

"Yes. He arrived about ten minutes ago with Harvey Collins and Earl Hucksley. Bruce Nickles brought them."

"They were running late too." I wanted to ask who else Tommy Lee had checked on, but I didn't want to bring it up in front of Kevin. Instead, I asked, "How many men have you got here?"

"Two less than I wanted. We had a burglary called in a couple hours ago and I sent two men back over the scene."

"Back?"

"Yeah, happened in the storeroom of Frank Mendle's pawn shop. He'd discovered a busted lock but wasn't sure what had been taken. Now he knows."

"Let me guess," Kevin said. "A thirty-aught-six."

"Not just any thirty-aught-six. A Springfield with a Weaver scope and some ammo. Our snipers in World War Two loved them."

I weighed the implications. "We've got someone who's very resourceful. He might not have everything planned out, but he reacts quickly. We call a meeting, and he gets the untraceable weapon he needs."

"That's why he's dangerous," Tommy Lee said. "Especially since we don't know what he wants."

Kevin laughed. "Oh, I think it's pretty clear he wants to kill somebody."

We found Weathers, Millen, and Talbert in a receiving line anchored by Archie at one end and the mayor at the other. Bruce

Nickles stood just behind the senator, not shaking hands, but listening to each remark. He took his job as Communications Director deadly seriously. Weathers, Millen, and Talbert appeared gracious with their smiles and comments as a growing number of guests left the buffet tables to meet the celebrities.

Kevin started toward the tables of food. "I'm starving. At least our famous friends cleared out the chow line."

The staples of roast beef and baked ham were accompanied by green beans and mashed potatoes. People stood and ate at high cocktail tables scattered around the ballroom. The food was too heavy for my taste, and if there had been any light hors d'oeuvres, they'd been devoured.

I left Tommy Lee and Kevin and searched for Y'Suom. I hoped to speak with him in private about how he wanted me to handle announcing the disappearance of his father's body. I found him and the two Lutherans at a table in a far corner. Collins and Hucksley were eating from generous portions. Y'Suom didn't even have a plate. His attention seemed concentrated on the receiving line and he didn't look happy.

"How are things at the VFW?" I asked.

Collins put his fork down. "Good. The churches have coordinated plenty of food. We didn't eat because we were coming here."

"But Y'Suom hasn't eaten at all," Hucksley said between bites. "We've told him he needs to keep his strength up."

"I'm fine," Y'Suom replied. "Any news, Mr. Clayton?"

"No. But I thought you and I might talk a moment."

He looked at his two companions. "In a few minutes. I'd like to thank the mayor first and speak to the others."

"All right." I realized I should have waited to catch him alone. He feared I was going to announce the stolen body while Collins and Hucksley were eating, bad form even in this country.

Y'Suom excused himself. To be polite, I spent a few minutes with the two men. We discussed the threatening storm front and how it would play havoc with the graveside tomorrow. Little did they know weather would be the least of their worries.

I'd positioned myself with my back to most of the ballroom. From the corner of my eye I saw a crew setting up microphones on a small stage against the wall. A long-haired local laid a guitar case on one corner.

"Ah, we're about to hear some music, I hope." Kevin walked up and placed a dish of apple pie and a cup of black coffee on the table. "Gentlemen, good to see you again."

"You like mountain music?" Hucksley asked.

"I'm Irish. I like anything with a fiddle."

"Then you're in good shape. The tunes have been handed down from our Scotch-Irish settlers."

Kevin took a sip of coffee and sighed. "I wish I had some scotch in this Irishman."

Harvey Collins laughed. "You're the victim of Wednesday night, my friend."

"Wednesday night?"

"Baptist church meeting night. The mayor's Baptist. It's bad enough he's throwing a party, but if he served alcohol, he'd catch hell."

Kevin shook his head in disbelief. "And you're Lutherans, right? Nothing dry about Wednesday for you?"

"No," Hucksley said.

"And a man of the cloth to boot. Well, I'm an old Catholic altar boy. You'd think the mayor could be more ecumenical. Even the Pope's recognized the Baptists have their good points."

Hucksley chuckled. "But here's the God's truth. The Pope might recognize the Baptists, and the Lutherans might recognize the Baptists, but in a liquor store, not even a Baptist recognizes another Baptist."

Kevin roared. "That's worth passing up a drink." He raised his cup. "Here's to Thursday."

"I need some coffee myself." I took the opportunity to leave the table. I saw Y'Suom with the thinning crowd around the mayor and figured when the band started we could slip into another room for our conversation. Meanwhile, a cup of coffee was a welcomed diversion.

As I pulled the handle on the urn, Melissa Bigham stepped close beside me.

"One for me?"

"Since when did you cover the celebrity beat?" I handed her the cup and reached for another.

"Since I learned not to let you and my story out of my sight. What's happened?"

I poured my coffee and edged away from a waiter replenishing desserts. Melissa followed me to a quiet alcove just off the main room.

"Nothing's happened."

"So all this security is just for show?" She cocked her head and gave me a hard eye.

There was no way I could tell her about the shooting. Even Melissa wouldn't sit on that story. "I guess the mayor asked for it. Makes the event seem more important."

"So, how was Mr. Action Hero? I hear you picked him up."

"Did you stick a global positioning transmitter on my jeep?"

"No. Just a phone call to the guardhouse at Crystal Cascades to confirm where Talbert is staying. Edith's quite chatty. She volunteered that you drove through a couple hours ago. Been pitching your life story?"

The woman was relentless. "Remind me to never get on your bad side."

"I don't have a bad side. Just a curious one."

"I took Talbert by to see the others before we came here." I neglected to tell her we'd been at my cabin. "He's all right, but too show-bizzy for my taste."

"What's he think about the disappearance?"

I moved to a love seat in the recess and motioned for Melissa to sit. From the ballroom, Mayor Whitlock began an official welcome over the stage mike. No one paid any attention to us.

"He was stunned, and I don't think he's a good enough actor to fake it. All of them were in Raven together, but Talbert's as in the dark as the rest."

She grabbed my wrist. "I can't wait, Barry. Letting you bury an empty casket was never part of our deal."

"I'm not asking you to wait. I'm going to break the news before the service tomorrow. You've still got the exclusive to my story."

I hoped she'd relax, but her grip tightened. "What about the others? What are they going to say?"

"That it's a police matter and Tommy Lee will be the only one commenting."

"But I've got you on the inside."

I heard Whitlock introduce General Weathers, Senator Millen, and Franklin Talbert. The round of applause almost drowned out my reply. "As much as I can divulge."

"You're holding back?"

"It's an ongoing investigation. I don't know what'll turn up. But you can print everything we talked about in the park yesterday."

She let go of my arm. "And new stuff? Off the record?"

"Possibly."

"That's not good enough, Barry."

My throat constricted to keep from shouting. "I came to you, remember? After tomorrow, I won't be involved."

Melissa winked at me. "Calm down. Just doing my job. And I sure as hell know you're not going to announce the theft of Y'Grok's body and then let it go at that. I'm not stupid."

"No. You're not."

"Then what are you going to do after tomorrow?"

The sound of a fiddle and banjo echoed from the ballroom. I looked down the hall toward the main doors where a deputy stood guard. "I don't know. Maybe I'll watch a movie."

This time Melissa took my hand with a gentler squeeze. "A movie? Which one?"

"Ever hear of *Operation Falcon*?"

I didn't catch her answer because at that moment the deputy opened the doors to admit a latecomer. Susan stepped inside. Holding an umbrella protectively over her, Dr. Ray Chandler nodded a thank you to the guard. I pulled my hand from Melissa's, but not before Susan's eyes had found me.

"Oops." Melissa stood up. "Maybe we can talk later. I'll want to check my facts before filing the story."

"You don't have to leave." I hoped my guilty blush was fading.

"This could be a little awkward." Melissa stood up and walked away.

I took a deep breath and got to my feet. Susan and her escort were halfway to the ballroom. "Susan." If she heard me above the music, she didn't react. I hustled after them. "Susan!"

Dr. Chandler looked back and then touched Susan's arm. She stopped and turned.

"Oh, hello, Barry. You remember Ray."

"Yes." I shook Chandler's hand and then looked at Susan. "I didn't know you were coming."

"That's because you didn't ask me. Ray was kind enough to pick me up when he got off call."

"How's the head?" Chandler asked.

I wanted to say mind your own business, but he was a physician and I guess that was his business. "It's fine. Frankly, I've been too pre-occupied to think about it."

Susan glanced at the vacant love seat. "So I see."

"Some things have happened. I'm here working."

"Me too. I'm completing the assignment you gave me." She stepped back and gestured to Chandler. "Here he is."

"Here who is?" I didn't like being on the outside of some secret joke, especially at my expense.

"The one who saw that Montagnard," Chandler said. "I was on call."

I felt like a dope. I'd asked Susan to get what medical background she could on Y'Grok, and, of course, it would have to be dashing Ray Chandler, doctor of mystery. She'd even delivered him to me.

"Let's step over here." I led them back to the alcove, made sure I sat by Susan on the love seat and left Chandler with an armchair. "When did you see him?"

"Tuesday. Two weeks ago."

"At the clinic?"

"No. The emergency room. A social worker brought him in. He was having difficulty breathing."

"Why didn't you admit him?"

"I insisted. He refused. Without evidence of mental incompetence, I couldn't force the man against his will."

"What could you do?" The challenge in my voice brought a glare from Susan.

"I ordered an x-ray to see what was going on. The cancer had spread to the point where his lung efficiency was severely impaired. The mass concentration pressed upon his esophagus which not only meant discomfort but made swallowing difficult." Chandler threw up his hands. "I pleaded with him to allow us to provide comprehensive treatment. He said that wasn't necessary. It would interfere with his mission."

"His mission?"

"That's what he said."

Susan smiled. She knew that piece fit into the puzzle somehow.

"Did you examine him all over?"

"You're talking about the tattoos?"

I tried not to show my excitement. "Yes."

"They couldn't have been more than a day old. The puncture wounds were still in danger of infection. I applied topical antiseptic cream and dressed them with a light bandage."

"Did you ask him about them?"

"Yeah. Wouldn't you? Here's a guy who I figure has a couple weeks to live and he carves a lifelong design in his skin. He told me they were insurance."

"Insurance?"

"I thought he meant some ritual of dying. I know Asians put travel money on a corpse for the hereafter. Something like that."

"It's a Buddhist tradition. Y'Grok was Christian. What was the name of the man who brought him?"

Chandler shook his head. "I don't remember."

"Harvey Collins?"

"Sounds familiar."

"Did he see the tattoos?"

"Y'Grok asked him to remain in the waiting area. I think he knew we'd gang up on him about being admitted. If this Collins saw the tattoos, it wasn't at the hospital."

The music from the band swelled. A penny whistle broke into a complicated solo and the audience applauded. I decided I'd need to be more direct with Collins later. He'd had the most contact with Y'Grok during his final days.

"Is any of this helpful?" Chandler asked.

"Yes." I didn't know what else to say. I could tell from Susan's expression that she hadn't told Chandler about the missing body, and he was expecting some sort of explanation for my questions.

"I'm sure Y'Grok's son will appreciate knowing you tried to help," Susan said.

I jumped on the bandwagon she'd provided. "Yes. Y'Suom was anxious to know about his father's final days."

"Tell him if his father had remained at the hospital, I could've done more to make him comfortable." There was a look of true compassion in his eyes. "As it was, I prescribed a strong inhalant to keep his bronchial tree as open as possible."

"Would being in the hospital have prolonged his life?" I asked.

"I doubt it. Frankly, I'm amazed he lasted as long as he did."

"He was a tough old bird."

"Yeah, something kept him going."

His mission, I thought. But what was his mission?

I forced a smile. "Thank you. I'll be happy to introduce you to Y'Suom if you'd like."

As we entered the ballroom, Chandler pointed to the far corner. "There's the man who came with Y'Grok. In the brown suit."

"Harvey Collins," I confirmed. At least our circle of contacts remained small.

Susan pointed toward the stage. "Isn't that the detective friend of Tommy Lee's?"

In the middle of a quartet of mandolin, banjo, guitar, and fiddle players, Kevin piped away on a penny whistle. He even added a jig step to punctuate his final flourish. The audience clapped while the other musicians egged him on for an encore. I saw Tommy Lee laughing at the foot of the stage.

"And he accuses me of being the center of attention." Franklin Talbert had eased up beside us and put his arm around my shoulder. "Kevin's one of a kind, isn't he?"

I enjoyed seeing the star-struck expression on Chandler's face. Even Susan was impressed. "Franklin," I spoke like we'd known each other for years, "meet my very special lady Dr. Susan Miller. And this is her professional colleague, Dr. Ray Chandler."

Talbert shook hands and turned on the charm. "You can operate on me any day, young lady."

Susan had heard the line a thousand times. "Great. I specialize in lobotomies."

Talbert laughed. "Okay. I deserved that. But, now I'm worried Barry will ditch me to go home with you."

Chandler put a hand on Susan's back. "Don't worry. I'm taking her home."

And I'd almost warmed up to the twerp.

I scanned the room and then turned to Talbert. "Have you seen Y'Suom?"

"Yes. Fifteen or twenty minutes ago. He greeted us in line. Then I passed him going into the men's room."

I scanned the room again. "Maybe the mayor's got him cornered. I'll check the hall."

"That would be a true public service." Talbert took a step closer to Susan. "Meanwhile I'll keep Susan hostage to make sure you don't forget me."

The hall to the restrooms was deserted. I checked the men's room and found Bruce Nickles washing his hands. I glanced at the stalls and saw a pair of black shoes beneath the door. Nickles wouldn't even let the senator sit on the john without being there. Maybe he proofread the toilet paper.

"Is the senator having a good time?"

Nickles tore off a couple towels from the dispenser. "Yes. He can let his hair down a bit. No national press trying to trip him up on every word."

"You always seem to be there to catch him."

Nickles didn't smile. "He does fine. I just help insure that the integrity of his context is preserved."

Integrity of his context? This man must sit in his suit by the senator's bedside in case Millen talks in his sleep.

"Have you seen Y'Suom?" I asked.

Nickles tossed the wadded towels in the trashcan. "Only when he went through the receiving line."

The commode in the stall with the shoes flushed.

"Maybe Senator Millen knows."

"I'll ask him." To my surprise, Nickles left.

The stall opened and Archie Donovan walked out.

"Great party, huh, Barry?"

"Yeah, great party."

Archie stuck his hands under the tap. "I heard you asking about Y'Suom."

"I'm looking for him."

"So was the mayor. Wants to make that plot offer one more time."

"Has Mayor Whitlock got him in one of the offices?"

"I don't think he found him. Must have gone back to the VFW."

I knew that wasn't the case. Collins and Hucksley were still here and Y'Suom had promised to talk with me before he left. "If you see him, tell him I need to talk with him."

"Sure. And mention the mayor if you run into him first."

That I definitely would not do. I left the men's room and tried an adjoining wing of the club. Along one wall, a display of Roland Foster bricks capped off an historical exhibit of the company and the creation of the golf course. Opposite the exhibit, a wall of glass separated the room from an enclosed courtyard popular for wedding receptions. I heard rain beating against the atrium's roof. None of the atrium's overhead lights were on and the starless sky cloaked the space in deep shadows. I didn't remember if Y'Suom smoked, but the courtyard would be the perfect place to stay dry and grab a quick cigarette. I found the door ajar and felt the chill in the air as I stepped in.

My eyes required several seconds to adjust to the darkness. Then I made out the shape of a few plants and a bench. "Y'Suom?" The question went unanswered. I inched forward, looking for any movement against the glow from the far wall. I'd gone a couple yards when my foot kicked a loose brick.

Bending down, I discovered a leg protruding from behind the bench. My stomach knotted. I peered over the edge, careful not to move my feet. In the gloom, I saw Y'Suom's face turned toward me. His eyes were closed, but his tongue hung from a corner of his open mouth. His head lay in a dark pool of blood. A thin belt encircled his neck. The belt was embedded so deeply that lifeless flesh nearly covered the taut leather.

Chapter Fifteen

"Monstrous. Absolutely monstrous." Kevin Malone stared down at Y'Suom's body. Kevin's eyes were reduced to slits and the vein in his forehead bulged like a snake trapped under his skin.

Weathers, Millen, and Talbert stood silently behind him. Weathers' face was drained to chalk white, while Millen's nearly exploded in a burst of red. "Someone will pay for this," he promised.

Talbert spoke through tears on his cheek. "The poor boy. After all he went through." He turned to the others. "Whoever couldn't kill one of us took his revenge out on Y'Suom. This smacks of terrorism. Persecute the Montagnards. Make examples of those who support them."

The atrium lights blazed and a wall of curious faces pressed against the glass. I stepped away from the corpse to join Tommy Lee at the door. Deputies had strung crime scene tape across the opening.

On the other side, Mayor Whitlock leaned against the jamb. A sheen of perspiration coated his face. "This is terrible." He stared at Tommy Lee. "You told me you had security."

"To screen people coming in. Not to patrol the grounds and building."

The beads of perspiration on Whitlock grew bigger. "What do we do now?"

"Nobody leaves here until we get a statement from them."

The mayor's mouth popped open so wide his multiple chins flattened against his chest. "What? You suspect one of the guests?"

Tommy Lee spoke calmly. "Listen, Mayor. This is going to blow up in the morning. Every news organization and tabloid in the country will be crawling over this town. You have the chance to look like a leader or a befuddled mountain hick. How do you want to play it?"

"But, but—"

"You wanted publicity," Tommy Lee said. "Well, you've got some. I've got a job to do and I expect your cooperation."

The mayor sputtered unintelligible syllables until his mind caught up with his tongue. "What do you need?"

"I need you to set an example, and you can do it with the help of your guests of honor." Tommy Lee pointed to the four men he'd cleared to view the body.

"Anything."

"My deputies are sealing the building. No one can leave until we've taken a statement about the evening—what they did, where they went, when they last saw Y'Suom."

"But there must be a hundred people."

"Then the sooner we get started, the sooner we finish. Get more coffee and food. People will understand, particularly after you and our celebrities make a personal request from the stage."

The light bulb went off in Whitlock's skull and he couldn't suppress a smile. "Of course. Can you get everyone back in the ballroom?"

"Yes, but you start telling them one on one. I'll have Weathers, Millen, and Talbert out in a minute. Barry and I'll stay with the body till the crime lab arrives."

"Okay." Whitlock's head bobbed with enthusiasm.

"Oh, and I'll keep Malone with us. He's a detective."

Mayor Whitlock couldn't have cared less about Kevin Malone. He waddled into the crowd, instructing people to return to the ballroom.

With the interrogative process underway, Tommy Lee returned to the atrium and joined Kevin and me. "I've phoned a request to Buncombe County. They have a new mobile crime lab and I want the first pass to be state of the art."

Kevin looked skeptical. "I'd be surprised if even the FBI found anything."

"Why?" Tommy Lee asked.

"You ever get prints off a brick?"

"Nothing usable."

"Our killer knew that." Kevin pointed to the brick beside the body. "Barry showed me the display in the other room. The example of Esquire Heritage is missing, but I'd say we've found it. No coincidence this type brick is the most porous of the unglazed styles."

"Maybe the lab can still get something," Tommy Lee said. "I've read about new sprays that have been tested."

Kevin nodded. "We got in on that. An information exchange team from Boston went to Australia last year. They're developing a formula they claim can get prints off of rocks. Trouble is the spray's so toxic you need protective gear and a scene cleanup the EPA would have to bless."

"And what if you do lift some." I bent down and examined the brick. "This was part of an open exhibit. How many hands have touched it? The killer could say he was just examining the display."

Tommy Lee crouched down for a closer view. "There's hair and a trace of blood on one edge. You two figure the brick knocked Y'Suom out first."

I stood back up. "The guy knocked me out. Seems to be his pattern."

Tommy Lee continued to stare at the brick. "Assuming this is the same guy."

"Why wouldn't he be?" Kevin asked.

"Barry was attacked at three in the morning on Tuesday. Since then, Y'Suom's been at the hotel, the town park, the VFW, and probably a few other places we don't even know about. Why's our guy wait till tonight at a crowded party with fairly tight security?"

"We were shot at tonight." I said. "There has to be a connection."

"I don't buy it." Tommy Lee stood up. "If Y'Suom had any idea that someone might be desperate enough to shoot at us, why didn't he say something?"

Neither Kevin nor I had an answer.

"We're either misreading something, or haven't a clue as to the motive," Tommy Lee said. "That's the big question I keep running up against. Why? Why steal a body? Why shoot at one of us? Why kill a dead man's son?"

"And any answer comes back to Y'Grok and those tattoos," Kevin said.

"His mission," I muttered.

Tommy Lee looked up at me. "What mission?"

"That's what the doctor said who treated Y'Grok at the emergency room two weeks ago. I spoke to him tonight. He'd noticed the tattoos right after they'd been made. Y'Grok told him they were to insure he completed his mission."

"That's clear enough," Kevin said. "What's unclear is what do the tattoos mean and what was Y'Grok's mission?" He pointed to Y'Suom's waist. "The killer stripped off Y'Suom's belt, probably holding it through a handkerchief or jacket sleeve." Kevin leaned over the body. "See the bruising on his cheek? That's where a foot went. The killer slipped the belt around his neck, stepped on Y'Suom's face, and then pulled with all his strength to strangle an unconscious man. Couldn't have taken more than a few minutes. Dollars to doughnuts your M.E. will find a crushed windpipe."

"Our M.E.'s a simple coroner," Tommy Lee said. "Old Ezra Clark. He's on his way with perfunctory paperwork, but then I'm sending the body to Asheville for a full forensic autopsy."

I studied the raw spot on Y'Suom's cheek. "Guess it's too much to hope that the sole of the killer's shoe left some distinctive mark."

Tommy Lee got to his feet. "We'd have better luck scanning everyone's hands for brick dust."

Kevin crossed himself before rising. "A little soap, a little water, and that trace goes down the drain. I need a drink."

A little soap, a little water. I saw Archie Donovan at the sink washing his hands, telling me the mayor wanted to make one final appeal to Y'Suom. The idea that flashed through my head was too absurd to mention.

Tommy Lee caught my arm. "We have to speak to the minister about postponing Y'Grok's service."

"Postpone the service? We've already delayed it two days trying to find his body."

"Then why have people turn right around and come back for Y'Suom? And you know they will. Can we go Friday?"

"If you release Y'Suom's body in time."

"Well, I don't have any reason to doubt what Kevin said about the cause of death. With a little pressure from a U.S. senator and a three-star general, I estimate you'll get the body by four tomorrow."

"That'll work."

As we ducked under the crime tape, I saw Melissa Bigham waiting in the hallway. She walked up to Tommy Lee, her notepad ready.

"Sheriff, can I get a statement?"

"We're too late for your press run, aren't we?"

"Not for the wire services."

"Then the Asheville and Charlotte papers will pick the story up and you'll scoop your own employer."

"That's my problem."

Tommy Lee winked at me. "I know. That's why you won't do it. Anyway, I really don't have time now. Talk to Barry. Just know if he says anything unauthorized and you print it, I'll jail him." He walked off.

Melissa pivoted to block my path. "So what's the deal?"

"Either off the record or my lips are sealed."

"Have we ever had a conversation on the record?"

"No. Why start now?" I led her back to the brick exhibit and showed her the empty spot for Esquire Heritage. Then I told how we suspected the murder was accomplished, but that no details could be released at this point.

"Someday this will make good copy, Barry, but what's the motive?"

"We don't know. Probably something to do with Raven and the disappearance of Y'Grok's body."

"The father told the son?"

"Y'Suom didn't know anything."

"That's what he told you," Melissa said. "Maybe someone else thought differently." Melissa's reporting instincts had zeroed in on an interesting possibility.

"You mean maybe Y'Suom knew more than he realized, and said something to the wrong person?"

"Which is why he wasn't killed the same night his father's body was stolen. Who'd he talk to since Monday?"

"Good question." I made a mental note to mention the theory to Tommy Lee. "I love hanging out with smart women."

Melissa didn't smile. "Your other smart woman left with that doctor. She told me to tell you goodbye."

"When?"

"Before you discovered the body."

"So she and Chandler didn't give statements?"

"No." Melissa looked around the crowded ballroom. "I wonder who else left before Tommy Lee sealed the building."

I was more concerned with why Susan had told Melissa to tell me goodbye. Women. "We're delaying the funeral for Y'Grok a day. We'll have a service for both of them on Friday."

"Your dignitaries staying till then?"

"I don't know. You're the first person I've told."

She jotted the fact on her pad. "You still releasing the story of the missing body?"

"That's Tommy Lee's call. I suspect he will in a briefing on the murder investigation. He'll have a zoo on his hands tomorrow."

"Reporters. We're such a pain in the ass. Anything else?"

What the heck. Let her be a pain in somebody else's ass. "The mayor and Archie Donovan had this party to get publicity for their Heaven's Gate Garden cemetery. Did you know that?"

"I knew they took Franklin Talbert up there this afternoon."

"Archie told me tonight Mayor Whitlock wanted to make one last pitch for Y'Suom to have his father buried there."

"So he killed him? Bring in customers by bumping them off?"

"No. But I can guarantee you they'll make another run at me and Pastor Hucksley, offering an extra plot to keep father and son together."

Melissa flipped the cover of her notepad closed. "So?"

"So, I'm curious as to how far out on a financial limb they might be. Who at the paper covers real estate and development?"

"Mannie Elwood."

"Maybe some information on their investors, leverage, and tax assessments could help me advise Pastor Hucksley on how seriously to take their offer. Perhaps they'd sweeten the deal with a nice donation to the Montagnard resettlement fund."

"Sure. I'll mention it to Mannie in the morning. I'll say there's a possibility the double burial could happen up there and I need background. He'll dig. Mannie's no fan of the mayor."

"Thanks." I walked with her back to the ballroom.

"I guess I'll give my statement and split for the newsroom. Can I call you in the morning to go over my story draft?"

"Try the cabin and then my cell."

Melissa took a step away and I couldn't resist. "Did Susan say anything besides goodbye?"

"No. Sorry, Barry."

From the tone of her voice, I wasn't sure if she was sorry Susan hadn't said more or sorry for me in general.

I gave my statement to Reece Hutchins in about ten minutes, and then Tommy Lee found me at the coffee urn where I was trying to clear my head with another jolt of caffeine.

"How'd things go with Melissa?"

"I told her what we know off the record. Nothing for print. I went long on our theories of how Y'Suom was killed and short on why."

"Because we are short on why."

"She had an interesting take. What if the killer thought Y'Grok had told something to his son?"

Tommy Lee's one eye narrowed. "That doesn't explain why he waited till tonight."

"It does if between Monday and this evening Y'Suom said something that spooked the killer."

"Confronted him?"

"Maybe, or maybe inadvertently revealed more than he should have."

Tommy Lee mulled the possibility. "We should have thought of that."

"We're not big enough pains in the ass."

"Don't sell yourself short, Barry. You're way up there on my Richter scale."

I didn't have a snappy comeback. All I could manage was an overpowering yawn.

"Why don't you get out of here," Tommy Lee said. "You're two days off a concussion, and I need you to stay alive a little longer."

I took a healthy swallow of coffee. "But we never got to talk. You were checking where people were during the shooting. There's stuff to go over."

"Not tonight, pal." He looked at his watch. "It's after ten. Promise me you'll go home, and I'll meet you at the Cardinal Café tomorrow morning."

"What time?"

"Better make it seven. Tomorrow's going to be non-stop."

He gave me a pat on the shoulder and I wobbled. God, I was tired. "Okay. I'll be there." I set down my cup and turned toward the door.

"Barry, you ready?" Franklin Talbert broke from Whitlock and Archie with a hasty goodbye.

I'd forgotten I'd promised him a lift.

Once in my jeep, I started the engine, looked in the rearview mirror at the red brick of the country club and thought about Y'Suom's body on the cold atrium floor. Maybe the mayor shouldn't have thrown a party on Wednesday night after all.

Franklin Talbert snapped his seatbelt. "Barry, can I ask a favor?"

Great, I thought. He wants to go bar-hopping. "Sure."

"This stuff tonight, the shooting and Y'Suom's murder. Well, it's got me a little rattled. I don't like the idea of being up at that strange house where I don't know my way around. And Whitlock's told everybody that's where I'm staying."

"You want to sleep at the cabin?"

"That'd be terrific."

"Okay." I shifted the transmission into drive and headed home.

What a funny world. My girlfriend tells me goodbye and leaves with another man. The woman who helped get me in that fix delivers the message, and then instead of comforting me, goes to write the story of how a body was stolen from my family's funeral home.

But, despite these setbacks, I wind up sleeping with a movie star.

Chapter Sixteen

Every morning but Sunday, the Cardinal Café on Main Street is the heart of Gainesboro, pumping caffeine through the veins and gossip through the ears of eager customers. I pulled open the front door at ten till seven and entered a room filled with clanking silverware and the steady drone of voices.

Six construction workers crowded around the cash register at the end of the Formica counter, anxious to pay their tab and get to the job site. Given the rain, I hoped they worked indoors.

Helen, the head waitress, grabbed tickets and made change so fast her hands never stopped. Even with all the commotion, she heard the three bells tinkle above the door. She flashed me a smile and jerked her head toward the back booth on the left.

I didn't see an occupant and figured I'd beaten Tommy Lee to the restaurant.

"Morning," Tommy Lee growled. "Nice day if you're a duck." He was hunched over a cup of coffee, his body shielded by the back of the pink booth.

"Why are you sitting on my side?" Tommy Lee routinely sat with his back to the wall and facing the customers. A habit all police had. "Did I miss a memo?"

"I'm hiding. Got here ten minutes ago and no less than eight people have already asked about last night." He motioned to *The Gainesboro Vista* and *Asheville Citizen-Times* newspapers beside his coffee. "Nothing there, but word travels fast enough. I'm going to have a ten o'clock press briefing at the courthouse."

"The courthouse?"

"Yeah. Thought the place would make me look more digni-
fied." He laughed. "Can't have a briefing outside in this downpour, and I'm afraid we'll have too many people for my little
department. Our halls of justice are more like closets."

Helen walked up and set a cup of black coffee in front of me.
"Somebody been beating on your face again?"

It's nice to have a reputation. "Yes. I paid them. An improve-
ment, don't you think?"

"You're still better looking than Tommy Lee, but then so's
my dog. What are you two heartthrobs having?"

Tommy Lee ordered an English muffin with grits on the side.
I decided to fill my empty stomach with pancakes.

When Helen had banged through the swinging door to the
kitchen, I got down to business. "Anything happen since last
night?"

"Not really. Y'Grok's memorial service has been pushed back a
day like we wanted. The Asheville M.E.'s got Y'Suom scheduled
first thing. Mobile crime lab finished about two this morning
and I squeezed in three hours of shuteye."

"What about Millen and Weathers?"

"They're hanging in. Don't know about Talbert."

"I took him home with me. He was nervous staying at Crystal
Cascades by himself. When he wakes up, he'll find a note I left
with my cell phone number."

"Anybody know he's there?"

"No. You think he's the target?" The knot returned to my empty
stomach. Maybe I'd made a mistake leaving Talbert alone.

Tommy Lee threw up his hands. "I don't know what to think.
Damnedest case I've ever had. Talbert was the last guy to arrive
in town and then the shooter appears."

"But Y'Suom's the one who's killed and he's been here all
week." An idea struck me. "What if Y'Suom and Talbert each
knew something that would make sense only if they put the
information together?"

"So killing one would eliminate the need to kill the other?"

"Something like that."

Tommy Lee looked skeptical. "If you were Talbert, would you bet your life on that theory?"

"Definitely not."

"Me either. We're trying to force connections without understanding why they connect."

"All right, we take them separately. Somebody steals a body. Why?"

"For the tattoos."

I waved my finger at him. "Now, now. Are you sure? At first we thought the theft was a political statement, then a ransom, and now a tattooed treasure map none of us can decode. Which one gets us closer to a suspect?"

"Look, Barry, I don't need you to run me around in circles. I'm doing a helluva job chasing my own tail."

"Right. The only people we know benefited from the missing body are Archie and Mayor Whitlock. By delaying the funeral, they at least got Talbert to take a tour of the cemetery and get a lot of free publicity."

"Fine. I'll arrest the mayor at the courthouse. He loves to be on TV."

"I'm just agreeing with you that we've been pushing too hard for motive. So forget motive. Who had opportunity to steal the body? Who had opportunity to fire the shot at the cabin? Who had opportunity to strangle Y'Suom?"

"You mean other than all of Laurel County?"

"All of Laurel County didn't know we were meeting at the cabin last night. What time was that break-in at the pawn shop?"

Tommy Lee grinned. "Okay. You know I was on that track."

"Yeah. So why are you running me in circles?"

"I'm trying to run you off. You look like hell, you nearly got shot last night, and you could have walked up on a murderer at the country club. I get paid to be stupid. You don't."

"And you earn every penny."

"Okay. It's your funeral."

"No. It's my funeral home, so let me help."

Tommy Lee pushed his coffee aside and rested his arms on the table. "I planned to go over this with you last night, but Y'Suom's death turned everything upside down, and I got thinking how you'd be safer on the sidelines. But I also realize if they were casting the remake of *Dumb and Dumber*, they couldn't choose between us."

"I could have told you that." Helen set our plates on the table. "Surprised those movie producers missed you two the first time."

Tommy Lee grabbed his muffins and grits. "You talked yourself right out of your tip, Helen."

"Oh, I'm sorry. I really needed that quarter." She gave my plate of pancakes a spin as she slid them in front of me. "Enjoy."

I swirled hot syrup over the melting butter. "If the pawn shop was being burglarized at the same time we were gathering at the cabin, then the shooter already knew where he was headed. He didn't follow any of us."

"Menkle thinks the storeroom was broken into between five-thirty and six. Someone could still have tailed me, but that would've been cutting things close."

"You can probably get directions to my cabin off the internet, or the shooter could've learned about the meeting and checked out the location in the afternoon. Picked his shooting spot in the daylight."

"Yeah. We made the plan yesterday morning and you didn't get back to your cabin till mid-afternoon. I've made a list of everyone who knew about the meeting." He set down a half-eaten muffin and pulled a small pad from his chest pocket. "There're the attendees, obviously. Plus Weathers' aide Randall, and Millen probably told Nickles."

"How about Y'Suom?"

"He was at the VFW when we made the decision, but I suspect either Millen or Weathers would have told him that afternoon."

"Which means the Lutheran minister Hucksley and Collins knew as well."

"Yes."

"Anybody in your department?"

"No. I let them assume I was going to the Grove Park. Same for the mayor."

"So who was where?"

"That's the problem. There are gaps in everyone's schedule. Weathers and Millen met over lunch about the upcoming senate hearing. Then they rode together to visit the Montagnards at the VFW, leaving Randall and Nickles free and unaccounted for. Collins had left the VFW to return home and was alone. Hucksley said he went to the library where he could work on his eulogy and next Sunday's sermon."

"How about any of the vets?"

"What do you mean?"

"They're fiercely loyal to the Montagnards. Must be at least ten staying at the VFW. Maybe somebody doesn't like Millen's politics or Weathers' war strategy."

"All right, I'll ask. I can't see any of them killing Y'Suom. But, I know, we're setting motive aside for now."

We then set aside our suppositions to do some serious eating. I was down to my last pancake when Tommy Lee asked, "What are you doing today?"

"I promised Melissa I'd review the draft of her story. Double check she doesn't put something in we don't want released yet."

"Good."

"Then I'll need to confirm funeral arrangements for tomorrow. Don't know what to do about the plot. We could bury Y'Suom in the one for Y'Grok, since without a body, Y'Grok's service was only going to be a memorial. But if we ever recover his body, they both might wind up at Heaven's Gate Gardens where they can rest side by side."

"So the mayor wins. Maybe you're right. He should be a suspect. Murdering people to fill a cemetery."

"I'm just kidding. That would require too much ingenuity."

"You got that right." Tommy Lee concentrated on his grits, mopping them up with the remnant of a muffin.

"Anything promising in the statements from last night?"

Tommy Lee shook his head. "To tell the truth, I was so whipped I only gave them a quick read. Nothing leapt out at me. I'm going back over them this morning."

"What's Kevin up to?"

"He wants to go to the country club. Look around the fence and see if anybody climbed over."

"In this rain?"

"Yeah, doubtful he'll find anything, but the daylight might reveal some clue we missed last night. Gives him something to do. He's taking Y'Suom's death pretty hard."

"He have any theories?"

"If he does, he's not sharing them." Tommy Lee looked out the plate glass window at the side parking lot. Rain pounded off the cars and pooled in deep puddles. "What a mess. We'll have roads flooding today, which will stretch my department even more."

"When it rains, it pours. Let me know if I can help."

He wiped the final traces of jelly from the corner of his mouth. "You'll have your hands full with tomorrow's service and preparing Y'Suom's body."

"Uncle Wayne and Freddy can back me up."

"I'll call if I think of something. Meanwhile try to keep Melissa Bigham from making me sound too baffled."

"Now you want miracles."

Tommy Lee got to his feet. "Maybe that's what it'll take to break this case." He picked up the check and tossed a ten dollar bill on the table.

"Generous."

"At least Helen will have a nice day."

After debating whether to return to my cabin or go straight to the funeral home, I decided Franklin Talbert still slept on Australian time and could use a few extra hours. Meanwhile I'd get an early start on the day and then run him back to his condo before lunch.

When I walked through the back door, Mom was placing a glass of orange juice beside my dad's cereal bowl. He sat at the table in his pajamas, watching her closely. He smiled at me but immediately returned his attention to his food. The sound of snap, crackle, and pop was more than just a Rice Krispies marketing slogan. Dad wouldn't eat till it quieted. Then Mom gave him a spoon and a straw and watched to make sure he knew what to do with them. One day these simple implements would be beyond his understanding.

"You want some breakfast?" Mom asked.

"No, thanks. I met Tommy Lee at the Cardinal Café."

"Any word?"

"Let me get a cup of coffee and I'll tell you."

I broke the news of Y'Suom's murder as gently as I could. Dad ate his cereal, oblivious to the tragedy.

Mom started crying before I finished. "That poor family. Is there no one left?"

"Y'Grok had to leave his wife back in Vietnam. Someone will get a message to her."

"What happens now?"

"Tommy Lee's investigating. We're delaying the service till tomorrow. It'll be for both of them."

Mom dabbed her eyes with a paper napkin. "How could somebody do this?"

Her question went beyond who or why to a more basic level. How could one human being stand on the face of another and pull a belt so tight it crushed his windpipe?

"I don't know, Mom. I really don't."

We sat for a few minutes without speaking. When Dad had finished, I took his bowl to the sink.

"I'll call Wayne for you," Mom said.

"The body won't be here till this afternoon."

"He'll want to get prepared."

"Okay. I'm going to phone the church." I rested my hand on my dad's shoulder. He reached up and patted it.

An answering machine at Grace Lutheran recorded my request for someone to call me. I also stressed the urgency for the church to coordinate things with Reverend Hucksley. When Wayne arrived, we'd go over the plan for the next day's service. Meanwhile, I turned my attention to business matters for the funeral home.

After no more than thirty minutes, Mom interrupted my paperwork to announce that Melissa Bigham was in the parlor. I found her standing by the fireplace, her hair still damp and a rain-splotched manila envelope in her left hand.

I bent down and flipped the starter switch. The logs blazed to life. I lifted the nearest armchair and moved it closer to the hearth. "Take this seat." I sat on the sofa opposite her.

"Thanks." She pushed her wet hair off her forehead. Her cheeks glowed pink from the morning chill. "I was on my way to the newsroom and thought I'd run by with the first draft. Anything happen since we spoke?"

"No. I've got a call into the church about the burial plot and service. Tommy Lee's holding a press conference at ten."

"Knew that. My editor called me at home to make sure I'd be there." She tossed me the envelope. "Here's the draft about last night's murder. I'll add whatever new comes from the briefing. And I spoke to Mannie about the mayor's cemetery deal. He's heard some of the investors want out, and the bank's not happy with the loan status."

"Not surprised. They've been peddling plots for three years with little success. Nobody wants to buy till they see the finished landscaping."

She looked at her watch. "Is Tommy Lee going to mention the missing body?"

"Yes, but the emphasis will be on Y'Suom's murder."

"People are murdered every day, Barry. Stealing a corpse is news. If you want me to be your only media outlet, you'd better plan on hiding."

"You're kidding?"

"The CNN stringer's on his way over from Asheville. He'd love to get your battered face on camera."

I heard a footstep in the hall.

"Here you are." Uncle Wayne nodded to Melissa. "Morning. Sorry to interrupt. Just wanted to say he doesn't look too bad for his trip."

"Who?"

"Why, the body, of course."

"They brought Y'Suom already?

Uncle Wayne stared at me like I'd lost my mind. "Didn't you check him in?"

I jumped to my feet. "No." I rushed past him. As I ran down the hall, I heard Melissa hurrying after me.

The door to the operating room stood wide open. A white shroud covered the body on the table. How had the Asheville M.E. delivered Y'Suom without my knowledge? I stepped to the head and yanked back the sheet.

There before me lay not the body of Y'Suom, but his father. Y'Grok Eban had returned.

Chapter Seventeen

Melissa gasped. "The father?"

Without answering, I went to the outside door. The jamb had been re-splintered and the latch broken. A thin trail of water was smeared over the threshold. "He was dragged in. Must have been during the night."

Uncle Wayne stared at the shattered latch. "I didn't notice the door. I was so glad to see him."

"We never had the chance to reconnect the alarm. Probably no prints." I stepped back to the body and removed the sheet. Melissa looked a little green around the gills, but she held her ground.

Uncle Wayne cleared his throat and nodded toward Melissa.

"She's okay," I said. "Reporters see it all."

"If you say so." He wasn't comfortable with Melissa observing a nude man.

"He's not wet." I tucked my hand under his back. "Dry here as well. But the floor's still damp."

"Must've had him wrapped," Wayne said. "Could've been a sleeping bag."

"Or a body bag." I glanced at my watch. Nine-forty. "We need to get word to Tommy Lee. He'll want to send the mobile lab. And there's no need now for him to announce the missing body at the briefing."

The color was returning to Melissa's face. "Can you catch him at the department?"

"I'll try his cell. He'll recognize my number."

Tommy Lee answered on the second ring. Without so much as a hello, I blurted, "Y'Grok's body's been returned."

"Where?"

"It's back on the table in the embalming room."

"How?"

"The door was broken in. Had to be the same guy who stole him. Y'Grok sure as hell didn't climb up on the table."

"Thank you, Sherlock." Tommy Lee covered the mouthpiece and said, "Reece, tell them I'll be there in five minutes." Then to me, "Sorry, almost time for the briefing. Are the tattoos defaced?"

I hadn't bothered to look. Setting the phone on the lip of the table, I moved Y'Grok's thighs apart. The tattoos showed no sign of damage. "They're fine. What do you want me to do?"

"Nothing. As soon as I get through this briefing I'll be over."

I remembered Melissa's advice. "Maybe you shouldn't mention the body to anyone yet. Unless you think it'll aid the investigation."

"Good point. That would be chum for the sharks. I'll see you around eleven." He hung up.

I turned to Melissa. "You'd better scoot. You don't want to miss rubbing elbows with the big boys."

She took out her notepad and stepped closer. "Can I see those tattoos?"

I draped the sheet to provide a semblance of modesty, and then showed her Y'Grok's handiwork. This time I noticed the 4KM under the number 2000. "We think the tattoos are a message for Kevin Malone. You can see how these letters spell Raven."

"But Kevin doesn't understand it?"

"No. We tried looking at the circle as a compass and a clock. We tried the number as yards, meters, feet. Nothing fit."

"Tried them where?"

"Where Y'Grok stayed. The old mill up at Redman Gorge."

"This has to mean something else." She leaned closer to the body. "You'd think it'd be tied to their military training. If the V is also hands on a clock face, what's so special about ten minutes till two or ten minutes after ten? And how would you know which time is right?"

I studied the circle. Time. Military training. Military lingo for a twenty-four hour day. "Twenty hundred hours," I whispered.

Melissa gave me a confused look. "Archie's time for the mayor's party?"

I laughed. "Archie gave us the answer." I pointed to the 2000 on Y'Grok's thigh. "Twenty hundred hours. Eight p.m."

Melissa stared at the number and then at the circle with the V. "But eight doesn't match the time on the clock."

"Because it's not a clock. The V's the center letter of Raven and we read too much into it. The circle is simply a circle and whatever Y'Grok hid, he hid at eight o'clock on the circle." I grinned at them. Maybe Tommy Lee was right. I was Sherlock Holmes.

Melissa and Uncle Wayne looked at me like I was Inspector Clouseau babbling French.

Then Melissa drew on her notepad and held up a circle with an X at eight o'clock. "Okay, genius. What and where is this circle?"

My grin faded. "Right. That's the million dollar question." I thought for a moment. "The circle has to be close to where he was staying. He wouldn't hide something that valuable where he couldn't keep an eye on it. And he was too weak to walk out of Redman Gorge. He'd have to stay close to the mill."

The mill. The same light bulb came on for all three of us.

As Melissa and Uncle Wayne opened their mouths, I stole their words. "The waterwheel. Twenty hundred hours on the water-wheel. Eight o'clock, but only recognized if you thought military time." I remembered the cut rhododendron branches with no trace of their ends on the ground. Had Y'Grok wedged his ammo case in the wheel and covered it with brush? Dead branches that would look like they'd been washed downstream.

The rain beat on the porte-cochere roof with renewed intensity. "I've got to leave right now. Uncle Wayne, tell Tommy Lee I may have broken the code, but not to tell anyone else. If I don't get up to Redman Gorge fast, everything Y'Grok worked for will be washed away."

I turned to Melissa. "You've got to sit on this."

"Hell no. The only thing I'm sitting on is your passenger seat. Like it or not, you've got a partner."

The wipers slung rain off the windshield in waves. Traffic flowed through town slower than the water racing along the pavement to the storm drains.

Melissa leaned forward as far as the seatbelt allowed and gripped the dashboard. If she could have outrun the jeep, I think she'd have jumped from the moving vehicle. "So this ammo case is stuffed with a million dollars?"

"Maybe. Maybe something else to do with Operation Raven."

"Aren't we ruining Y'Grok's efforts if we recover the money?"

I didn't follow her logic. "You've lost me."

"The money comes to light. The government steps in and confiscates it. End of any chance the cash goes to Montagnard resistance. End of story."

"What's your solution? Keep the money for ourselves?"

She laughed. "No, not that I wouldn't be tempted. I do need some new tires."

"We could tip off Kevin Malone, but I still don't totally trust him. Besides, look at this deluge. There's no time. If we don't get to that waterwheel soon, somebody downstream's going to get a very nice surprise."

Melissa's grip tightened on the dashboard. "Just doesn't seem fair."

"I agree. The Montagnards did everything our government asked them. But there's more than money at stake."

"What?"

"A possible solution to Y'Suom's murder. That's the fairness I'm interested in."

She leaned back. "And that'd be a great story, wouldn't it?"

"An exclusive." I kept my eyes on the road, but I knew she was smiling.

Once on the back road to Redman Gorge, I made better time. Everyone else had the good sense to stay indoors. I hadn't thought through exactly what we would do when we reached the mill, but I'd thrown a rope in the back of the jeep in case I needed a lifeline. If conditions were too dangerous, I'd phone Tommy Lee for help. I hated to drag him and his deputies on a wild goose chase if the ammo case contained nothing more significant than a dying man's foolish dreams. Then I remembered my cell phone was useless between the gorge's ridges. I couldn't call out and no one could reach me, including Franklin Talbert, stranded with my dog and guinea pig.

The rickety slat bridge over the stream to the farmhouse looked even narrower in the gray downpour. I stopped and made sure the jeep was lined up to roll across the center. The water already boiled a foot higher than normal and the force of the rising current could eat away the bank supports. I opted for faster rather than slower, and heard Melissa's sharp intake of breath as I gunned us to the other side.

Once over, I skidded to a halt. "That wasn't so bad."

"Why don't you try backing over when we leave? I'll be glad to watch."

I parked between the farmhouse and the log footbridge. Out in the clearing, the wind roared down the gorge, hammering the rain into horizontal streaks. Before stepping out of the jeep, I pulled the hood of my slicker over my head and tightened the drawstring. "This is going to be nasty."

Melissa wore a light parka more suited to a spring shower than a monsoon. She zipped the jacket up to her neck and snapped the hood strap under her chin. The fit was loose and when she turned her head, her face slid into the side of the fabric.

"Great. Am I going to be your seeing-eye dog?"

"Don't worry about me. You're the one who's always being patched up."

I opened the door and the wind whipped the handle out of my hand. The rope would be a necessity.

We stood on the bank opposite the waterwheel. The stream rushed by, carrying broken limbs and uprooted plants. The water frothed a murky brown and the current tore at the lower third of the broken paddles. The axle had been locked in place to keep the wheel from turning. I could see some withered rhododendron branches crammed into a section just above the rising water line. Eight on a clock face.

Melissa shouted above the storm. "How are you going to reach it?"

"I'll climb down from the top of the wheel and stand on the spokes. I should be able to get the case from there."

"And the rope?"

I'd brought the rope as a safety line, but the thought of dropping the ammo case in the raging stream created another use. "If the handle is strong enough, I'll loop the rope through it. Then if the case falls in the water, you can retrieve it."

Melissa looked at the powerful current. The body of a drowned squirrel hit a paddle, and then disappeared below the surface. She shook her head. "Tie the rope under your arms. The case can't drown."

I studied the trees on the far bank till I found what I wanted— a large poplar with a branch extending over the stream. "All right, but we'll throw the rope over that limb. Otherwise, if I tumble, you'll be yanked in after me."

"And this way I'll be hoisted in the air?"

"The limb should bear the weight." I managed a smile. "If I'm wrong, you'll only fly up till you smack your head." I lifted the coiled rope to my shoulder. "Let's go."

The wind blew too strong to dare cross the foot log standing up. I straddled the worn wet bark like riding a horse and scooted across. Melissa followed my example.

The poplar was about twenty feet from the mill. My selected limb angled toward the wheel and over the stream. The height of the branch would take an additional fifteen feet of rope. I hoped there'd be enough slack for me to maneuver on the wheel.

I triple knotted one end of the rope so I could throw it like a ball. I needed the rope in as straight a line as possible from Melissa to the wheel. The wind blew the rope back but enough made it over the branch to fall within my grasp. I handed Melissa the coil. "Hold onto this and feed it out as I go. It looks like you might end up directly under the limb if we use every foot."

Melissa held the rope in both hands. "Make sure you tie the rope tight under your arms."

The knotted rope end dangled from the limb. I stretched to reach it and pulled as Melissa dropped a loop. I wrapped the rope around my upper chest, knotted it snug, and slid the safety line to my back. "If I fall in, I'll float downstream feet first so I won't crack my head on any rocks. The anchored rope should force me to the shore."

"What about the case?"

I held up the loose end of rope. "I've allowed an extra yard I can use to attach the case so I can swim without holding it."

Melissa looked doubtful. "Why do I feel like I'm about to hang you?"

"Don't worry. I'm much more likely to drown." With those words of comfort, I walked slowly to the mill. Melissa kept the rope from snagging by feeding slack only as fast as needed. I felt like an astronaut venturing outside the space shuttle.

The stone foundation of the mill had been built along the natural edge of the stream. The water was less than three feet beneath it, but if the level rose much higher, the spillover would happen on the other bank first. That meant my footing on the foundation ledge should stay passable, but Y'Grok's hiding place was below the foundation and would soon be submerged.

I stepped up on the smooth stone outcrop and looked back at Melissa. A gust of wind blew the hood from her head and plastered her hair to her skull. She gave me a thumbs up. I had about a dozen feet to the circumference of the wheel. The six-inch ledge had looked bigger when I wasn't perched on it. Now I pressed myself flat against the rough sideboards and dug my fingernails into the decaying wood. I slid my feet along a few inches at a time. Wind whistled through the paddles of the wheel, varying in pitch with each gust.

The diameter must have been close to ten feet, and I didn't know if Y'Grok had stashed his case nearer the paddles or the axle. I approached the wheel from the left, bringing me to a horizontal spoke at roughly nine o'clock. I gripped the spoke with my right hand and pulled down. The beam felt rock solid. The paddle blades were much thinner and their splintered condition promised little hope that they could support my weight.

Stepping around the blades, I clung to the spoke with my left hand while testing my footing on the spoke below. Water splashed over my shoe, but the tug wasn't strong enough to trip me.

I bent down, still holding the beam above my head, and yanked at the mass of rhododendron branches. A few broke loose and the current swept them away. I could see behind the paddles clear to the foundation wall. No case. Y'Grok must have wedged it closer to the axle. I took a step farther. The rotted spoke angled at a steep incline toward the hub. The rope at my back tightened and I looked back to see Melissa wrapping the last foot around her wrist. She stepped directly beneath the branch, giving me as much slack as she could.

Climbing a few more feet, I removed another section of brush. Then I saw it. A gunmetal corner stuck out over a mesh of gnarled branches. Y'Grok had woven a makeshift cocoon to hold his treasure. I had to be careful not to tear into the branches so rapidly that the ammo case toppled before I could find the handle.

"I see it!" The wind carried my voice to Melissa. She nodded vigorously. "Just another foot!"

I strained against the rope, groping with my left hand till I felt cold metal beneath my fingers. I ran them along a dented edge to a corner. The handle wasn't facing me. I pulled the rope up to my armpits, stretching for every last inch. I poked one foot through the branches and lightly struck the case with the toe of my shoe, searching for the handle. I must have looked like a crouching Russian dancer, kicking a leg in time to unheard music.

The case moved, slowly at first, but then gained momentum as the box slid down the spoke toward me. Without thinking, I bent down to grab the handle with one hand. The rope pulled at my back and then loosened as I snared the handle. A half second later and the case would have tumbled into the churning stream.

Suddenly, the rope jerked taut with such force that I fell backwards, clutching the upper spoke with one hand and Y'Grok's case with the other. What the hell was Melissa doing?

My hand on the beam slipped. Splinters pierced my skin. Then the rope yanked me like a team of horses was hitched to the other end. Gray sky and bare branches swirled overhead. I hit the water flat on my back and plunged beneath the icy surface.

The current tore at me, digging the rope into my armpits. I floundered in the water like a hooked bass, spinning around as the powerful torrent tried to wrestle the case from my grip.

My head broke the surface and I rolled onto my back, tucking up my knees to wedge the case against them. I looked downstream and saw Melissa in the water, clinging to her end of the rope. I knew what had happened. In my lunge to grab the case, I had pulled her off her feet. She had fallen into the stream, dragging me after her. Now we were tethered to each other, hanging from the branch.

Hydraulic physics began to take effect. I was heavier and the larger mass—a barge compared to Melissa's slender kayak body. The current exerted greater pressure on me, and as I was driven downstream, the rope pulled Melissa upstream.

"Hang on!" I got a mouthful of water for my efforts.

I fought to maneuver toward her. The point at which the rope segments became equal would bring us briefly together. If we could hold onto each other, we might be able to make it to the bank. I clutched the case to my chest and spread my legs. She came to my right, and I caught her with my heel and wrapped my legs around her waist in a scissor grip.

She sputtered a few words. "Can't hold on."

"Don't let go. Kick to shore."

I felt her legs moving, but we only traveled a few feet diagonally, then stopped. I looked up at the branch and saw the problem. The rope had slipped farther out until it reached a fork over the stream. The plumb of the line was no longer on the bank. We were trying to swim against the current, a hopeless endeavor.

"We're going to have to ride it out," I shouted. "There's a bend downstream."

Melissa shook her head. "Too tired."

"No. Fill your lungs with air and I'll hold you. Paddle towards the shore. Ready?"

She took a deep breath.

"Let go!"

She released her grip and twisted free of the rope. Immediately, the current snatched us. Melissa kicked and clawed for the bank. I used my right arm like a canoe paddle, reaching toward the shore in short furious sidestrokes. We hurled downstream at a speed that would have gotten any amusement park sued. I hoped that by staying together, our combined weight and effort would break us out of the current's force as the stream curved into the forest.

We must have bodysurfed several hundred yards when the stream suddenly broadened. We were spit to one side and I felt my butt bouncing along bumpy ground. The current weakened and I could see we'd crossed into a lower clearing, now flooded into a small lake. The water still flowed rapidly, but it was no longer deep. I grabbed Melissa's arm with my free hand and unlocked my legs. She tumbled clear and staggered to her feet.

Her parka was wadded up over her shoulders. The buttons from her blouse were somewhere downstream and her bra was more outside than in. Her pants had stayed on thanks to my vise-grip, but she lifted a foot to show her shoes had been ripped from her feet. She bent over, hands on her knees, gasping for breath. The state of her wardrobe didn't concern her.

I struggled to my feet, checking to see if all my parts were there. The water was about eight inches deep and rising. "We'd better get out of here." I looked in the direction of the mill. The building was out of sight, but the higher pasture promised drier ground.

Melissa laughed and cried at the same time. "I've never been in a wet tee-shirt contest before."

"Obviously. You're supposed to wear a tee-shirt."

She tucked her blouse together as best she could and then rapped on the metal case in my hand. "I'm glad you could save both of us. I'd hate to think where I'd be if you had to make a choice."

"I would've asked the new reporter to dedicate the story to you."

She grabbed the rope still knotted around my armpits and pulled me over. "And I'm throwing you back."

We slogged through the flooded field, me carrying the case and Melissa toting the frayed rope. Our progress was slow, not so much because of the water but because Melissa's shoeless feet found each step a potential hazard. I offered to carry her on my back, but she found the prospect too humiliating.

The euphoria of survival gave way to the aches and pains of the ordeal. Melissa's wrist had been burned raw where she'd wrapped the rope around it. My left hand bled from the barrage of splinters and I suspected we'd both find bruises over the next few days like the aftermath of a car wreck.

The rain continued to pour and I decided the shelter of the mill offered the best place to examine the case. After our harrowing adventure, I didn't want to take a chance on crossing the log without first knowing the contents of what we'd risked our lives to retrieve.

Y'Grok's room was dark and damp. Water blew in under the eaves and trickled down the wall that faced the brunt of the wind. I remembered the matches on the stove and lit the kerosene lamp on the table and the two hanging from the beams.

Melissa turned in a full circle, taking in the illuminated space, and then sat in the straight-back chair. "This is where he lived?"

"And died." I set the ammo case on the table. The handle on the top was twisted to one side, but the clamps holding the lid seemed firmly in place. Dents and rust marred the metal finish. The box looked like it had survived a war. I guess it had.

Melissa gripped the near corner. "I'm amazed Y'Grok was able to smuggle this out of Vietnam."

"I don't think they know exactly how Y'Grok got out of Vietnam. He didn't come through any resettlement agency." I looked at Melissa. "Ready?"

She withdrew her hand and I snapped the clamps free. The lid flipped back and revealed a dirty oilskin. No water beaded on its surface. I lifted the bundle and found a second oilskin underneath. I laid the first on the table. The cloth had been wrapped lengthwise around an object about six inches by four inches and an inch or two thick. The ends had been tucked in and the whole parcel tied with cord. The knot had been pulled so tight that time had merged the strands into a solid mass.

I found a knife on the stove and cut the cord away. Melissa leaned closer as I unraveled the oilskin down to a manila envelope slightly larger than a business letter. A clasp had long ago broken off and the flap was simply stuffed inside. Carefully, I probed a finger under the edge and opened the envelope. I lifted the other end and a stack of dirty hundred dollar bills slid onto the table.

Melissa stood up. "You were right. He brought back the money."

I looked at the grungy stack of bills. "But we're not talking anywhere near a million dollars."

"Maybe there's more bundles."

"If they're all hundreds, we'd need ten thousand of these bills." I lifted out the second oilskin. It had filled the rest of the case. The cloth's contents felt lumpy and hard. I smiled. "Unless he converted the money to gold or diamonds."

"Now you're talking."

Our pain and exhaustion were forgotten. I pushed the money to one side and made plenty of room for the larger parcel. I cut the cord and Melissa helped me unravel the cloth. Neither of us wanted to dump nuggets or jewels onto the mill's rough plank floor.

No loose treasure appeared. The cloth protected a sack of coarse muslin, the neck of which was bound by a military dog tag. Although the metal was stainless steel, years had turned the chain and plate black. I held the tag against the globe of the lantern.

Melissa's wet hair brushed my cheek. "What's it say?"

"Raven, James A. There's a serial number and no pref."

"Raven? Raven is a person?"

A queasy feeling came over my stomach. "I don't think we're looking at nuggets of gold." I used my fingernails to pry loose the knotted chain, and then folded back the neck of the bag.

The flicker of the lantern danced over pieces of human bones.

I clutched Melissa's hand. "Raven's come home."

The door to the mill flung open. Kevin Malone stood dripping on the threshold, the rain blowing in around him. He looked at us, and then the case on the table. His face turned hard and grim.

Chapter Eighteen

"I'll thank you to give me my property."

The first thought flashed through my mind—watch his hands. He's carrying a pistol. The second thought—he shot his partner. I stepped aside. "This is evidence."

"No. Whatever's in that case is mine. That's what Y'Grok wanted and that's the way it's going to be."

"James Raven's family might have something to say about that."

Kevin's mouth fell open. "Jimmy? Jimmy Raven?"

"James A. Raven. His dog tag sealed this bag of skeletal remains."

Kevin rushed forward, his drenched face pale and his eyes wide in disbelief. He laid a hand on one of the bones. Then he picked up the dog tag, read the stamped words, and clutched the tag to his chest. "Sweet Jesus. Y'Grok brought Jimmy back. All those miles and all those years. He brought Jimmy back."

I slid the envelope toward him. "There's some money too."

Kevin snatched the envelope. He looked at Melissa and then at me. "A dying man brings the remains of a dead comrade halfway around the world. You can't buy that kind of loyalty." He leaned on the small table for support, and then crossed to the bed and sat down. He clasped the dog tag in one hand and the money in the other.

I realized the bones changed everything. "So Y'Grok's message has nothing to do with money from Operation Raven."

"The message has everything to do with Operation Raven. Jimmy Raven started the operation. At first we called it Yard Guard. It was a small underground network that linked some Montagnard villages together. The Yards would pass word along if they were hiding one of our boys. That's how Ryan Millen got rescued."

"And the operation got more elaborate?"

"The war escalated, which meant we had more downed pilots and stranded grunts. The Yards were so trustworthy we didn't worry about betrayal. Stormy Weathers wanted the operation expanded and he brought in Military Intelligence operatives to run things."

"Like Franklin Talbert," I said.

"Yeah. Franklin came in and worked with Jimmy. By then I was down in one of the lower provinces."

"Was the operation changed to Raven because of Jimmy?"

"Stormy renamed it Raven when Jimmy got killed. Jimmy died in a firefight, and the enemy overran the position. His body wasn't recovered."

"Y'Grok must have gone back."

"He never forgot. I guess when he decided to come here he recovered the remains. A matter of honor."

I looked at the bone pieces. There was no skull or femur, nothing that wouldn't fit into the ammo case. I picked up the envelope. "And returning the money would've been a matter of honor as well?"

"Yes. He would've wanted to look us in the eye and return what he considered ours." He looked at the envelope and read the scrawl on the back. "Received from U.S., $10,000." As if to verify the statement, Kevin thumbed the stack like a deck of cards. "Where's the rest of the money?"

"That's all that was in the case."

Kevin shook his head. "No. Y'Grok had been entrusted with ten times that."

"And I'm telling you, that's all we found. We'd just opened the case when you stormed in."

"Then there must be a second case." He looked at us like we were suspects in a line-up.

I glared back at him. "Then you jump in that torrent and find it. This case and only this case was right where the tattoos placed it. There was nothing else there, and there was nothing else in the case but that packet of money and the bag of bones."

Melissa sat down in the chair and sighed. "You're barking up the wrong tree, Kevin. If there's more money, we don't know where it is. You should be asking why Y'Grok didn't just turn these remains over to the MIA investigators."

Kevin shrugged. "Personal duty."

I looked at the bag. Somehow it seemed irreverent exposing the bones to the damp chilly air. I tucked the fabric closed. "Just strange he'd have gone to such lengths—the letter to you, the tattoos. Wouldn't personal duty have been served by getting the remains to the family?"

Kevin walked to the table and wrapped the money in the oilskin. "If Y'Grok could find the family. Jimmy was killed back in the Sixties. He had a young wife and infant son. I'm sure she remarried. Without access to army records, Y'Grok had no way of locating her."

"Did he ask you where she was?"

"No." Then Kevin thought a moment. "He might have asked about the son once."

"In the letter you got last week?"

"No. That would have been years ago. About the time he smuggled Y'Suom out as a boy."

"How'd you stay in touch?"

"Letters. I'd send duplicates mailed a week apart and hope one of them would make it. We knew they were censored. I had various addresses for him—names of friends or sympathizers who had ways of getting the letters into the central highlands."

"Did he ever write anything in code?"

"Hell, yes. But more of reading between the lines than code. Things were bad. By the Eighties, most of the Raven network had been wiped out."

"Revenge?"

"Partly. Mostly to crush any chance for organized Yard resistance to the persecution."

Melissa leaned forward, breaking into the conversation. "Wouldn't your letters have fingered him?"

"If they'd been addressed to him. That's why they always went to a Vietnamese. There are sympathizers who believe their government's policy is wrong. I never mentioned Y'Grok by name but he could read between the lines as well."

"Did you help Y'Suom?" I asked.

"There were retired Special Forces families around Fort Bragg who took care of him. I sent a check now and then. Should have done more. When Y'Suom was old enough, he enlisted."

I looked at the bag of bones on the table and the oilskin of money Kevin clutched in both hands. "But Y'Grok sent for you, even though others had personally aided his son and Tommy Lee was nearby. Were you that much closer?"

Kevin mulled the question. "I guess we were. I got the letter."

"And it came to your work? Is that where all the correspondence had been sent?"

"No. That surprised me. Since I've had my recent trouble with the department, my mail's been forwarded. I got the letter at home, but the address had been to work."

"So he knew you were a policeman?"

Kevin laughed. "Oh, yeah. I'd even sent a photo of me receiving the award for Boston Detective of the Year. Wanted him to know I was still after the bad guys."

A light flickered in the back of my brain, but I wasn't sure what was being illuminated. "And he sent his letter to your work," I repeated to myself.

"Even had detective underlined." Kevin cocked his head. "Damn. That's it, isn't it?"

Melissa stood up, trying to make sense of our incomplete phrases. "What are you talking about?"

"A crime," I said. "A crime Y'Grok wanted solved. A crime that might have cost Y'Suom his life."

"And been behind last night's shooting," Kevin added.

"Shooting?" Melissa stepped between the two of us. "What shooting?"

I gave Kevin a sharp stare. "Now you've done it."

"There was a shooting after the murder?" She patted her wet pockets, futilely searching for a notepad.

Kevin said nothing.

Melissa wheeled on me. "Okay, Barry. No games. What happened?"

"Someone took a shot as we were coming out of my cabin. Before the party."

"Who's we?"

"Talbert, Millen, and Weathers."

Her eyes widened. "Someone shot at a U.S. senator and a three-star general?"

"And a two-bit actor," Kevin said. "And don't forget me, Tommy Lee, and Barry. What are we, chopped liver?"

"Why didn't you tell me?"

"Tell you what?" Kevin asked. "For all we knew the shooter could have been some drunk deer hunter."

Melissa fumed. "Even I know you don't hunt deer in April."

There was no use trying to hide the truth. "We made a decision to investigate without creating a media frenzy."

"Barry, I'm not sitting on this. At the rate we're going, I'll be retired before this story breaks."

"And what's the story? We have pieces of evidence and we have bodies, but what connects them?"

"Y'Grok connects them." Kevin met Melissa eye to eye. "And if you print what you know, our killer might bolt. I think he was trying to keep us from finding this case. He took Y'Grok's body, he killed Y'Grok's son, and he fired a shot at one of us. We have a better chance of catching him if he thinks we're still in the dark."

"But you figured the code out," Melissa said.

Kevin shook his head. "I didn't crack the tattoos. Tommy Lee confided that the body had been returned. I went to the funeral home and spoke with Barry's uncle. All he said was the two of you left in a hurry. I tried your phone and got no answer. I knew this spot was out of cell range and our prime contender for where Y'Grok would have hidden something. I played a hunch."

Melissa bit her lower lip. She wasn't comfortable holding back so much explosive information.

I weighed in with the best argument I could muster. "Look, we're the only ones who know about this. I'm not saying we withhold evidence because we'll tell Tommy Lee as soon as we can reach him. But Kevin's right. The killer could disappear if he thinks we've found the evidence. I don't think we should tell anyone else. Y'Grok must've had a damned good reason for trusting only Kevin."

"So how can you proceed?" Melissa asked.

"That's Tommy Lee's call. But I'd like to get an unofficial examination of these bones, something that doesn't generate a report from the medical examiner."

Kevin looked skeptical. "Will the M.E. do that?"

"No. But Susan Miller will, and a surgeon's eye might be enough to shed some light."

"That's your girlfriend?"

I nodded, smothering my uncertainty.

"How do we know the theft of the body and Y'Suom's murder aren't all about the money?" Kevin asked. "I was expecting a lot more and someone else could have as well."

"We don't know," I said. "But I'd at least like to rule out the possibility that there's more to Raven coming home than a simple return of money and remains."

Kevin separated the dog tag from the money. He looped the chain around the closed bag. "All right. But we keep both things secret, the money and the remains. For now we leave everybody in the dark except Tommy Lee. You head straight to Susan and after she's had her examination, we'll talk about the next step."

"I'm in," Melissa said, "but I'm in all the way. No more withholding little tidbits like last night's shooting."

Kevin took her hand. "Fair enough."

They looked at me. I trusted Kevin about as far as I could swim against the stream raging outside. What choice did I have? I placed my hand on top of theirs. The three musketeers. I hoped I didn't get a sword in the back.

Fortunately, I'd had the good sense to leave my cell phone in the jeep before my plunge into the stream. The instrument vibrated as soon as Melissa and I cleared Redman Gorge. It wasn't a caller but a notice that I had two messages. Since I hate fooling with the phone while driving, especially in bad weather, I asked Melissa to read me the numbers.

"I know this one by heart. It's your cabin."

I slapped the steering wheel, and then winced as the splinters in my left hand dug deeper. "Franklin Talbert. I forgot about him. He's been stuck up there all morning."

"Do you want me to call him?"

"No. What's the other number?"

"The funeral home."

"Dial, and then give me the phone."

Uncle Wayne answered. As soon as I spoke, he interrupted.

"People been looking for you all day. That Talbert fella called. You know he's at your cabin?"

"Yes. I'll get him later."

"Don't bother. Mayor Whitlock came by. When I said Talbert was at your cabin, the mayor fell all over himself to be the one to pick him up."

"Good. Saves me a trip."

"That Yankee detective fellow find you?"

"Yes."

"Sorry. I didn't know what to do."

"It's okay. Just don't tell anybody where I've been or that the detective was with me."

"How about Tommy Lee? Can I tell him?"

"No. I'll tell him." The phone went quiet and for a second I thought I'd lost the signal. "Uncle Wayne?"

"Well, he's sorta standing here."

If Wayne had been a spy, he'd never have lived long enough to come in from the cold.

I rolled my eyes at Melissa. "Put him on." I could imagine my uncle passing the phone like it was a hot potato.

"So what are you going to tell me?" Tommy Lee didn't sound amused. "How big's this sling you're about to put my ass in?"

"Big, even for your ass."

"Is Melissa Bigham with you?"

"Yes."

"She gonna be okay?"

I winked at Melissa. "If she gets her exclusive."

"I'm afraid you and I are going to owe her big time." He paused. "Okay, I'm sitting down. What is it?"

I didn't trust myself to concentrate on what I was saying and keep the jeep in my narrow lane. I pulled off the curvy road into the muddy lot of a seasonal roadside fruit stand. Its shuttered front would be dormant until South Carolina peaches were hauled up the mountain. I could park and talk to Tommy Lee for three months.

"Y'Grok brought back the remains of Jimmy Raven. That's what he meant by Raven's come home."

"What?"

"Dog tag. Bones. Kevin's shook up. I take it they were close."

"I never knew Raven, but Kevin told me about him. Weathers named the operation after him."

"I know. We think Y'Grok might have been bringing the remains to Kevin because Y'Grok knew he was a detective. Otherwise, there were far easier ways to get Raven home."

Tommy Lee gave a soft whistle. He understood the implications immediately. "So the bones could be the motive for Y'Suom's murder."

"But for who? And who had both motive and opportunity? Kevin and I want to keep the discovery a secret so as not to spook the killer. If he learns the remains have been discovered, he might make a run for it."

"And there's a chance the medical examiner's office could leak the information," Tommy Lee conceded.

"I planned on taking the remains to Susan for a first look. She's not a forensic examiner, but her knowledge of anatomy's better than yours or mine. Then—"

Tommy Lee cut me off. "Then we don't have time to talk. Get going." He hung up.

I lowered the phone.

"What happened?" Melissa asked. "Did you lose the signal?"

"No. I got the signal. A green light to proceed."

Melissa turned in her seat to face me. "Shouldn't you call Susan?"

"It's after lunch. She'll be at the clinic."

"Do you really think I should go with you?"

Her question surprised me. Melissa's journalistic zeal had never been restrained before. "Why not?"

"I could check some things at the paper. Background on James Raven." The blush in her cheeks said there was more to the story.

"I want to get these remains to Susan right away. We're going to drive past the clinic on the way to the funeral home."

Melissa looked away from me. "She won't have to bring anybody else in on this, will she?"

"I'm not asking her for any tests, just an educated opinion. I'll stress the confidentiality."

Melissa's cheek muscles tensed, but she said nothing.

"What's the matter? Don't you trust her?"

She snapped her head around and gave me a piercing stare. "What matters is that you trust her."

I felt the blood rush to my cheeks. "I know things have seemed strained. She's just worried about me. I haven't been a good patient since I took that blow on the head. That's all."

Melissa's fingers fidgeted with her seatbelt. Then she took a deep breath and squared her shoulders. "Let me just say this, and then we'll drop the subject. This is a big story, maybe the biggest I've ever worked on. We don't know what kind of dynamite we're toying with. There could even be some cover-up that involves Millen and Weathers. Confidentiality is all we've got right now. This Dr. Chandler who came with Susan to the party last night, you said he'd examined Y'Grok so he knows something's up."

"Just that the tattoos were recent."

"Stress to Susan not to mention anything about the remains to him."

"Okay, but why do you think she would?"

Again, Melissa hesitated, and then plunged ahead. "Barry, I don't know how to say this any other way. Tuesday morning, before we met in the park and you told me about Y'Grok Eban, I went to the clinic for a routine physical. When I walked back to my car, I saw Susan and Chandler across the parking lot. They didn't see me. She gave him a hug and a kiss. I don't know what that means, but it certainly wasn't a handshake."

Chapter Nineteen

I turned into the clinic's parking lot and saw Susan's Subaru in her usual spot. Melissa and I had ridden the last five miles without speaking, the swish of wiper blades and steady pounding of rain filling the silence. I knew there had to be an explanation for the scene Melissa had witnessed, but at the moment I couldn't create one that I believed, let alone try to sell to a skeptical reporter.

Melissa unsnapped her seatbelt. "There's her car. You think she'll interrupt her patient schedule?"

I raised my bleeding left hand. "I'm a patient. I hope to jump to the head of the line."

Melissa held an umbrella over us as I carried the ammo case from the jeep to the clinic's door. I recognized the steel-haired woman at the appointment desk, guarding the passage to a half-filled waiting room.

"Good afternoon, Natalie."

Natalie Golden looked up from her computer screen. "Barry. Did you fall off the ark?" Then she noticed my hand. Her smile faded as she looked from me to Melissa. "This isn't a social call, is it?"

"Can you let Susan know I'm here?"

"Yes. But she's in an examination room and has two appointments waiting." Natalie scowled at her computer as if demanding the screen to delete the other patients. Then she winked at me. "Okay. Go back to her office. I'll let her know you're here."

I knew my way around the clinic enough to lead Melissa across the waiting area and down a side hall that bypassed the examination rooms. Susan rated a corner office large enough to accommodate a sofa and chairs for patient consultations. I set the ammo case on the floor, but remained standing, reluctant to perch my soaked butt on her furniture.

Melissa tucked her damaged blouse in as best she could and leaned against the desk, careful not to drip on the paperwork. "What do you think she'll say?"

"Not much. Susan has a temper when she thinks I've done something really stupid."

"If nearly drowning doesn't qualify as stupid, what does?"

"That's what I mean. She'll be angry, but she won't explode with you here."

"Don't be so sure. I might be the fuse." Melissa walked to the window and stared at the rain pelting the parking lot.

Susan's office had the feel of a cozy den rather than a medical clinic. No diplomas hung on the wall; no skeletal models to remind the patients what parts needed repair or replacement. Instead, framed mountain photographs, many by the celebrated Hugh Morton, lent an air of tranquility to what at times could be a space of bad news and worse options. A box of Beanie Babies offered distraction for kids, and the magazines on the end tables covered upbeat, positive topics from kayaking to crocheting. A few personal mementos complemented the décor. Susan's collection of ceramic frogs had spilled over into her office. Poised leapers and squatters adorned the shelves. Three family pictures in small gold frames sat on her desk: individual portraits of her father, her deceased mother, and a sixth-grade school photo of her brother Stevie. Twelve-year-old Stevie had been killed by a drunk driver while teaching his younger sister to ride a bicycle. I knew the tragedy haunted Susan and had been the major reason she'd pursued a career in medicine.

The only other personal photograph stood on the credenza behind her desk. I'd shot the picture with a timer so that Susan and I could pose together in front of Looking Glass Falls in

Pisgah National Forest. We both beamed in one of those rare instants when eyes are open and expressions are natural. Beside the pewter-framed tribute to our relationship sat a warty, porcelain bullfrog on a lily pad. Was I in danger of undoing the fairy tale?

"Natalie said you were hurt." Susan walked in and set her clipboard on the desk. "What happened?" She looked from me to Melissa as if the reporter was more likely to give the straight answer.

I bent down and picked up the ammo case. "We found Y'Grok's secret. He'd hidden this case in the waterwheel át the mill. Seeing the tattoos again helped me break his code."

"You found his body?"

I'd forgotten Susan knew nothing of Y'Grok's return. "Someone returned the body during the night, right back to the embalming table."

Now Susan showed genuine concern. "Your parents?"

"They're okay. I figure the thunderstorm covered the noise of the break-in."

"Have you told Y'Suom?"

If Susan had been in surgery since early morning, she hadn't heard. "Y'Suom was murdered last night at the party. I discovered his body about the time you left with Chandler." Chandler's name tasted sour in my mouth.

Susan's face paled. Again, she looked at Melissa for confirmation.

"Y'Suom's murder must be all over the radio and TV," Melissa said.

"I didn't get out of surgery till thirty minutes ago and had to rush here. Was he shot?"

"No," I said. "The killer knocked him unconscious with a brick and then strangled him. Used Y'Suom's own belt. Probably took only a few minutes. I found him in the atrium."

"Oh, good God." Susan sat on the edge of her desk. "Who would do such a thing?"

"We don't know." I raised the case higher. "But his death must involve this."

Her eyes moved from the case to my hand. "You're bleeding."

"Not that bad. Looks worse than it is. Melissa and I fell into the stream trying to get this before the current swept it away. I got a palm full of splinters for my trouble."

"I'll get my nurse to tend you. So, you found the money?"

"Some. But Kevin Malone says there should be much more. We need your help, Susan. Y'Grok smuggled the partial remains of a U.S. serviceman out of Vietnam. His name was Raven and his bones are in here."

Susan stared at the ammo case, speechless. In less than a minute, I'd dropped three bombshells: Y'Grok's body, Y'Suom's murder, and Raven's return. I'd have been speechless too.

I pressed on. "There has to be a reason Y'Grok wanted Kevin Malone to have them. Other channels could have accomplished the task of getting the remains back to the United States without all this secrecy."

"Why are you bringing them to me?"

"Because the killer doesn't know we've found them. And we don't want him to know until we have a better idea what's going on."

She shook her head. "I'm not a forensics expert."

"We know. But you work cheap and you can keep a secret." I wondered just how many secrets she was keeping.

"And Tommy Lee?"

"He knows and he agrees."

She pursed her lips, stood up from the desk, and stepped back from me. "What am I supposed to be looking for?"

"I have no idea."

"Ray Chandler had some forensic experience in med school."

My words came harsh and sudden. "No way that hotdog gets near this."

Susan flushed. "I thought you wanted answers."

Melissa interrupted in an effort to keep me from sabotaging the whole deal. "I'm sitting on this story, Susan. My job's at stake if someone else scoops me and I've withheld information from the paper. I'm willing to do that because I trust Barry. I hope you do too. If anyone else becomes involved, I'm yelling stop the presses."

Susan clenched her teeth. "I don't need a lecture about trust. Not from you."

This was going nicely. I decided the truth should be stretched to preserve the peace. "But Tommy Lee requested you. At least conduct the first unofficial exam. Then we can bring the sheriff in for any decision on who else should be involved."

Susan didn't have an argument with Tommy Lee. She sighed. "Okay. Take the case to 3B, first room on the right. I'll get through my appointments as quickly as I can, and I'll send in Loretta to look at your hand." She turned to Melissa. "Are you injured?"

"Just my pride."

"Didn't know you had any." With that barb hanging in the air, Susan left the office.

"So, she doesn't talk much when she's angry," Melissa said.

"Must be the weather."

At ten minutes after two, I was sitting on the edge of the examination table with my left hand coated with ointment and wrapped in gauze. Nurse Loretta had also applied fresh antiseptic and a bandage to my forehead stitches and given me a lecture on the importance of following the doctor's orders. She'd been well coached.

Melissa had bummed a legal pad from Natalie and sat in the one metal chair, jotting down the details from our morning adventure. Forty minutes had passed since the confrontation in Susan's office. I was worn out and talked out.

There was a knock at the door and Susan entered. "I've got about thirty minutes."

Melissa stood up. I hopped off the table and set the case on the damp spot left by my pants. Neither of us spoke. I flipped up the clamps and lifted out the sack. Then Melissa and I stepped clear to give Susan room.

Susan pulled a magnifying glass from her lab coat. "At least I thought I'd look the part of Sherlock Holmes."

Her smile eased the tension a little. She pulled latex gloves from a box on the wall and tugged the cuffs over her wrists.

"Is it all right if we stay?" Melissa asked.

"Fine by me." Susan held the magnifying glass over the dog tag. "At least we've got a blood group listed. A-positive. At some point, tests should be run to determine a DNA match, if there's a family to match the bones with."

"I was told he had a son," I said.

"That should be enough." Susan untangled the chain and removed it from the neck of the bag.

"What's no pref mean?" Melissa asked.

"No preference," I said. "Religion. But skeletons don't display religious affiliations so that won't help."

"No skeletons I've met," Susan agreed. "The TV cop shows would have you believe they can determine if he was Catholic and how many times he knelt at mass." She spread the bag open. "Even without a skull, maybe there's a mandible."

Melissa looked to me for help. "I flunked biology."

"Lower jaw. For dental records."

"Did you see one?" Susan asked.

"I only looked at a few pieces to determine if they were human."

Susan carefully began to extract fragments. "Certainly has taken a lot of punishment."

Melissa jotted on her legal pad. "Before he died?"

"No. If Y'Grok lugged this case around, the jostling and pounding would have knocked the bones against the metal walls with sufficient force to destroy the fragile calcified cartilage that holds a skeleton together. Ah, here's an ulna."

"The smaller bone in the forearm," I clarified for Melissa.

Susan grabbed her magnifying glass. "Looks like there was a break. Probably when he was a teenager."

I looked over her shoulder. "That's good. Gives us something to check against a medical record."

Susan set the ulna down and picked up a thoracic vertebrae. I knew because part of one of the ribs was still attached.

"Hmmm." Susan held the fragment closer to her eyes. "This is strange."

Melissa and I edged closer.

"What do you see?" I asked.

"A piece of tape's been stuck to this vertebrae."

"Thoracic, right?"

"Yes. Middle range. Probably level with the heart."

"What kind of tape?" Melissa asked.

"Shipping. Some type with filament reinforcement running through it. Would they have that in Vietnam?"

"They would now," I said. "Tesa International."

Susan and Melissa looked at me for an explanation.

"They have a headquarters in Charlotte. I was the first officer on the scene of a break-in there once. I spoke with a manager and got the company spiel. They're a big tape manufacturer with a global market. Vietnam is part of their Asian Pacific operations."

Susan peered through the magnifying glass. "Well, there's no Tesa logo, and though the tape's discolored with age, it certainly doesn't date back too far, otherwise the adhesive would have dried out."

"Why tape that particular bone?" Melissa asked.

"Maybe to keep the vertebrae intact. But there's something under the tape. Might be soil." Susan opened a drawer and found a small scalpel and a pair of tweezers. She laid the bone on the table. "I'll see if I can remove the tape without damaging the fragment."

Susan worked the blade under a corner of the tape, and then picked at the edge with the tweezers. Meticulously prying and plucking, she separated the tape so that only a thin layer of dirt adhered. She set down her surgical instruments and examined the bone through the magnifying lens. "That explains the tape."

"What?" Melissa and I asked in unison.

"There's a bullet fused in the bone. It's mangled, but in one piece."

"That fits," I said. "James Raven was killed in a firefight in the central highlands."

Susan grabbed the tweezers and pinched a rough extrusion of the metal. "That's a surprise." She dangled the slug above the bone. "No wonder he needed the tape."

"What do you mean?" Melissa asked.

"I mean this bullet has been dug out once already. Then somebody taped it back in place."

I turned for the door.

"Where are you going?" Susan asked.

"To call Tommy Lee. I think you just found the key to this whole mystery. Now all we have to do is figure out what that key unlocks."

Chapter Twenty

When I returned to examination room 3B, Susan was wrapping the bone and bullet in gauze. Melissa watched her from the corner. I got the sense neither had spoken while I was phoning Tommy Lee from Susan's office. Susan sealed the gauze with a single strip of surgical tape and placed our discovery in the ammo case on top of the bag of skeletal remains.

"Did you reach him?" Susan asked.

"Yes. He wants to see the bones and the bullet right away."

"Is he coming here?"

I could tell Susan wasn't thrilled at the prospect of patrol cars descending upon the clinic. "No. He asked me to bring them to the back entrance of the Sheriff's Department. He doesn't want anyone to know yet." I turned to Melissa. "I'll drop you at the funeral home for your car. I can't have you walking into Tommy Lee's office with me."

Melissa frowned. "You'll let me know what's happening?"

"Yes. You too, Susan. And this part's been off the record."

"Of course," Melissa agreed. "Thanks for including me." She slipped past me into the hall before Susan and I could say anything.

Susan handed me the case. "I hope this helps."

"It's got to. We're running out of options. Can I call you later?"

She shrugged. "That's up to you. If you can find the time."

Not exactly an enthusiastic invitation, but I resolved to make sure I'd be back in touch before the afternoon got away from me.

After seeing Melissa safely on her way to the newspaper, I hurried into the funeral home to check on the status of the next day's service. Uncle Wayne was in the viewing room, which we called the Slumber Room. I'd tried to get away from that title since everyone knew the guests of honor would never wake up, but old traditions die hard, meaning Uncle Wayne would have to die first.

He was bent over the casket, holding a brush in one hand and a can of hairspray in the other. The short bursts from the aerosol nozzle meant he was applying the finishing touches. I circled to the other side where I could admire the meticulous grooming. According to Montagnard custom, Wayne had dressed Y'Grok in regular clothes and rested his head on a rolled ceremonial blanket the Montagnards of his tribe had provided. Its delicate multicolored embroidery ran in narrow vertical stripes down the dark blue fabric. I didn't understand the tribal significance, but the artistry created an expression that was both somber and celebratory.

My uncle looked up from his handiwork. "What the devil happened to you?"

"The usual. I got in over my head."

"Don't let your mother see you. You got any clothes to change into?"

"No. I just came in to see if Y'Suom's body had arrived from the Asheville morgue. I've got an errand to run for Tommy Lee."

Wayne capped the hairspray and stepped back from the casket. "He looks pretty good. Too bad he can't tell us where he's been."

"Yeah. Too bad he can't tell us a lot of things."

Wayne gave me a critical glance. "I'd say you're in over your head all right. I've got Freddy coming at four. That's when the other body will be released."

"I'll be back by then."

"Don't worry, we'll be fine."

"Uncle Wayne, you and Freddy don't have to take up my slack."

He walked to a side table and tucked the brush and hairspray into our leather touch-up kit. Then he turned and fixed me with one of those stares that prefaced a pronouncement. Over the years, his hair had gone from brown to white and his face cracked into more creases than wadded linen, but the stare had never altered. "No slack. A question of priorities."

Pain shot through my left palm as my hands reflexively balled into fists. I didn't want to get into an argument over a dead body—literally over a dead body as Y'Grok lay between us—but I'd made more than my share of sacrifices. My father's Alzheimer's had brought me back to this town. Then I'd passed up the chance to sell out to a big chain so that Mom and Dad could remain in their own home, and I continued to tolerate my uncle's old-fashioned ways. My frustration boiled over. "This funeral home is my priority!"

"That's what I'm trying to tell you, Barry. Don't let it be."

Once again my uncle's logic defied penetration, and I couldn't respond to what I didn't understand. Y'Grok's corpse probably had a better idea what Wayne meant.

"You've had police training. Even I can see how Tommy Lee depends on you. His deputies just carry out orders, but you've got a good head on your shoulders and a nose for the truth."

The first twinge of guilt surged in my chest as I suspected I'd misjudged where my uncle was taking this conversation. "Thanks."

"Don't thank me. Ain't none of my genes in that recipe. But Freddy and I can handle things here. We can do that in our sleep. Your priority's to find this rampaging lunatic. You'll be doing the town more good, and from what I gather this poor fellow went through, you'll make sure his efforts weren't in vain."

I stepped to the casket and looked down at the Montagnard. "You'll never find someone with a greater sense of loyalty."

"I don't know about that."

I looked up and caught the glint of a tear in my uncle's eye.

He turned away, fiddling with the zipper on the makeup kit. "I've seen your loyalty, Barry. To your mom. Your dad." His voice cracked. "Even me. More than I deserve. By a long shot."

I didn't know what to say. The words, so heartfelt and genuine, coming from a man who spoke so few, caught me off guard. I realized how much I loved the old coot, even though he could be exasperating at times. "We're family, Uncle Wayne. That's what families do."

He cleared his throat, turned, and nodded. "Well, you best get out of here before your mom comes downstairs. She sees you all bandaged up, she might get the wrong impression."

I didn't know what the wrong impression could be. It was only April and I'd already met the yearly deductible on my health insurance. The simple truth was her son had a talent for getting beaten and battered. Bandages were just another wardrobe accessory. "Okay. Tell her I'm safe at the sheriff's office. And you call me if you need me."

"I will. But don't worry. If I wasn't here, I'd just be sitting on my back porch watching the leaves grow."

Tommy Lee escorted me quickly through the back halls of the department. Only the dispatcher saw us enter the sheriff's private office.

Tommy Lee shut the door and closed the blinds covering the interior window to the bullpen. Kevin Malone leaned against a filing cabinet, sipping a cup of coffee.

As I set the ammo case on Tommy Lee's desk, Kevin asked, "Did Susan give an opinion on how he was shot?"

"No. As soon as she found the bullet, she stopped her examination. She wasn't comfortable making forensic interpretations."

Kevin smiled. "I told Tommy Lee about the money."

"Okay." I guessed Kevin had decided to head off any revelations I might make.

"And he knows I'm on suspension from the Boston police force."

Tommy Lee returned to his desk. "With things escalating like they have, Kevin figured he'd better tell me in case his name got linked to the events. He doesn't want it to appear like he's part of the investigation."

Kevin set his cup on the corner of the desk. "But I'd like to see the bullet. What's the caliber?"

"I don't know. I didn't look that closely."

"You're not trained in M&M forensics? My God, Tommy Lee, I thought you said he was a professional."

Tommy Lee frowned. "I'm a professional, and I don't know what the hell you're talking about."

Kevin's shocked expression broke into a grin. "An inside joke. One of my fellow detectives got forced on a diet by his wife. He had a terrible sweet tooth and she caught him with a bag of M&Ms in his pocket. Billy's one hell of a detective but scared to death of his Mrs. So he told her carrying M&Ms was official police policy."

"To carry M&Ms?" Tommy Lee asked.

"Yeah. To determine the caliber of a murder weapon at a crime scene. He told Ann the plains matched a thirty caliber bullet hole, the peanuts a thirty-eight, and the almonds a forty-five."

"Fast thinker," I said. "She believe him?"

"Hell, no. That's why he asked the rest of us to back him up. We started carrying M&Ms in case we ran into her on the street or saw her at some social function. I was the designated peanut."

Tommy Lee opened the ammo case. "Well, let's see what your friend's sweet tooth says about this bullet." He lifted out the gauze-wrapped bone and laid it on the desk. Then he took a pair of scissors from his drawer and carefully cut the tape. Kevin's impish face turned grim as he watched the gauze unravel.

When only the final layer was left and we could see the dark surface of the bullet, Tommy Lee held the vertebrae over his open palm, removed the last strip of gauze and let gravity do the rest. "It's blunted like you'd expect, but not fragmented." He held the deformed lump between his thumb and forefinger. "Hmmm. I think we've got an almond."

"Don't kid about that." Kevin leaned in for a closer look. "A forty-five?" I asked.

"Judging from the size, that would be my bet." Tommy Lee handed the bullet to Kevin.

Kevin stared at the bullet like he'd discovered a tumor growing on his palm. "I don't believe this. Y'Grok figured out what happened. This is what he wanted to show me."

Tommy Lee nodded. The two men shared some understanding that I couldn't comprehend.

I stared at the bullet. "What's it mean?"

"Friendly fire," Tommy Lee replied.

"Friendly fire, my ass. More like murder." Kevin held out the bullet. "This came from an M1911." He shot me a glance. "You familiar with it?"

"Yes. Some of the older officers in Charlotte carried 1911s. Automatic forty-five."

"And I bet they were vets. They liked the stopping power. I hear soldiers in Iraq are dumping their nine millimeters and going back to them. Damned suicide bomber coming at you, you want to stop him cold."

I lifted the slug from Kevin's hand. "Wouldn't the Viet Cong feel the same way?"

"Probably," Kevin answered. "But they didn't have the choice. The Viet Cong and North Vietnamese regulars carried a TT33 pistol. Its 7.62 millimeter round equates to a thirty caliber. Same as their AK-47s. So, by all odds, you should be holding a bullet more like the thirty-aught-six you dug out of your cabin last night."

I handed the bullet to Tommy Lee. "What do you do now?"

"The hard part. I have to think."

I looked at Kevin. "We're in real trouble. But we ought to be able to get more information. A forensics lab might determine the angle of the trajectory and distance from the victim. That could rule out friendly fire."

Kevin shook his head. "Come on, even I can see from the position of the rib that this forty-five slug was taken in the front. We know enough already. Jimmy Raven's remains lead us back to Vietnam where something happened that Y'Grok knew was wrong. If you're willing to give me a pass based not on my word but Y'Grok's message to me, then we have to look at Stormy, Ryan, and Franklin."

"One of them killed Raven?" I asked. "Why?"

"Money's a possibility. Jimmy carried his share of the operation's funds. Or maybe some personal argument."

Tommy Lee shook his head. "Seems like General Weathers would have been too high up the command to have been on the ground."

"Stormy wasn't afraid to get his hands dirty. You'd be surprised where he showed up."

"We know Franklin Talbert was working with Operation Raven," I said. "What about Senator Millen?"

"Ryan was there a couple months," Kevin said. "First of all, it took time to arrange the escape route for our boys. We varied each one. And then he'd been injured. He's got that cocked eye because he couldn't get proper medical treatment."

Tommy Lee fidgeted with the bullet. "Millen crossed paths with James Raven?"

"Yes. Jimmy was reported killed while Ryan was still in the central highlands."

"And they all carried M1911s?" I asked.

"Everyone I knew. Maybe an M19 which was even heavier. A few of the special ops preferred 357 Magnums, but they were rarer."

I gave Kevin a hard stare. "What did you carry?"

"An M1911. So, I'm counting on Y'Grok's message to me as my defense. He obviously didn't think I was the killer. Now I prefer my thirty-eight revolver. Once you've had an automatic jam in a tight situation, you learn you'd rather shoot slower than not at all."

Tommy Lee finally laid the bullet beside the vertebrae. "Then we've got to look at who of the three had the opportunity to take Y'Grok's body and not try to reconstruct a murder from nearly forty years ago."

"Millen was the only one here," I said.

"Are we sure Franklin was in Australia?" Kevin asked.

Tommy Lee nodded. "Yes. Harvey Collins told me Franklin was on the list of people Y'Grok had asked to be notified. Franklin's donated money and spoken out against Montagnard persecution. Collins reached him at the Australian studio. He definitely got off that plane in Asheville yesterday. He's in the clear unless he snuck into Gainesboro on Monday, stole the body, and managed to get down to Charlotte for the final leg of his supposed flight from Los Angeles."

Kevin walked to the filing cabinet and drummed his fingers on the metal surface. "I don't like our options. I can't see a three-star general sneaking back from Iraq either. Randall'd have to be in on it too. He picked Stormy up at Fort Jackson."

"Which brings us back to Millen," Tommy Lee said. "And they all had an alibi last night at Barry's cabin. We're the witnesses. They couldn't have stolen the thirty-aught-six or fired it from the woods."

I could think of only one other option. "We're missing a possibility."

Kevin and Tommy Lee looked at me for an explanation.

"Two people are involved."

"Ryan and Stormy are working together?" Kevin asked.

"No. But what about Millen and Nickles. It's pretty obvious Nickles will say or do anything to protect the senator."

The silence told me they were considering the possibility.

I continued off the top of my head. "We don't have an accounting of Nickles' whereabouts, either for Monday night or yesterday. Right before I found Y'Suom's body, I saw Nickles washing his hands in the men's room."

"That doesn't tie him to the killing," Kevin said.

"No, but don't you think Nickles bears investigating? He must have a rental car of his own. Or maybe the big trunk of Millen's Grand Marquis transported Y'Grok's body."

Tommy Lee looked doubtful. "They kept a body in the trunk since Monday night?"

"I'm not speculating on details, and I know you can't go charging into a U.S. senator's hotel room with a search warrant unless you're damned sure of what you're going to find."

"You got that right," Kevin said.

"But that doesn't mean you can't set a trap."

Tommy Lee picked up the bone and bullet. "With this?"

"With the possibility of the case's discovery. No one knows what's been found except the three of us, Melissa, and Susan. You call Nickles and tell him the body's been returned, and you've figured out the key to the code. See what he does."

Tommy Lee frowned. "Why not just tell him the secret's at the mill and we're hightailing up there?"

"Because you haven't decoded the tattoos yet. Don't give yourself credit for being so smart."

"This boy's got you pegged," Kevin said.

Tommy Lee grinned. "I've gotten a lot of mileage out of being dumb. So it takes me the rest of the afternoon to break the code. Then I call Nickles and say we're going to the mill after the rain stops tomorrow. That'll be after the funeral and I'd like the senator to know in case he wants to delay his departure."

"Sounds good," Kevin agreed. "What about Stormy and Franklin?"

Tommy Lee turned to me. "What do you think?"

"Tell Nickles to pass the word to them, but stress the information's confidential. If he tells, then it's less likely he's our man. If he doesn't, then you'll have a tail ready to follow either him or Millen."

"Up to the mill?" Tommy Lee asked.

"Why not? The location lends credence as to why you're not going there till tomorrow. We can change the exact site of the ammo case if the waterwheel's been washed away." I thought a second. "Tell Nickles the circle means the gristmill stone inside, and you think 2000 is eight o'clock, with north being noon."

"I like it," Kevin said. "Damned close to the truth. That's the best kind of lie."

Tommy Lee stared at the blinds as if he could see into his bullpen. "What if Nickles does pass the word to Stormy and Franklin? I don't have enough manpower to tail everyone."

Tommy Lee raised a good point. "Then stake out the mill. That's where the chickens will come home to roost."

"We can help with the tail," Kevin said.

"Definitely not. I don't want either one of you near this operation. Kevin, you know yourself you're damaged goods right now. And, Barry, you're standing there in bandages, itching to get some other part of your body mangled. You've done enough already. Just make sure Y'Grok and Y'Suom have a funeral worthy of them."

Kevin shrugged. "You're the sheriff. I guess Barry and I could spend the time trying to find out more about Nickles."

And I knew exactly how to do that. "Let me call Melissa. She was checking out his background."

Tommy Lee swung the phone around on his desk. "Go ahead."

My call went right through.

"What's up?" Melissa asked.

"What have you got on Bruce Nickles?"

"Is he a suspect?"

"We're trying to rule people out."

"Yeah, right. I've got some info. Whatcha going to give me?"

Reporters. I rolled my eyes at Tommy Lee.

He shrugged. "Tell her what she wants."

I gave her a brief sketch of the plan.

"That's great. And this is going down tonight?"

"Maybe, but not with you or me anywhere around. You get involved and Tommy Lee will have both of us sitting in a cell."

"I get the message. Well, if Millen's dirty, then Nickles' job would be to keep his image squeaky clean. You ever hear of Charles Colson?"

"Charles Colson?" I repeated.

"One of Nixon's lackeys," Tommy Lee said.

"Tommy Lee says Nixon."

"Right," Melissa said. "Colson once said he'd walk over his grandmother to assure the president's re-election. Nickles has the reputation for that kind of loyalty. Been with Millen since the start of his political career. He's known for shouting matches with members of the press who reported stories he didn't like. You want access to Millen, the door goes through Nickles. And there's probably nothing the senator doesn't discuss with him."

Even a murder, I thought. "Thanks. That helps Tommy Lee know what he's dealing with."

"Tell Tommy Lee not to forget my number. I'll see what else I can find."

"Good plan. Keep on with Weathers and Talbert as well." I hung up, feeling better knowing Melissa would be chained to her computer with busy work.

Tommy Lee rewrapped the gauze around the bone and bullet. "I'm going to get this case up to the mill. We'll rig it under the floorboards by the grindstone like you suggested. I'd better replace the money too. Something goes wrong with every plan, but I doubt if Nickles or Millen would destroy the money if they get their hands on it. I'll record the serial numbers and then we'll have something to link them to the ammo case."

"What about the bullet?" Kevin asked.

"That's going under lock and key in my evidence room. I'm not taking a chance with it."

"Good. Then I guess that's it for now." Kevin extended his hand to me. "Smart plan. You should've stayed a cop."

I didn't say anything.

"I'd rather Barry stay alive," Tommy Lee said. "He seems to be allergic to investigations."

I started for the door. "I'll be at the funeral home for awhile, and then up at the cabin. Call me if something breaks."

I ducked out the back door of the department and ran through the rain to my jeep. I sat for a few minutes before starting the engine. Kevin had punched my button. I did want to be part of the investigation. Tommy Lee knew that, but he also knew I had my responsibilities. That didn't mean I couldn't do a little investigating on my own. I decided it was time to get to the bottom of the case of Susan Miller and Ray Chandler. Tonight, I hoped to interrogate my chief suspect, Susan, over dinner and wine.

Chapter Twenty-one

Uncle Wayne and Freddy arrived with Y'Suom's body shortly after four. After we'd moved the corpse from the hearse to the embalming table, Uncle Wayne handed me a manila envelope.

"What's this?" I asked.

"It came with the paperwork." Wayne turned his attention to the body. "The M.E. did a nice job. He didn't stick us with a lot of cosmetic reconstruction."

Sometimes an autopsy can leave the funeral home with a real challenge. The Asheville medical examiner was exceptional in his respect for the dead, but he'd never sent me a personal message before. He'd written my name on the envelope and added the script, "per Sheriff Wadkins—Laurel County." Inside I found a copy of the autopsy report.

The information parroted what Tommy Lee and Kevin had said last night. In summary, a blow from a blunt object consistent with the brick had rendered the subject unconscious, but hadn't inflicted sufficient trauma to cause death. The force of the garroting belt crushed the windpipe, making survival extremely unlikely even if the victim had received immediate medical attention.

"What's the manner of death?" Wayne asked.

"Cold-blooded murder. Given his neck injuries, you might need to dress him in a high collar."

"Freddy and I'll take care of Y'Suom. You've got other priorities."

This time I didn't argue. I also didn't confess that I'd been relieved of my unofficial investigative duties.

Once in the office, I called the clinic and asked Natalie to put me on hold until Susan had a chance to pick up. Ten minutes elapsed before she came on the line.

"You'll be glad to know I'm off the investigation."

"They find the murderer?" She sounded excited.

"No, but there's a plan in place. A trap actually. I don't want to talk about the details on the phone. How about dinner at the cabin?"

She hesitated.

"Not a late evening," I assured her. "I'm leaving the funeral home now. I could have steaks and wine on the table by six-thirty."

"But I've got early rounds in the morning."

"How long's it take to eat? You can leave by eight if you need to."

A briefer hesitation, and then she agreed. "All right. I'll see you at six-thirty."

I hung up and took a deep breath. For the first time since the attack in our operating room, I relaxed. I was back on familiar turf. Uncle Wayne and Freddy would have everything ready for the funeral, Tommy Lee had baited the trap, and I could surely handle a romantic dinner with Susan.

I turned the steaks over and slid them beneath the broiler. Four more minutes and then they could sit under foil, self-cooking to a perfect medium. I'd started the broccoli steaming, timed to finish with the steaks, and fed Democrat early so that he wouldn't be tortured by the aromas. He'd been relegated to the guest room with George, who munched on the lettuce trimmings.

I set the bowl of tossed salad and a small plate of crumbled bleu cheese on the dining table. Linen napkins, two place settings of china and silver I'd salvaged from my divorce, and crystal wine goblets elevated the meal to four-star status. I uncorked a bottle of Malbec, Susan's new choice in red, and laid a long-stemmed rose across the base of her glass. Even I was impressed.

At six-twenty-five, I flipped on the front porch light to offer a welcoming harbor in the storm. I remembered that last night I'd unwittingly signaled a sniper that his quarry approached. I hoped the weather discouraged any second attempts and that Tommy Lee would soon have the culprit in custody.

Since I'd had no phone call from Susan, I knew she'd be prompt. At six-thirty, I heard tires on the gravel. I lit the two candles on the table, poured wine in each goblet, and hit play on the CD. Linda Ronstadt's torch songs softly filled the cozy space of the open living and dining rooms. My single regret was the wood had been too wet to build a fire and complete the mood.

I heard the tires again. Susan must be maneuvering to get as close to the porch as possible. I could score a few early points for meeting her at the car with an umbrella. I grabbed one from the stand and opened the front door. There stood my worst nightmare.

Kevin Malone clutched a wet paper bag to his dripping Boston Red Sox jacket with one hand and held a six-pack of Killian Red in the other. His damp curly hair was matted to his scalp and trickles of water arced around his wide grin. Behind him, Susan jumped from her Subaru and dashed through the rain. She'd had to park beyond my jeep and the Taurus Kevin borrowed from Tommy Lee.

As Kevin turned to watch her, I shook my head and threw up my hands, showing Susan I had nothing to do with this.

"Hello, I'm Kevin Malone." He bowed like a Japanese diplomat. "Sorry, it's against my religion to set down alcohol."

Susan brushed her wet hair from her face. "Barry's told me about you. I'm Susan Miller."

"You found the bullet." Kevin looked at me. "I hope I'm not interrupting anything."

"Susan and I are having dinner." I left it there, figuring Kevin was savvy enough to take the hint.

"But come in," Susan offered. "I'm sure we've got enough."

"Really, I don't mean to intrude."

Behind Kevin's shoulder, Susan glared at me and nodded to the door. Just my luck to have a girlfriend with manners.

"Yeah. We'll have enough. Looks like you brought supplies." I stepped back to let them enter.

"Guys' rations," Kevin said. "Pizza, beer, and a movie."

"We can use Barry's TV trays," Susan said as she followed the man who'd ruined my evening.

They both stopped. Linda Ronstadt's sultry voice rose above the rain. In the ell off the living room, the dining table sparkled with candlelight refracting through wine prisms. Shadows flickered across the blood-red rose and fine china. I envisioned the romantic scene mutilated by flimsy trays on rickety metal stands, and instead of gazing into Susan's lush brown eyes, I'd be watching Jean-Claude Van Damme kick somebody's face in.

"My God, pretty special for a Thursday night. I'm definitely intruding."

"Just my typical dinner for Susan." One silver lining was Kevin could be a witness to my efforts and say nice things about me.

Susan walked over to the table and picked up the rose. She didn't say anything.

"Would you get the TV trays, dear?" I was careful to keep the sarcasm out of my voice. "I'll fix the plates. Kevin, what's the movie?"

"*Operation Falcon*. Franklin Talbert's first film. A VHS tape. The store didn't have it on DVD. Not exactly a big renter."

My derailed evening suddenly jumped onto an unexpected and interesting track. "Why the urge to see Talbert's movie now?"

"Because I've never seen it before."

Still holding the rose, Susan turned to Kevin. "You and Talbert served together in Vietnam and you haven't seen all his movies?"

"I haven't seen any of his movies. I didn't like the idea of Franklin exploiting what we went through. I refused to put a dime in his pocket."

"What changed your mind?" I asked.

"A bag of bones named Raven. If Franklin modeled his movie *Operation Falcon* after Operation Raven and if Franklin was the target of last night's shooting, then maybe there's a clue in the film."

"But this came out nearly twenty-five years ago," I said. "Why kill him now?"

Kevin smiled. "Good question. But Y'Grok Eban only died last week and I think his death changed everything for somebody."

I took the china plates back to the kitchen, added a third, and then cut the steaks into strips. The portions were small, but adequate. We could always cook Kevin's pizza for a second course.

My television sat on a stand in the corner near the edge of the stone hearth. The lower shelf held the combination VCR/DVD player. Susan rolled the unit in front of the fireplace where we could all see. I placed my subdivided romantic meal onto the three TV trays and we snuggled together on the sofa with Susan in the middle. At least she kept the rose by her plate as a token of what might have been.

The movie opened with a pilot ejecting from a crippled jet-fighter tumbling out of control. As his parachute drifted down, title credits appeared that included "starring Franklin Talbert." The last credit, the film's director, gave the unpronounceable name of an Asian. The music reeked of a cheap Seventies score that could have been under a variety of action movies—from spaghetti westerns to knock-off Bond flicks.

"Well, at least the steak is good," Kevin said. "Don't know if I can swallow this Kung Fu crap."

The pilot hit the ground hard, rolling down a slope and becoming entangled in the parachute. Gunfire drew closer. The pilot freed himself from the lines and ripped off his helmet. A close-up of Franklin Talbert filled the screen. His rugged face, absent the wrinkles twenty-five years can carve, grimaced. The camera cut to a high angle showing North Vietnamese regulars climbing the hill behind him.

Kevin set down his beer. "Damn. The terrain sure looks real."

Despite the cheesy music and over-the-top acting, the story proved intriguing. Talbert played Jack Falcon, and that first miraculous escape from the hostile forces—he must have fired an impossible thirty rounds from his sidearm—ended with his rescue of a Montagnard boy being held captive by the enemy soldiers. The teenager led Falcon to his village where the boy's grateful father welcomed the downed pilot. The son would have been tortured to reveal names in the Montagnard resistance.

Of course, the boy had an older, beautiful sister who fell in love with Falcon. The romantic subplot was minor compared to the shoot-em-up sequences. The main story line concerned establishing an organized resistance that performed the rescue and smuggling functions of the real Operation Raven. One of the Americans who joined Falcon was named Kevin O'Reily.

"I'll be damned," Kevin said. "He put me in the movie. Ten to one he makes me an asshole."

The odds weren't high enough. By the end of the film, Kevin O'Reily had betrayed the network, skimmed money from the funds, tried to frame Falcon, and shot his Montagnard girlfriend. The climax came in a mano-a-mano confrontation amidst a firefight with the North Vietnamese along the Ho Chi Minh Trail. Franklin Talbert, aka Jack Falcon, triumphed and Kevin Malone, aka O'Reily, got his just and deadly desserts.

A sweeping panoramic aerial shot and the swell of orchestral music cued the final credits. Kevin got up from the sofa and crouched down closer to the screen.

I handed Kevin the remote. "You can slow or freeze them."

Something caught Kevin's eye. He paused the tape and the picture jittered on a single frame. Squinting, he read aloud, "The producers would like to thank the Office of Cultural Affairs, the Socialist Republic of Vietnam for their assistance in filming on location in the Central Highlands." He looked back at Susan and me. "This movie came out years before we'd re-established diplomatic relations."

"That's probably why the film was produced by a Hong Kong production company," I said.

"But the story's pro-American."

"I'm sure the money spent by the crew more than made up for any misguided political slant."

"How much of the movie was true?" Susan asked.

"None of it." Kevin clicked off the TV.

I couldn't let go of the final scene. "Except Falcon killed a traitor, and we've got evidence James Raven died from an American bullet."

"Jimmy Raven was no traitor," Kevin said. "Otherwise Y'Grok would have left his remains in Vietnam."

I knew Kevin was right. My neck tingled as the other possibility suddenly came to light. "What if we're looking at this backwards? The story's true except the bad guy won."

Kevin stood up. His eyes burned. "Franklin Talbert?"

"Who was alive to contradict his story? You said most of the Montagnards in Operation Raven had been wiped out by the mid-eighties. Talbert pays some money, sells out a few names, and his production crew's on location with the government's blessing. He probably expected Y'Grok to be eradicated years ago."

"But why'd he make the Montagnards his celebrity cause?" Susan asked. "Why come to the funeral?"

I shrugged. "Guilt?"

"No," Kevin said. "The bastard used the Yards as cover. And he came to the funeral because Y'Grok gave the Lutheran social worker his name. He was on a short list with Stormy and Ryan. His ego would want the world to know he stood shoulder to shoulder with them."

The picture crystallized. I slapped my hand on my TV tray so hard the legs buckled. The goblet and china plate shattered on the floor. "God damn it. We missed the whole point." I stood up, crunching over the broken fragments as I walked to the fireplace. "We thought stealing Y'Grok's body was about the tattoos."

Susan looked at me like I'd lost my mind. "Wasn't it?"

"No. I'd been right but as a joke. I said Archie and the mayor might have stolen the body to get all the celebrities in town at the same time. The body was stolen to get Franklin Talbert in town."

"He was coming anyway," Susan said.

"Not at the same time General Weathers would be here. We put the finger on Bruce Nickles thinking he was protecting Senator Millen for killing James Raven and that they were afraid of what Y'Grok could prove. Our suspicions fell on them because they were here on Monday. Weathers was still on his way from Iraq. But if the motive were revenge. If Weathers had learned about Talbert's betrayal—"

"From Y'Suom." Kevin shook his head. "Y'Grok ran twin operations. He trusted me to find his hard evidence, but he also told his son who he suspected."

"And Millen told us during that first interview that Y'Suom and Captain Randall were together Monday." I ran the time-frame in my head. "Randall could have gotten word to Weathers that night and received his instructions to do whatever he had to do to delay the funeral."

Susan held up her hands. "You guys are moving awfully fast. I'm neither a policeman nor a lawyer, but the evidence all sounds circumstantial. Why are you suddenly ruling out Nickles?"

"We're not," I said. "But both motives fly. One covers up a murder, the other avenges the same murder."

"Yeah, and turns a three-star general into a vigilante." Susan frowned. "You're jumping to conclusions, Barry."

"Am I? Seems to me I've turned a blind eye to too many things lately." That dig came from some place I should have left bottled up.

Even Kevin heard the accusatory tone and looked away. Susan colored and said nothing.

I headed for the kitchen phone. "Maybe I can get some hard evidence."

"Are you calling Tommy Lee?" Kevin asked.

"No. Fort Jackson."

I got the main number from information, and then went through several transfers. Each time I gave my name and the explanation I was calling from Clayton and Clayton Funeral Directors. On the third hold, I heard Susan tell Kevin that she had early rounds and to tell me goodbye. Two nights in a row that message had been delivered by a third party. Before I could call after her, I heard "Morgue, Lieutenant Crawford speaking."

"This is Barry Clayton with Clayton and Clayton Funeral Directors in Gainesboro, North Carolina. We're handling some arrangements at the request of General Weathers."

"Is there something wrong?" Apprehension laced his question. "We didn't do anything other than store the body."

His candid revelation stopped me. I'd been thinking Captain Randall might have picked up a body bag. I took a breath and tried to sound casual. "No. I just wanted to thank you."

"Good. You scared me for a second. Glad to help. My dad has a small funeral home in Beaver Falls, Pennsylvania. I know how it is when you get that unexpected surge in business."

"Do you need any paperwork from me?"

"No, sir. Captain Randall explained the situation. No sense upsetting the family just because you ran out of room. What they don't know can't hurt them."

I thanked Crawford again and promised to give his regards to the general.

Kevin read the shocked expression on my face. "What'd you find out?"

"Weathers had Randall store the body in the morgue at Fort Jackson. The lieutenant in charge thought we'd run out of room and was only too happy to accommodate his superiors."

Kevin ran his fingers through his curly hair. "What a bitch of a mess. Stormy Weathers couldn't prove Talbert's guilt so he arranged to take him out the old fashioned way."

"And Y'Suom must have said something to Talbert last night. Maybe Talbert thought Y'Suom fired the shot at him. I can't see any reason Weathers would want Y'Suom killed."

"Neither can I, but if Stormy knows Talbert killed Y'Suom, he's got to be so pissed he might order an air strike on that condo. Can't say as I blame him."

"We've got to get to Tommy Lee. This is far more than circumstantial evidence." I glanced at Susan's TV tray. The rose lay with the stem snapped in half. I'd been right about Weathers' guilt, but I wished I could take back my sharp words.

"What the hell's Tommy Lee going to do? Arrest a three-star general?" Kevin walked to the front window and stared into the dark. "And if Franklin did what we think he did, why save his ass?"

I didn't answer. Nothing I could say would make a difference. The rain beat against the window. While Tommy Lee kept his eye on Nickles and Millen, Weathers and Randall were on their way to settle an old score. And the projector cranked the final reel for action hero Franklin Talbert.

Chapter Twenty-two

I reached for the phone. "I'll try Tommy Lee's cell first, but reception is so spotty in the mountains I might have to be patched through the department's radio."

Kevin followed me to the kitchen. "I hope not. You'd have to speak in code. Too many people monitor police frequencies."

Fortunately, the Grove Park Inn made sure its guests wouldn't be cut off from the pressures of the world they tried to escape. Cell phone coverage blanketed the resort including Tommy Lee's stake-out car in the parking lot. He sounded like he was in the next room with Democrat and George.

"It's Weathers and Randall." I shouted the accusation without saying hello.

"What?"

"I have proof. A Lieutenant Crawford in the morgue at Fort Jackson stored Y'Grok's body for Weathers. Randall delivered the body and then picked it back up last night."

"Shit."

"They aren't going to the mill. Their target's Franklin Talbert. We think he killed James Raven. Y'Grok told Y'Suom and he told Randall. Kevin was insurance that the proof would be found."

"Shit. Shit. Shit." Tommy Lee sounded like a broken rap record.

"Shift your surveillance to Weathers and Randall."

"No good. Randall left ten minutes ago. Reece tailed him for a few miles, and then radioed me that he lost him in the rain. I alerted Wakefield up at the mill, but now you tell me Randall's not going to the mill. I've got the wrong suspect and the wrong damn place staked out."

"Are you sure Weathers isn't with him?"

"Yes. I watched Randall walk out of the Grove Park and get in the SUV alone. He didn't stop the vehicle at any other entrance before leaving."

Kevin stepped closer to me, sensing things were falling apart.

"We've got to get word to Talbert," I said.

"He'll bolt."

Kevin jumped in. "For God's sake, what's wrong?"

"Randall's given them the slip. He's probably on his way to Talbert's condo right now."

"Can we beat him?"

"Yes." I knew there were few options left. "Tommy Lee, Kevin and I can get to Talbert first unless you've got somebody closer."

"Shit." Tommy Lee sounded like he really meant the word this time. "No, I don't."

I didn't press him for a decision.

"Okay. You and Kevin go armed, but see if you can get Talbert in the car and away from there without pulling a gun. He doesn't need to know he's a suspect, just that we think he was the target last night and we want to keep him safe. Bring him back to your cabin."

"What are you going to do?"

"Confront General Weathers. I'll have a man with me. Maybe I'll get Millen and Nickles there as well. The more witnesses the better and the less likely there'll be a scene." He paused, quickly making his plan. "Who was the guy at Fort Jackson?"

"Lieutenant Crawford."

"I'll phone Crawford from Weathers' room and verify his story in front of everyone. When the general sees the score, maybe he'll call off Randall. You'd better get going, and don't do anything foolish. Call me when you've got Talbert." He lowered his voice. "And watch Kevin. He'd probably like to kill Talbert with his bare hands."

We'd put about ten miles behind us when the rain slackened. I pushed the jeep faster, knowing my lead on Captain Randall would evaporate if he exceeded the speed limit along his stretch of the interstate. I took some comfort knowing my knowledge of the shortest route would buy us even more time. I estimated a margin of fifteen minutes.

Kevin repeated the plan we'd discussed since leaving the cabin. His nerves must have been kicking in, and talking about the scheme made its success seem all the more possible.

"I'm telling you, Franklin won't trust me so you're going to have to convince him."

"I know. We've been over that." I didn't like talking the plan to death because then I'd deliver my lines like the worst actor in one of Talbert's movies. "I'll emphasize the request came from Tommy Lee and the cabin offers better protection."

"Don't be surprised if I disagree."

"What?"

"Psychology."

I wanted to take my eyes off the road to see if he was kidding. "Are we playing good cop, bad cop?"

"No. Good undertaker, bad Vietnam vet. Hell, I've got to say something. Yes, you've got to convince him, but if I'm too quiet, he'll smell a rat for sure. I'll say the stuff we don't want him to do."

His logic carried a ring of truth. Score one for the Boston detective of the year. Then I remembered he'd also accidentally shot his partner. "All right. But we can't get into a debate. We need to get out of there."

"Understand me, Barry. I only have one goal for this mission."

"Yeah, protect a man we can't stomach." I reached in my jacket pocket and felt the cool steel of my unholstered thirty-eight.

Kevin smiled. "It'll be hard enough to nail the bastard without letting him wrap himself in the cloak of victim."

When I was a police officer, I'd testified enough in court to see slick attorneys weave a story that buried the truth under a cloud of maybes. "First let's get Talbert and keep Randall and Weathers from becoming killers. We'll talk about the rest with Tommy Lee."

"Fair enough. Are we getting close?"

I turned the jeep onto the last leg. Another mile on Cletus Owens road and we'd be at Crystal Cascades. "Just up ahead. Damn. I should've called the guardhouse. We could block Randall at the entrance."

"We can warn the guard not to let anybody through. I'm banking on Franklin being too scared to argue. He'll want to leave if he's in danger." Kevin laughed. "Maybe he'd feel more secure at the jail than the cabin."

Spotlights illuminated bronze letters embedded in a rock wall. The three-dimensional words *Crystal Cascades* shimmered behind an artificial waterfall spilling over the stones. The sign and landscaping cost more than most mountaineers' houses.

Warmer air had moved into the valley, and as the rain diminished, mist rose from the soaked earth. The guardhouse appeared suspended over a wispy blanket of white. I pulled alongside, careful to steer wide of any hidden curb.

Edith Delaney slid back her glass window. "Mr. Clayton, what brings you out on a night like this?"

"We're here to pick up Franklin Talbert."

She flipped through a few pages on her clipboard. "I don't see your name. Is he expecting you?"

"I was on the list. You checked me through yesterday."

"That was yesterday's list."

"They just put me down for one day?" I turned to Kevin. "Mayor Whitlock screwed up and now Edith will get the blame."

"That's not fair," Kevin said.

"What do you mean?" Edith's forehead wrinkled, pulling her cap closer to her eyes.

"I'll have to call Mr. Talbert and tell him you won't let us through. You and I know the screw-up is the mayor's fault, but do you think he's going to admit that?"

"No," Edith said. "He'll cover his own fat ass."

"Couldn't have said it better myself. No sense a big movie star like Franklin Talbert getting the wrong impression of you."

"Well, you did pick him up last night." Edith made her decision and the crossing bar rose out of the ground fog.

"Thanks." I inched the jeep forward and then stopped. "Oh, Edith, you can do Mr. Talbert a big favor."

"Really?"

"There's a fan who's been bothering him, not giving the poor man a moment's peace. Showing up everywhere."

"I know the type." She leaned out the guardhouse window, eager to please.

"There's a chance he might come here, try to see Mr. Talbert."

"He won't get past me."

"I'm sure he wouldn't, but just tell him Mr. Talbert's not here, even if we haven't left yet."

"No problem. What's he look like?"

"About my age. Black hair. Drives a dark SUV."

Kevin spoke up. "Don't forget he likes to make believe he's a soldier."

Edith's mouth dropped open. "I think he was here this morning."

"You saw him?" I asked.

"Bert Metcalf had first shift. He told me a guy in a black SUV tried to get in to see Franklin Talbert. He didn't say nothing about him being a soldier."

Randall probably would have been dressed in non-descript clothing—dark like my attacker's in the funeral home. "What else did Bert say?"

"That he told the man Talbert wasn't in his condo. The mayor had already been by and found him gone."

So Talbert had been smart to stay at my cabin. My stomach tightened. Randall had been here before. He wouldn't have to find his way.

"Thanks, Edith. Remember, Talbert's not here. That's all you need to say. This man might be mentally unstable so don't push him. If he threatens you, let him through. Then call the condo and the police." I didn't want an overzealous security guard on my conscience.

Edith blinked. "You mean he's crazy?"

"No, I mean he's determined. But, if he thinks Talbert's gone, he should leave."

I drove on.

"You played that about as well as you could," Kevin said.

"It didn't buy us much. Randall won't care that Talbert's out. He'd rather lay in wait, and then pick him off when he comes back." I noticed a grin on Kevin's face.

"You'd have made a good detective." Then he turned toward the side window. "I just hope you're a good driver."

The narrow road existed only in the beam of the headlights. We traveled up a tunnel of darkness, but this tunnel twisted and turned like a writhing copperhead. The developers of Crystal Cascades should have spent more on reflector-studded guardrails than fake waterfalls and polished bronze letters. I didn't want to be the driver to literally cascade down the mountainside.

"Should we check in with Tommy Lee?" Kevin asked.

"We can't. We're in a dead zone. If we have to call, we'll use the phone in the condo."

Although I'd picked up Talbert only yesterday, I might as well have been on a different planet. Nothing looked familiar. Mailboxes materialized at the edge of the road and then vanished. Kevin started calling out addresses.

"Look for a black mailbox on a wrought-iron post."

"Great. Why not a white mailbox in a snowstorm?"

From the number of switchbacks the jeep had negotiated, I figured we were getting near. I cut our speed to a crawl.

"There it is." Kevin leaned close to the dashboard. "Man, I can't see a driveway."

"It's there. We park by the garage on the lower level." I eased the jeep down the slope. For an instant, the headlights shot out into space.

Kevin gripped the armrest. "Jesus."

"You must be tons of fun in a high-speed car chase."

"At least then I can see the god-damned road."

Somewhere, a motion detector tripped and floodlights pierced the darkness. The empty parking apron outside the garage indicated we'd find Talbert alone. Small lanterns mounted about six inches above the ground marked the brick walk to the front door. A blue glow flickered through the high glass windows, probably from a television. The rain had withered to beads of mist hanging in the air.

Kevin opened his door. "If he's watching one of his old movies, he won't want to leave."

I stepped out and waited for Kevin to walk around the front of the jeep. His right hand patted the small of his back where, underneath the Boston Red Sox jacket, he carried his holstered version of the Louisville Slugger. Our eyes locked. Nothing needed to be said. Franklin Talbert had slain a comrade-in-arms and the truth of that crime cried out through the unwavering loyalty of an old Montagnard and the strangled body of his son.

I paused before ringing the bell. Kevin moved to the right and I realized he'd taken the position to avoid catching me in a crossfire. I eased to the left of the door. When it opened, a scene would begin and I had no clue as to how it would end.

My finger hovered over the glowing button, but before I could press it, footsteps sounded on the other side. Talbert snapped the door open.

"Has something happened?" He looked from me to Kevin. He wore jeans and an open-collar, blue-checked shirt with the sleeves rolled up to the elbows. His casual attire clashed with the tension in his face.

"No," I said. "Not yet. But Sheriff Wadkins didn't like the idea of you being alone up here. He wants you to spend the night at my cabin."

Talbert frowned, and then stepped back. "Come in. No sense standing outside." He led us into the great room where the TV was now off. "Have a seat." He pointed to the leather sofa. "I'm sure the sheriff is being overly cautious. I'll be all right. I've asked the guard to call if anyone comes."

"Did the guard call you about us?" Kevin asked.

Talbert froze. His tongue flicked over his lower lip. "No. I saw your Jeep pulling in."

Kevin shrugged. "There you go. If we can get by the guard, who's to say our mystery sniper can't?"

"The sniper won't look for you at the cabin. And we won't be dealing with windows two stories high." I swept my arm across the front of the condo. "Even with the drapes drawn, you make a target every time you cross in front of a light."

Talbert started toward the bedroom, but stopped. His eyes narrowed as if he saw something about me he didn't like. "I don't want to put you out two nights in a row."

"No problem. I'll drop Kevin in town on the way. You can bring your suitcase. I'll get you to the funeral tomorrow and you won't have to deal with the mayor." That was an offer I thought he couldn't refuse.

Talbert didn't budge. Something had spooked him.

"Or Barry and I can camp here if you're too much of a pansy to give up your luxuries." Kevin drenched the pitch in sarcasm, confident his Psych 101 ploy would do the trick.

"All right," Talbert said. "Let me call the guard and say you're here. And she'd god-damned better not let anyone else through."

He turned for the back bedroom.

"Stop." Kevin shouted the words as he snatched the pistol from his back. "You're going with us and you're going now."

Talbert pivoted and took a step closer to me. "What's going on?" He held out his empty hands. "Are you taking me hostage?"

"We're taking you where we can protect you," I said.

"At gunpoint? How do I know I won't be shot by the sniper as soon as we walk out that door? No. I'm going nowhere with you. You'll have to shoot me yourself, Kevin. Would you do that to an old combat buddy?"

The phrase "throwing gasoline on a fire" doesn't begin to describe the incendiary explosion created by Talbert's taunt. Kevin's face blazed red. He cocked the pistol, rotating a loaded chamber under the hammer. His finger wrapped around the trigger.

"I could put a bullet in you as easy as you put one in Jimmy Raven. Easier, because I'd be killing vermin, not murdering someone who trusted me."

A tremor ran through Talbert. The long-buried secret erupted in an uncontrollable shudder, rushing to the surface with damning conviction. "You're crazy. Jimmy died in an ambush. I saw him go down."

For an actor, Franklin Talbert delivered his lines right out of a bad high school play. The tremor returned and his fingers twitched by his side.

"Really?" Kevin inched closer, the gun pointed at Talbert's chest. "That's interesting. Then how do you explain the forty-five slug we found in Jimmy's backbone?"

If Talbert was acting now, he'd gone from high school to Oscar nomination. His breath came in short, guttural wheezes. He looked to me. "I don't know what he's talking about. Jimmy Raven died in Vietnam."

"I'm talking about loyalty," Kevin said. "Y'Grok Eban brought Jimmy Raven home. That's what his message to me was about. Bringing a comrade's remains home. And bringing me the proof that Jimmy had been murdered."

"I didn't kill Jimmy. Why would I?"

"You cocky prick. Watch your own movie. Skimming the Raven funds. Selling out the network. Along with Jimmy's bones is an envelope containing ten thousand dollars. Y'Grok signed the envelope like a receipt. You were his pay drop, and there was a hell of a lot more than ten thousand."

"I don't know what happened to the money." Talbert's voice husked in a dry whisper.

"You can tell that to General Weathers," Kevin said. "If he doesn't kill you first. Who do you think's behind all this?"

"Stormy?" Talbert looked at me for an answer.

"He had his aide Randall steal Y'Grok's body to delay the funeral. That gave Weathers an excuse to stay in town till you arrived. Then he planned on having Randall kill you, but Randall missed at the cabin."

"You strangled the wrong man," Kevin said. "Y'Suom didn't shoot at you. And a little while ago, Randall slipped the sheriff's tail in Asheville. He's probably on his way here."

"You've got to do something," Talbert pleaded.

"I don't want to do anything. I'm on Stormy's side. But the truth is you're not worth either Randall or Stormy going to jail."

"Okay. Let me —"

The front door crashed open. Like a cat, Captain J.R. Randall landed on his feet, a pistol in one hand, a military flashlight in the other. Kevin whipped his gun around, but held his fire.

I stood paralyzed. Then I sensed Talbert lunging for me. Before I could move, he hooked his left arm around my neck and dug his right hand into my jacket pocket. Too late, I understood he had seen the bulge of my pistol.

He jammed the cold barrel in my ear and hid behind me. "Drop your guns or I'll shoot him. I swear to God I will."

Chapter Twenty-three

Three guns in the room. Two were pointed at me and the third kissed my eardrum.

Kevin lowered his revolver but kept the hammer cocked. "Let him go, Franklin. You can't shoot both of us."

"No, but Clayton and I can walk out that door and nobody gets shot."

Kevin cut his eyes to Randall. "It's over, Captain. Sheriff Wadkins knows about the morgue at Fort Jackson and he's confronted Stormy. You can do the general a big favor by abandoning his orders before someone gets hurt."

Randall's rock-steady hand kept his gun level with my chest. The mouth of the barrel looked like a black hole, sucking the life out of the room.

"What orders?" Randall spoke the words without moving his lips.

"You don't need to fall on your sword," Kevin said. "Barry talked to Lieutenant Crawford. We know he held Y'Grok's body for Stormy."

"General Weathers has nothing to do with this. This is between me and Talbert."

Talbert's hairy forearm dug into my Adam's apple. His breath blew hot on my neck. "You and me? What have we got to do with each other? I don't even know who you are."

Randall nodded. "Then maybe it's fate I missed you yesterday. What's the pleasure in sending you to hell without you knowing why?"

Talbert shouted at Kevin. "Who is this guy? You said he was working for Stormy."

"I'm Captain J.R. Randall. J.R. stands for James Raven. You murdered my father."

Talbert's body stiffened. His weight bore down on me. I was as much a support as a shield.

Kevin looked at Randall in amazement. "You're Jimmy's son?"

"My mother remarried. The jerk gave us his last name and then took off."

Talbert angled me toward Randall. I could feel his sweat dripping on my neck.

"I didn't kill your father. You've got to believe me."

"I believe in actions, not words. Y'Grok wouldn't have spent his dying days coming here if his story weren't true. He told his son what he suspected and Y'Suom told me a year ago when General Weathers put us in contact with each other. He wanted me to meet the son of one of my father's most trusted allies."

"So Stormy is involved," Talbert said. "Can't you see he's trying to frame me?"

Randall's tight mouth curved into a cold grin. "General Weathers knows nothing about this. I handled the arrangements to smuggle Y'Grok out of Vietnam. Y'Grok knew he was dying and I knew his funeral would be the one chance I'd have to avenge my father's murder. But then you were late so I had to take matters into my own hands."

Kevin looked doubtful. "Why didn't Stormy tell us you were Jimmy's son?"

"When I picked General Weathers up at Fort Jackson, I said I wanted to surprise my father's friends after the service. He believed me. When I talked to Y'Suom Monday night, he told me Y'Grok had brought proof you killed my father."

"Y'Suom let you steal his father's body?" Panic rose in Talbert's voice as the magnitude of Randall's obsession dawned on him.

"No. That was my idea. Y'Suom thought the proof would be enough for a trial, but he didn't know where or what it was. My plan depended upon us crossing paths. I didn't tell Y'Suom what I did, but I'm sure he knew. I owe him because he kept quiet. Now I'll settle two scores for the price of one."

Randall's zeal terrified me as much as the gun pressed to my head. The military phrase "collateral damage" popped into my mind. Had security guard Edith Delaney been the first casualty? "Listen." My voice croaked and Talbert loosened his grip slightly, hoping I would talk sense to Randall. "I didn't know your father, but I can't believe he would condone murder. I know Y'Grok wouldn't. He trusted Kevin with the evidence because he wanted Talbert to be tried, not assassinated."

Kevin raised his revolver, only now he aimed at Randall. "That's right. Otherwise, why give the proof to me? Y'Grok wanted justice, not revenge." Kevin's voice hardened. "And I sure as hell won't let you sacrifice Barry."

"Then you'll have to kill me because Talbert's not weaseling out."

Kevin softened his tone. "We have the evidence. I've seen it. And we'll nail Talbert for Y'Suom as well."

Randall's lips curled in a sneer. "The LAPD had O.J. Simpson nailed. A celebrity with slick lawyers trumps truth every time."

Kevin edged closer to Randall. He held his gun in both hands. "Stand down or I'll take you down. Is that the way you want this to end? I suspect Stormy's been as much a father to you as anybody. Do you want to face him with Barry's blood on your hands? How does killing an innocent man honor your father and everything I know he stood for?"

Duty and honor. Kevin had pitted two virtues against each other. If Randall felt he had a duty to avenge his father's death, he must also feel compelled to honor his legacy. Randall's jaw muscles twitched. Then he slowly lowered his pistol.

Talbert exhaled. He pressed against me. I refused to move.

Kevin stepped back where he could see Randall from the corner of his eye and swung his gun toward Talbert and me. "Let him loose, Franklin."

"We're going out that door," Talbert shouted. "I'll let Clayton go as soon as I get in his jeep. In here, I've got nothing to lose because I don't trust either one of you."

Kevin looked at me and then at Randall. He stepped between us, using his own body as a shield to keep Randall from having second thoughts. "All right. Get out of here. But if you don't let Barry go unharmed, I'll hunt you down myself."

Again, Talbert pushed me. I walked toward the front door, letting him swing me around to face Kevin. When we reached the threshold, Talbert stopped. "Stay inside. Clayton will be back in a minute."

Kevin's face was as hard as a granite bluff.

Behind him, Randall smiled. "Be seeing you."

Talbert stepped outside and tugged me after him. The pistol sight ripped my ear as he yanked the gun away from my head. "To the jeep, and fast." He shoved me along the walk. Halfway down, our motion triggered the spotlights.

I fumbled through my jacket pocket for the keys. At the driver's door, I turned and held the keys up to Talbert's face.

He laughed. "Get in. You're driving."

"That wasn't the deal."

"The deal's changed. You know the back roads out of these hills. You'll get me to Atlanta."

Hot blood trickled from my ear to my jaw. "For what? To catch a flight in the middle of the night?"

He jammed the gun in my chest. "Get in the damn jeep!"

As I opened the door, Talbert circled around the front, keeping the pistol trained on me. He climbed in the passenger seat. "Start the engine and turn around."

I looked up at the condo and saw Kevin standing in the doorway. "They'll come after us."

"Let them. You're going to lose them." He chuckled. "The first thing you learn in military operations is always have an escape route. This afternoon I reserved a plane in a small private airport outside Atlanta to be readied at a moment's notice. I've shot movies all over the world and I learned to fly years ago. I'll be out of the country before daybreak."

"Then you did kill Raven and Y'Suom. Why else an escape route?"

"Drive, or the next body your funeral home buries will be yours."

I shifted into reverse and jolted us backwards. Then I shot up the driveway.

"Shit!" Talbert screamed as the headlights swung up the side of a black SUV parked across the driveway entrance.

The second thing you learn in a military operation is cut off the enemy's escape route. No wonder J.R. Randall had smiled.

I braked hard, rocking us forward.

"Go around," Talbert ordered.

"The slope's too steep."

"Drive!"

I backed up and shifted into four-wheel drive. I had to leave the driveway at an angle to avoid Randall's vehicle, but not so great an angle that we'd roll over. The landscaped slope was drenched by the storm and the jeep's wheels immediately started sinking. The jeep lurched toward the road and faltered. I pressed the accelerator and the tires spun deeper into the soaked soil.

"We're down to the axles. Nothing's moving this jeep short of a tow truck."

Talbert glared at me. In the wash of the dashboard, his face became a demonic mask. He grabbed my collar and pushed the gun in my face. "Open the door and get out slowly."

As I did, Talbert crawled across the seat, never releasing his grip. We sank in the muck churned up by the wheels.

"Up the hill," he growled.

"Franklin! Give it up." Kevin's voice rang from the bottom of the driveway.

I struggled forward, climbing through the beams of my headlights with Talbert's gun at my back.

I stepped on the wet pavement and turned around. Talbert pushed but I refused to budge. I heard a siren rapidly approaching.

"Move, damn you." Talbert snaked behind me and again wrapped his arm across my throat.

"I'll bet that siren's Tommy Lee." Kevin spoke from the dark shadows beside Randall's SUV.

Again, Talbert stuck the gun to my head. "Stay back."

The clouds drifted clear of the moon. The pale light showed Kevin and Randall side by side, twenty feet away. Each man had his gun leveled at me.

I realized I had nothing to lose. If Talbert took me with him, he'd have no qualms about killing me. "He's planning on flying a plane out of Georgia. I'll be dead in a ditch between here and there."

"Shut up." Talbert tightened his grip.

"Why should I? Shoot me, and then who will you hide behind?"

A patrol car sped around the curve, blue lights flashing and tires squealing. The vehicle's headlights turned Kevin and Randall into dark silhouettes before blinding me.

I didn't need to see to take control. "You're on your own, Talbert." I pressed to my left, against his arm and away from the pistol.

For a second, Talbert struggled against me. "Damn you." He stayed behind me for a few steps, and then let go. Without me as a hostage, he knew the situation was hopeless. He dropped the gun on the road and put his hands over his head. "Don't shoot. I give up."

I made a foolish mistake. I should have walked toward Randall, as insurance that honor would win out over duty, like Kevin had done in the condo. But I stepped clear, anxious to escape the blinding headlights.

Randall walked forward and brought up his gun. "This is for my father."

In the cross light from the jeep, I saw Kevin's eyes widen. "No!" His gun fired with a deafening roar. Talbert pitched backwards, landing flat on the asphalt.

Randall stared ahead, stunned. He looked down at his pistol, a cold hunk of steel. He no longer had a target.

Kevin reached out and took the gun from Randall's hand. The captain gave his weapon up without resisting.

I heard a car door open as I ran to Talbert. Blood spread across his blue-checked shirt. His eyes fluttered.

"Help me," he whispered.

"Radio for an ambulance. He's still alive." I ripped off my jacket and shirt and wadded them into a compress. I knelt beside Talbert and pressed against the chest wound. Talbert's breath came in gasps. He lost consciousness.

Out of the corner of my eye, I saw Kevin and Randall beside me.

Randall looked up from Talbert and stared at Kevin in disbelief. "Why?"

Kevin's eyes never left Talbert. "He wasn't worth it. I couldn't let him destroy you too."

"An ambulance will be here in ten minutes." Tommy Lee crouched down on the other side of Talbert. "How's he doing?"

"Depends on what that bullet did. Went in on the upper right side nearer the shoulder, but there's so much blood. Maybe you'd better call the hospital, give them a heads up."

Kevin knelt beside me. "You call. Tommy Lee's got work to do. I'll keep the pressure on." He slid his hands alongside mine.

I hesitated.

Tommy Lee didn't. "Go on. Use the phone in the condo. I'll handle things here."

I got to my feet. Randall stared at me, his face drained of color. When hate burns out a man, there's nothing left but ashen cinder.

I touched Randall on the shoulder. "What did you do to the security guard?"

"I knocked her out. But I checked her. She'll be all right."

"That's assault." I stared down at Tommy Lee. "The line's been crossed."

Kevin looked up. "I'm not going anywhere. I'll face the consequences."

I found the cordless phone lying on the marble top of the kitchen island. I dialed a number I knew by heart. Pain seared as I pressed the receiver to my ear. I switched to my left, noting the blood smear on the cream-colored plastic.

"Hello?" Susan sounded tired.

"I'm sorry to bother you. There's been a shooting."

"Barry! Are you all right?"

"Yes. Franklin Talbert's been shot and it's bad."

"James Raven's son?"

Her question stopped me cold.

"Captain Randall," she added.

"How did you know?"

"Melissa Bigham just called looking for you. She found out doing a background check."

I didn't want to get into an explanation of what happened. "Yeah, Randall. Tommy Lee has him. The ambulance should be there with Talbert in less than twenty minutes. He needs a good thoracic surgeon."

"I'll call the hospital. Ray's there."

Of course. Mr. Wonderful. "Okay. Tell him the wound's a right lung entry but where the bullet went after that's anybody's guess. He's bleeding like crazy."

"I'm coming in, Barry. Ray's only a resident. I'll want O'Malley as well."

O'Malley was the chief surgeon and founder of Susan's clinic.

"Thanks. We'll be there as soon as we can." I left the blood-smeared phone in the designer kitchen.

Kevin knelt over Talbert, still trying to stem the bleeding. Randall sat in the patrol car, slumped forward with his cuffed hands covering his face. Tommy Lee stood by the car, talking into his radio.

Faint gurgles sounded each time Talbert took a shallow breath. Kevin's crimson hands applied steady pressure to the wound. "Live, damn you."

I flashed back to that moment in the atrium when I stumbled over Y'Suom's body. Franklin Talbert had strangled the young man by cinching a belt so hard the leather crushed Y'Suom's windpipe. I had no doubt of Talbert's guilt. I had every doubt that he'd be convicted.

As for the murder of Jimmy Raven, I could hear the defense lawyer painting the horror of combat and the reality of friendly fire. "Yes, that might be my client's bullet, but could any member of the jury condemn a good soldier for a tragic accident in the fog of war?"

As Randall had raised his pistol, I'd seen only two choices— Kevin shoots Randall, or he lets Randall execute Talbert. Had the gun been in my hand, I don't know what I'd have done. But Kevin's third choice never entered my mind. He'd saved Randall from throwing his life away by shooting Talbert himself. Now, Kevin swore at him to live.

I heard an ambulance racing through the night. The wail of the siren echoed along the valley. At Laurel County Memorial Hospital, Ray Chandler would be rallying the trauma team for Talbert's arrival. Susan and O'Malley were headed for the O.R.—they would be scrubbed and ready. A transport helicopter would be en route from Charlotte—airborne as a backup if Talbert could be stabilized enough to benefit from the resources of a major medical complex. Professionals all, performing lifesaving duty with honorable dedication. Duty and honor for a man who knew neither.

Tommy Lee stepped beside me, his uniform etched by the blue light strobing from his cruiser. "General Weathers told us Randall is Jimmy Raven's son, but he didn't know anything about Talbert's involvement in Raven's death."

"Randall told us."

Tommy Lee stared at my bloodied ear. "Are you all right?"

"Yes. Talbert got my pistol. He tried to take me hostage. He had the gun to my head, stuck it in my ear. The gun sight tore the skin."

"Took guts to walk away from him."

"Yeah," I muttered. I didn't feel like a hero. "And I may have cost him his life."

Tommy Lee put his arm around my shoulder. "We all make our own choices. You can't bear the burden for someone else's actions."

"But you saw what happened."

Tommy Lee cocked his head and his one eye widened. "From the car. You broke away from Talbert. Then Randall stepped in front of him. I saw Kevin fire."

A siren swelled to ear-splitting intensity and then abruptly ceased as an ambulance pulled behind Tommy Lee's patrol car. Two paramedics rushed to attend Talbert.

Kevin stood up. "It's going to be touch and go."

Tommy Lee held out his hand. "Better give them up."

Kevin reached in his jacket and gave Tommy Lee the two pistols. "Mine's the only one that's been fired."

My thirty-eight still lay on the pavement where Talbert had dropped it.

"I've radioed Reece to come secure the scene. As soon as they've taken Talbert, I'll drive Kevin and Randall to the station."

"What about the guard?" I asked.

"I called for two ambulances." Again he looked at my ear. He yelled to the paramedics. "Got room for Barry?"

One looked over his shoulder. "He can ride up front with me."

"I'm fine."

"Fine, hell. You're collecting more stitches than a rag doll. You ride with them or you walk out of here. I'll have them tow your jeep to the funeral home."

Kevin held out his wrists. "Better do this by the book, old pal."

"Arrest you for shooting an armed killer?"

Kevin looked at me. We both knew Tommy Lee had missed Talbert dropping his weapon. I started toward the ambulance.

Tommy Lee caught my arm. "I want a statement from you. Tonight. Come by the department later. We're going to have more press crawling over us than chiggers in a blackberry patch. I'll want to get the facts out in the open as fast as I can."

"What about Melissa Bigham?"

"Tell her everything."

The paramedics loaded Talbert on a gurney. Plasma hung from an IV pole.

Kevin watched the paramedics retreat to the ambulance. He turned to me. "You tell the truth. You're too good a man."

Chapter Twenty-four

Two miles from Crystal Cascades, my cell phone came within range of a signal. I called Melissa.

As the connection rang, the ambulance driver turned on the siren.

"Barry?"

"Listen." I held the phone away for a few seconds so she could hear the wail. "I'm in an ambulance with Franklin Talbert headed for the hospital. He's been shot. Meet me at the emergency room and you'll get your story."

"Are you all right?"

"A minor cut. No big deal."

"I'm on my way. Any restrictions?"

"Restrictions?"

"Can the story go to press?"

"Yes, the sooner the better." I wanted my version in print. Let Talbert be the one who had to change public opinion.

"I'll call the paper and stop them from putting the front page to bed."

"And bring some makeup because you're probably going to be on TV." I hung up.

My last remark would set Melissa's mind whirring. But she'd be the source reporter. I had no intention of letting any of the media chiggers dig into me. Melissa was welcome to as much credit as she could stand. And she'd discovered Randall's identity on her own.

The ambulance pulled up in front of the double doors to the emergency room. I remained in the front seat until the attendants whisked Talbert deep inside. I walked in the hospital and stopped at the desk.

A young nurse was on the phone. "Yes, I'm sure it was him. Gunshot." She looked at me and dropped her voice. "Call you later."

I realized I must have been a sight, standing there with no shirt and a bloody ear. "Hello. I'm Barry Clayton."

"Oh, Mr. Clayton. We've been expecting you. Dr. Miller said you might be injured. Please have a seat in the waiting room." She pointed to a door on her left.

The beautiful people have standing reservations at classy restaurants where they're always expected. My fame starts and stops with the local emergency room. "Thank you. A woman named Melissa Bigham is meeting me here. If I'm in treatment, please send her back."

No one else was in the waiting room. I sat facing the door, assuming Melissa would arrive shortly and we could at least talk in private for awhile. I figured the staff would have their hands full with Talbert.

In less than two minutes, the door opened. Ray Chandler smiled at me. "I hear you've had quite a night."

"Why aren't you in surgery?"

"I'd just be in the way. Susan and O'Malley are doing all they can. Talbert's lost a lot of blood."

"We did what we could at the scene."

"He wouldn't have a chance otherwise." Chandler bent down and looked at my ear. "Nasty rip through the cartilage."

"I got a little too close to a gun barrel."

"Bleeding a lot. Have you been taking something for that first head wound?"

"Yeah. Tylenol. Thinned my blood, didn't it?"

"Let's get you back where I can numb your ear. Then we'll patch you up."

I stood and felt a little wobbly.

"You okay?"

I sure as hell wasn't going to have Chandler be my crutch. "I'm fine. Please tell the desk where we've gone. I'm expecting someone." I took a step and regained my strength. Outside the door, Chandler told me to walk to the end of the hall while he spoke to the admittance nurse.

When he rejoined me, his smile was gone. "We'll take this room at the end."

Chandler led the way and then closed the door behind him. He pointed to the patient table. "I want you to lie down so I can clean the wound and apply a topical anesthetic. Then I'll fully deaden your ear with a hypodermic."

"Does Susan know I'm here?"

"Yes. I had the desk call up to surgery. She was worried about you."

I looked around the small space. "Kinda tight. Will you have a nurse too?"

He glared at me. "Look, I don't know what's going on, but you have a hell of a nerve bringing that woman back here."

"I have a nerve?" I didn't need an anesthetic. The pain in my ear was forgotten. "You're the one butting in."

"Because I care about Susan."

"Good. So we're out in the open." I stepped away from the table. We were no longer patient and doctor.

Chandler crossed his arms over his chest and puffed himself to a half-foot height advantage. "I told her not to worry. That you probably weren't serious."

I couldn't believe this guy. He had the gall to tell Susan what I felt about her. "You're wrong. I am serious. She means the world to me."

"Well, your timing's for shit. Susan's up there struggling to save a man's life and you're down here only thinking about yourself."

My throat constricted and I had to shout the words to get them out. "You pompous asshole. Stay away from me. I'd rather my ear fall off than have you touch it."

The door snapped open. "What's going on?" Susan still wore her scrubs. A surgical mask dangled from her neck and tears glinted in her eyes. "Keep your voices down. The whole hospital can hear you."

Chandler and I both took a step back. I didn't know what to say. I didn't know what she'd heard.

Chandler spoke first. "What happened?"

"We lost him. The bullet hit a rib and fragmented. Bounced around like a pinball. We couldn't control the bleeding." She wiped her eyes. Talbert may have been a murdering son of a bitch, but he'd also been her patient.

Chandler was right about one thing. My timing was for shit.

Chandler put his arm around Susan's shoulder. "You did what you could."

Susan took a deep breath. "Now would someone explain to me why you're screaming at each other?"

I wasn't going to wait in line behind Ray Chandler, especially while he stood with his arm around my girlfriend. "I'm not giving you up without a fight."

"Giving me up? To who?" She looked at Chandler for an explanation.

Chandler dropped his arm to his side. "I don't know what he's talking about."

A commotion broke out in the hall. I recognized the voice of the nurse from the front desk.

"Stop. You're not allowed back there. Dr. Chandler gave me strict orders."

"I've got a deadline, and Barry Clayton's expecting me." Running footsteps drew closer. Then Melissa Bigham saw us. "Barry, Chandler barred me from coming back."

The nurse appeared behind Melissa. "I'm sorry, Dr. Chandler. She wouldn't listen."

Chandler flushed. "That's okay, Janice. I'll handle this."

The nurse gave a final glare at Melissa and left.

I gave the same glare to Chandler. "Looks like you're trying to handle everything."

Chandler looked at Susan and then Melissa. "I don't think this is the time."

"This is the perfect time. Admit you told Susan I wasn't serious about her."

Chandler swallowed like his mouth had suddenly filled with sand. "All right. I told Susan I didn't think you were serious about this woman." He nodded to Melissa. "Obviously, I was wrong. You are serious about her and I didn't want Susan to find her with you."

The deck was being reshuffled and I wasn't sure of my cards. "What are you talking about? I'm serious about Susan. I wanted Melissa here because I need to tell her what happened. She's working under deadline for a story that's got to make the morning paper."

"Oh." Chandler's blush deepened. "I thought your relationship was personal."

The pieces of the puzzle still didn't fit. "Why would you care? Seems like you win if I'm involved with Melissa."

"I didn't want to see Susan hurt."

Susan looked at Chandler, then at me. "Barry, do you think there is something going on between Ray and me?"

"Melissa saw you kissing him in the parking lot." I blurted out the words like I was exposing a junior high romance.

"Kissing Ray?"

Everyone turned to Melissa. Standing in the doorway, she clutched her notepad like a shield, and then met Susan eye to eye. "Tuesday. I was at your clinic and I saw the two of you."

For a second, both Susan and Chandler were speechless. Then Chandler sighed. "She's right. Tuesday. That's when I got the news about the job and I told you at the car."

Susan smiled. "Barry, don't believe everything you hear from a reporter. Ray's been offered a position at the clinic when he finishes his residency. I'm thrilled for him and the town. I gave him a kiss and a hug." She frowned at Melissa. "I didn't realize I was under surveillance."

I wanted to shrink into the toes of my shoes. Then I remembered Chandler had started the argument. "So what did you mean when you said you told Susan not to worry?"

Chandler looked like he hoped for an emergency page. "I didn't mean anything."

"That's my fault," Susan said. "I confided in Ray that I thought Melissa was coming on to you and you seemed to like the attention."

"What?" Melissa stepped into the room. "Me coming on to Barry? I'll admit I felt sorry for him. I thought you were dumping him." She shook her head as if she'd rather have a root canal. "But please, coming on to him?" She turned to me. "I'm sorry, Barry. You're just not my type."

Not exactly the phrases I'd have preferred to hear, but I saw my escape and challenged Susan. "So Melissa's attention threatened you?"

"Did Ray threaten you?"

She had me. "Yes." I offered Chandler my hand. "Sorry. I was way out of line."

Chandler took my hand with a firm grasp, but he didn't say Susan wasn't his type. He turned to Melissa. "I hope I haven't caused you to miss your deadline."

"Not if Barry starts talking."

Susan stepped close to me and looked at my ear. "His wound needs cleaned and stitched, but he should be able to carry on a conversation while I work. Let me check one thing before he starts talking."

Susan removed her surgical cap and mask. She bent down and kissed me. Then she turned to Melissa. "You'll make your deadline. His lips are working perfectly."

It was close to midnight by the time Susan had stitched my ear and I'd told Melissa about the shooting. Susan insisted on driving me to the Sheriff's Department, where we found Tommy Lee in his office. He looked at the hospital gown I'd commandeered as a shirt and then the pointed bandage covering my ear.

"You look like the German shepherd pup of someone who could only afford to crop one ear. Do you want a loan to do the other one?"

"No. This is more distinctive. Like wearing one earring."

"I always figured you for an earring kind of guy." Tommy Lee walked around his desk and extended his hand to Susan. "Sorry about Talbert."

"So is Court TV. That would have been quite a show."

"Where's Kevin?" I asked.

"I sent him home. You just missed Weathers and Millen."

"They have anything to add?"

Tommy Lee walked back to his credenza and poured two cups of black coffee from his pot and gave one to each of us. "Millen only came to keep the general company. Weathers is upset. Randall's actions shocked him. He knew that Randall idolized his father and Weathers admitted he contributed to that glorification. He'd kept up with the boy out of a sense of loyalty to Jimmy Raven. Got him in West Point and eventually brought him on his staff."

I rolled the cup between my hands. "What will happen to Randall?"

"We've got several local charges. Assault on you and Edith Delaney. Two counts of B and E at the funeral home. I'm not sure how to handle body snatching. Technically, who owns a body?"

"I'm not going to press any charges. Will he face a military court?"

"Definitely. He took Y'Grok's body to Fort Jackson under false pretenses. There'll also be a military inquiry into Jimmy Raven's death. I'm turning the remains over to Weathers."

"And the money?"

"As far as I'm concerned the money belonged to Y'Grok."

I sipped the coffee. The scorched taste would have offended a Starbucks palate, but caffeine was all I cared about. "What did Randall and Kevin say about tonight?"

Tommy Lee looked exhausted. He turned away to refill his own cup. "Not much about those last few seconds. All Randall will say is Kevin shot Talbert and that Talbert deserved to die. I think he's disappointed he didn't pull the trigger." Tommy Lee took a slow sip from his cup. "And Kevin's being unusually tight-lipped. Just keeps saying he's prepared to take the consequences."

"Of killing Talbert?"

Tommy Lee faced me. "You tell me." His expression showed no signs of conspiracy or complicity. "From what I saw, Kevin had no choice but to shoot. If he hadn't, Talbert could have killed all of you. So what consequence is he talking about?"

I hesitated. "I don't believe Kevin meant to kill Talbert."

"Kevin knows better than any of us that you can't call back a bullet."

I couldn't argue with him. I walked to the credenza and set down my drained cup. "So, how much of a statement do you need?"

"Pick up from when you got to the condo and carry through the shooting." Tommy Lee shifted his eye to Susan and back to me. "Shape your statement how you want. Just cover all the facts. You're all set up in one of the interview rooms. And we got your jeep to the funeral home. One of the deputies even ran it through a car wash."

"Thanks. Did you fill the gas tank?"

Tommy Lee ignored me. "Susan, I can have a deputy run you home if you want to leave Barry your car."

"I'll wait. I want to make sure Barry gets home without hurting himself."

Tommy Lee laughed. "Man, that's a full-time job." He headed for the interview room. "Come on, Barry, the sooner you get started, the sooner I can get home."

I followed him down a corridor to one of two small rooms used for interviews and interrogations. Tommy Lee opened the door and flipped on the overhead light. A table sat in the middle of the room with one chair behind it. A blank yellow legal pad and ballpoint pen lay on the surface.

"Write, sign, and date your statement. Tear off the pages and bring them to me. I'll have them typed in the morning and you can sign that copy tomorrow afternoon."

I walked around the table and sat down. The blank paper stared back at me. I picked up the pen.

Chapter Twenty-five

The morning sun shone with double intensity, as if making up for two days in hiding. As I drove through a residential section on the outskirts of Gainesboro, the light green of spring burst brilliant from lawns, hedges, and flower gardens. My spirits soared. I wore a dark blue suit, burgundy tie, and clean white shirt that matched the newly dressed bandage on my ear. Uncle Wayne and Freddy Mott were meeting me at Grace Lutheran Church at nine, a full two hours before the service, and I was grateful to be back on familiar ground.

Grace Lutheran stood at the corner of Church Street and First Avenue. For funerals, the lane nearest the front door was reserved for the hearse and family car. With a double burial, I'd arranged to borrow a second hearse from Williams Funeral Directors in the neighboring county. Wayne and Freddy would each drive one and I'd go back to our funeral home for the family limo as soon as we had the caskets positioned in the sanctuary. Family limo. The only planned family member would now be riding in the second hearse. Instead, I'd offer to take Senator Millen, General Weathers, and Bruce Nickles.

Half a block from the church, I noticed that cars filled the normally empty spaces. Several television vans and a satellite uplink truck were parked in the lot adjacent to the sanctuary. Logos for area stations, CNN, and NBC were splattered across their sides. Over two hours to the funeral and reporters were already jockeying for position.

Uncle Wayne and Freddy stood in the street, arguing with a network soundman holding a microphone attached to what looked like a fishing pole. A minivan blocked the spaces where the hearses should park and I could tell this media maggot didn't want to lose his spot.

I braked behind a hearse and hopped out. The church's pastor, Dan Swanson, and the guest minister, Earl Hucksley, hurried down the front steps. For a man of the cloth, Swanson looked like he wanted to belt the news crewman. Flanking the sidewalk were groups of Montagnards and veterans. The banner proclaiming *United Dega People* was held aloft beside the Rolling Thunder flag.

I faced the soundman. "You've got to clear this van out. Show a little respect."

"I told the old man we'd move it," the man snapped. "I'm just the soundman, and I don't have the keys."

Uncle Wayne shook his finger in the guy's face. "That's a lie. He's stalling so his cameraman can get some shots of the caskets. And he tried to get me to say something on TV."

Getting Uncle Wayne to talk on camera would be harder than getting Republicans and Democrats to balance the budget. I looked around and saw a cameraman and reporter breaking away from Harvey Collins.

Pastor Swanson forced his way between my uncle and the sound-man. "Barry, I called the sheriff. We'll get this vehicle towed."

"Barry? Barry Clayton?" The reporter hustled toward me. He clutched the morning edition of the *Vista* under his arm. "This is the guy. Roll, Phil. Mike him, Nick."

The fishing pole swung over my head and the camera lens flared in the sunlight.

"Pull him around," yelled the cameraman. "He's a silhouette."

The reporter reached out to grab me.

In the past few days, I'd been knocked unconscious in my own funeral home, nearly drowned at the mill, and had a loaded pistol jammed in my ear. Being manhandled by a gung-ho news team shoved me over the top.

"Get the hell away from me!"

The man's hand grabbed my left forearm. I slashed down with my right, pounding his wrist with my fist. He yelped and stumbled backwards, falling against the cameraman. The videographer had crossed one foot in front of the other as he tried to circle me while shooting, and he tripped over his own feet. Reporter, cameraman, and camera toppled into the soundman. The fishing pole flew up in the air high enough to mike a gaggle of geese and all three pillars of journalism crashed to the ground.

Other cameras approached, capturing the wrath of Barry. Reality TV comes to Gainesboro. A bearded vet holding the Rolling Thunder flag gave me a thumbs-up.

A short blast from a police siren drew attention from my carnage. Tommy Lee jumped from his patrol car. Kevin Malone raced from the passenger's side. The newsmen floundered on the lawn, trying to disentangle from one another.

The vet waved his flag. "Three men decked with one blow, Sheriff. Sign him up."

Pastor Swanson pointed to the reporter, now on his knees. "That man grabbed Barry first." The good reverend turned his clerical collar to the nearest camera. "I saw the whole thing and I'll swear to it."

To my astonishment, Uncle Wayne leaned over Swanson's shoulder and yelled at the camera, "That's my nephew. He'll teach people to respect the dead."

Kevin slapped me on the back. "And you're not even drunk. By God, I'm impressed."

In a short time, Tommy Lee cleared the way and we were able to roll the caskets up the handicap ramp and into the sanctuary. The public had a ringside seat as no less than ten cameras documented every inch of the journey. Just before entering the church, I looked down over the sea of the respectful and the curious and saw Kevin slip a brown envelope to one of the Montagnards holding a *Free The Dega People* banner. Y'Grok's funds would be used at last.

At the funeral service, mourners packed the pews so tightly one sneeze would have disgorged a whole row. More stood in the back and along the side aisles. Pastor Swanson banned all but one camera from the interior, and that videographer had to make his footage available to all.

Everyone in the church had read Melissa's story. The article was one of the longest ever run by the *Vista*, and she must have written the story in record time. She indulged no puffery or sentimentality, but her clear prose captured the enormity of Y'Grok's heart. Her description of the events in the condo painted a scene of Talbert's villainy unmasked. Both Randall and Y'Suom came across as victims of Talbert's greed and betrayal.

She wrote how I'd broken free of Talbert's grip and how Kevin Malone had shot him before he could shoot me. Just as I'd said in my statement. She posed the question as to where Talbert had acquired the financing for his first movie and she asked how many other Y'Groks might be hiding in Vietnam. A smart network producer would already be tracking those angles.

Melissa concluded with a promise to follow up because Y'Grok's story was a local story and our community now had a link to the Montagnard community. In a sense, Gainesboro had adopted the Montagnards.

During the service, General Weathers and Senator Millen spoke in elegant, personal ways that transported everyone back to the central highlands. I heard a few sobs, more male than female, as their words rekindled memories of loyalty, duty, honor, and fallen comrades. Comrades who, for the rest of us, were only frozen names on a black wall in Washington, D.C.

The scene at the burial erased my irritation with Archie and the mayor. There hadn't been room for both Y'Grok and Y'Suom to be interred at Grace Lutheran's small cemetery. General Weathers and Senator Millen had accepted the mayor's offer of a double plot at Heaven's Gate Gardens overlooking the valley. The clear blue sky complemented the landscape with a purity and serenity that touched the spirit.

Tommy Lee's son Kenny was home on spring break. He concluded the graveside ceremony by playing "Amazing Grace" on his bagpipes. Funny to think a man and his son, born in the wilds of Southeast Asia, would be laid to rest in the Appalachian hills under the haunting melody of an ancient Scottish instrument. But, as my father always told me, and probably still remembered in some corner of his diseased mind, funerals are not for the dead but for the living.

As the bagpipes' final note faded on the breeze and the mourners turned away, Kevin Malone walked to Y'Grok's casket and touched it one last time. I stood still, and then looked away when I saw the tears rolling down his cheeks.

"Life is funny, Barry." Kevin looked at me, unashamed to be weeping. "Just when you think you've got life figured out, something twists you by the neck and makes you think again."

"What's that?"

"I'd say hope." He smiled. "You think I'm speaking nonsense, don't you?"

"I believe in hope."

"Yes. I know you do. But I didn't. For me, hope had died with my divorce, my partner, even my will to live. And then I got Y'Grok's letter." Kevin glanced back at the two coffins. "Y'Grok was a man who had seen a thousand times more pain and injustice than me. He'd witnessed members of his family murdered. He'd seen his way of life destroyed as his so-called American allies left his people to the retributions of the North Vietnamese. Yet something kept him going. With all he had been through, the betrayals and hardships, he still believed in justice, and he hoped to have justice done for a man who died over thirty-five years ago. You can't see that kind of hope and not be touched."

"No, you can't. Y'Grok put his hope in you, and you didn't let him down. That hope should stay with you."

Kevin rubbed his hand along the casket and then stepped close to me. He gripped me by the arm, the same arm the reporter had grabbed. "Tommy Lee let me read your statement.

I haven't had a chance to thank you. What wasn't written tells me you understand why I did what I did. Not that I was right, not that I was wrong. Maybe that's all any of us can hope for. To be understood." Kevin loosened his grip, but held onto my arm. "What about you? Are you going to be all right with what you did?"

I'd asked myself the same question a hundred times since handing Tommy Lee a sworn statement that Talbert would have killed me if Kevin hadn't fired first. The fact that Kevin now stood before me, concerned for my well-being, provided the answer. I gave a slight shrug. "I'm prepared to face the consequences."

Kevin turned and walked toward Tommy Lee standing by the patrol car. Suddenly, he stopped and wheeled around. "At funerals my granny often quoted a tombstone she remembered from her native village in Ireland. 'Death leaves a heartache no one can heal, Love leaves a memory no one can steal.'" The impish grin broke across his face. "So I won't be forgetting you, my young friend. And something tells me I'll be seeing you again."

With that remark, Kevin left with Tommy Lee. I gave a wave as the patrol car disappeared into the trees.

"He's a good detective, isn't he?" Archie Donovan walked up beside me.

"The best. Boston Detective of the Year."

Archie looked around at the graves. "This worked out real well. I hope everyone was pleased with the way things looked."

I felt magnanimous enough for even Archie. "Very nice. And your kindness won't go unnoticed."

He beamed. "Do you think there's any chance we'll get Franklin Talbert?"

"Sorry, Archie. Frankfort, Kentucky and Daniel Boone outbid us."

Archie didn't realize I was kidding.

Chapter Twenty-six

Baby leaves on the oaks and dogwoods rippled in the light breeze. The temperature promised to ascend to the seventies, and spring ruled from the highest peaks to the deepest valleys.

Through this pastoral paradise, I drove with Susan beside me and a loaded picnic basket on the floor behind me. She held the Asheville Sunday morning paper in her lap and nursed a cup of coffee. Just the two of us in a perfect world. I'd left poor Democrat moaning at the cabin. His dark brown eyes had begged me to let him come, but today I didn't want to worry about what he'd chase or roll in.

Susan glanced out the window as we passed the road leading to our usual spot. "Didn't you miss your turn?"

"No. We're not going to Pisgah. I'm afraid it'll be too crowded."

"Too crowded?"

Susan and I had a secret place in the national park that lay in the fork of two streams. Rarely did we encounter others.

"On a day like today, everyone not in church will be outside. I've got a new spot I want you to see."

She patted my thigh. "Okay. I like surprises." She set her coffee in the cup holder and flipped the paper to scan the stories on the front page below the fold. "Here's an article about Montagnards."

"Another follow-up?" More than a week had passed since the Friday funeral and the revelations about Franklin Talbert. I'd shunned repeated requests for interviews, granting only one to Susan's aunt, Cassie Miller, who produced a local TV newscast in Asheville. That had been given under the condition that Cassie not run the footage of me knocking down the news crew.

"No. This has an AP dateline from Vietnam." She read the article to herself, punctuating the silence with an occasional sigh.

"What's the matter?"

"Reports trickling out of the central highlands claim the Vietnamese government broke up Easter services last Sunday as Montagnards gathered to worship. Official sources deny the allegations of beatings and imprisonment, but added that the so-called religious services are often fronts for politically subversive rallies."

"On Easter Sunday? Is there any day with the exception of Christmas when they wouldn't have more desire to worship?"

"The article says there have been credible accounts in the past of persecution and abuse on holy days. Senator Millen is requesting the President summon the Vietnamese ambassador and he's calling for hearings."

"Hope," I murmured.

"What?"

"Hope. Y'Grok had hope. Maybe something good can come out of his death. Funny. We buried Y'Grok and Y'Suom on Good Friday. Do you think that story would have been on the front page if Y'Grok hadn't done what he did?"

"No." Susan set the paper on the backseat. "So, where are we headed?"

"To a rendezvous with destiny."

I steered the jeep carefully over the slat bridge and parked between the old house and the stream.

"Is this the place?" Susan asked. "Is that the mill?"

"Yes. I hope you don't mind. I thought you'd like to see where Y'Grok lived. The field's got some smooth rocks where we can spread our picnic blanket."

We stopped at the foot log and I pointed upstream to the waterwheel. "You can see how high the level came. Those broken branches are above where I found the ammo case."

Even I was shocked at the sight. The bottom part of the wheel had been washed away up to the section where Y'Grok had hidden Raven's remains. Debris showed that the stream had crested a good foot higher.

Susan trembled. "You went in water that high? It must have been a torrent."

"More than I bargained for. But if I hadn't, the ammo case would have been lost."

She turned to me. "That was about the most foolish thing you've ever done. You could have died."

"No. I had a lifeline."

Before she could remind me that I'd pulled Melissa and the rope into the swollen stream, I bounded across the log to the other side. I turned and called to her. "Set down the basket and come over."

"What about our picnic?"

"Just humor me."

Susan started across and I stepped on the log to meet her.

As she carefully put one foot in front of the other, she kept her eyes on mine. "You're crazy."

"I thought you said foolish. Make up your mind. But for me this is a beautiful day for foolish undertakings."

She looked down at the flowing stream. "For foolish undertakers is more like it."

I reached out and clutched her hand. "This undertaker needs you to meet him halfway."

"Don't even think of pushing me in."

"No. I just wanted to show you what I discovered up here."

She looked around. We stood on the middle of a narrow log six feet above the water. "Okay. What have you discovered?"

"My true lifeline. The only woman who can keep me from falling."

The sparkle of the ripples on the water wasn't half as bright as her smile. "Barry. This is so corny. I love it."

"I love you. And I'm sorry if I haven't always shown my love. But twice I came close to dying, once in this stream, and once at the wrong end of a gun. Both times made me think about the fragility of life and what's really important to me."

Her eyes moistened. "And what is important?"

"You." I squeezed her hand and pulled her closer. "I've seen how easily I could lose you. And as if death weren't bad enough, I nearly lost you over something as silly as a petty misunderstanding. I don't want either to happen."

She kissed me. "Neither do I."

For several moments, we stood on the log in silence, holding each other. Then Susan laughed.

"What's so funny?"

"Barry, do you realize one of us is going to have to walk off this log backwards?"

"Walk? We'll dance." I grabbed Susan around the waist. "And I'll lead."

To receive a free catalog of Poisoned Pen Press titles, please contact us in one of the following ways:

Phone: 1-800-421-3976
Facsimile: 1-480-949-1707
Email: info@poisonedpenpress.com
Website: www.poisonedpenpress.com

Poisoned Pen Press
6962 E. First Ave. Ste. 103
Scottsdale, AZ 85251